SINISTER CENTURY

THE COMPLETE SERIES

SINISTER CENTURY

H. DAIR BROWN (ED.)

Published by Disturb Ink Books, an imprint of 79 Franklin Press, LLC. www.79franklinpress.com

First North American paperback edition September 2024

First North American ebook edition September 2024

ASIN (ebook):

ISBN (paperback):

Cover Images: Aden Lumbley

Designed by: H. Dair Brown

❀ Created with Vellum

SINISTER CENTURY

SINISTER CENTURY

BELVISO   DORING   MALANOCHE   MITCHELL

ESCAPE

EDITED BY H. DAIR BROWN
A DISTURB INK BOOKS ANTHOLOGY

ESCAPE

SCARY CINEMA | THE 1920S

DISTURB INK BOOKS

EDITED BY
H. DAIR BROWN

Published by Disturb Ink Books, an imprint of 79 Franklin Press, LLC. www.79franklinpress.com

First North American ebook edition September 2024

ASIN (ebook): B0DF6WRPDF

Designed by: H. Dair Brown

For everyone whose idea of escapism comes with jump scares and shivers

NOTES

Because we are fortunate enough in this collection to have writers from all over the world contributing to *Sinister Century*, you'll see a variation in the spelling of some words from story to story. The editor has chosen to respect the spelling of the country in which the author writes.

––––

"The cinema is an invention without a future."

—LOUIS LUMIÈRE

THE GIRL WHO SMILED

MEG BELVISO

RUBY'S FATHER started taking her to picture shows when she was a little girl. Even then, he rarely stayed to watch them. "Off to see a man about a dog," he'd whisper when he handed her a ticket. "I'll come and get you later."

Ruby was small and smart enough not to be noticed by the ushers when they cleaned up in between shows. Only when the lights went down once more did she sit up in whatever seat she'd been hiding under and watch the picture again.

Ruby wasn't quite so little now, but she still loved the picture shows. By now, the theater on 13th Street felt more like home than any of the tenements she and her father rented. She always felt a little sad when it was over and she found herself back on the sidewalk waiting for her father. She felt even sadder when she recognized his silhouette lurching down the street. The father who picked her up from the theater always walked, talked, and most of all, smelled different from the one who dropped her off.

"What'd you watch today?" he asked her as they walked home one night in the rain. "I like the cowboy pictures best."

It was never easy for Ruby to describe the film she'd seen, no matter how many times she'd sat through it. Today, there'd been a young man who got involved with gangsters in an effort to save his father's farm—no, his father's grocery store. Ruby rarely paid attention to the details of the plot. She got used to doing that when she was too young to read the title cards. She'd been happy enough just listening to the music and gazing at the images that flickered on screen, like a whole other world, more magical and manageable than her own.

And then she saw the Smiling Girl.

That's what Ruby called her to herself. She wasn't named in any picture, never did anything of note. She just appeared—in nightclubs, on streets, at train stations, mixed in amongst the crowd. Sometimes she was glamorous in an evening gown, sometimes down and out in rags. But no matter what she wore or what she was doing in the picture, Ruby always recognized the smile that spoke of secret joy, all the more obvious thanks to the white powder makeup and dark lipstick.

In this picture, she'd been a guest at a fancy party to which the hero had somehow gotten invited. There was a champagne toast, Ruby remembered, and just before she drank, the Smiling Girl looked right at her. Right at Ruby, as if she could look right through the movie screen at Ruby in the twelfth row, looking back.

She was so surprised she didn't even notice when a man a few seats away from her moved closer. Not until he put his hand on her knee. Then she froze.

Once, when she was younger, a man in the theater suggested Ruby sit on his lap for a better view. She had run away then. She ran away now, and waited in the lobby until the theater closed and her father turned up.

"Why didn't you find some nice lady to sit next to?" her father said when she told him about it.

"You said I shouldn't let anyone notice me too much, because I..."

"Looks like you got noticed all right. What a goof. Shoulda moved away before the sap sat down. What a bunny."

They walked in silence for a moment. "'Course, there was no reason to be rude about it," he said thoughtfully. "Maybe the fella just wanted to chat. You're too old to be a baby about everything. You're almost grown up."

She didn't dare ask her father's opinion on the Smiling Girl. That would really make him think she was a goof. So she thought about it on her own that night, while her father snored across the room. And the next day at school. And in the afternoon, mending a pair of socks for a nickel. *Had the Smiling Girl really been looking at her?* She desperately wanted it to be true.

The Smiling Girl was beautiful, she realized, with pale white skin and dark eyes full of bright movie lights. Ruby allowed herself to imagine being in a movie herself as she darned. Perhaps she would meet the Smiling Girl in person. They might become friends, and Ruby's own eyes would be as bright as her smile.

———

The next morning, Ruby saw her. Right on the sidewalk, standing beside a crate full of oranges at the grocer's on Bleeker Street that Ruby passed by every day on her way to school. As usual, she was dressed like everyone else around her, in a plain pale coat over a dark dress. But Ruby knew it was her, because she glowed black and white, even after Ruby blinked her eyes fast and shook her head. Even after she told herself it was impossible.

"Pardon me!" a man said, stepping around Ruby where she had stopped short on the sidewalk.

"'M sorry, sir."

The man paused, looked into her face, then stepped forward and blocked her view. "Fancy meeting you here."

Ruby leaned sideways to look around the man, but the Smiling Girl was gone, if she'd ever been there at all.

Ruby shifted her gaze to the man's face, then looked at his hands. He'd laid one of them on her shoulder.

No need to be rude, she remembered her father saying. She shifted her weight onto her other side and leaned slightly away. She hoped he wouldn't notice. She hoped he would.

"We've met before," the man said. "At the movie theater."

Ruby said nothing.

"Are you on your way to work?" He glanced deliberately at the books in her bag. "No? Still in school? I thought you were grown up. You look grown up."

"I'm going to be late."

He stepped aside theatrically to let her pass. "I'll see you again!" he called after her as she hurried on. "At the theater!"

By the time she turned the corner, Ruby's heart was beating fast. She tried to tell herself that running into the man was a coincidence, but something deep inside her knew it wasn't true. The man knew where she lived. He knew she went to school. He'd promised to see her again at the theater.

She looked helplessly around her until her eyes went blurry with tears. The street was full of people, but there was no one she could ask for help. She didn't even really know what help to ask for.

She could never go to the picture house again, she decided. On Friday night, when her father handed her a ticket, she would stay out in the lobby or hide in the ladies' room.

She remembered being a little girl, that first time at the pictures. How the screen was like a whole world she wanted to crawl into and wished she still believed it. Then she could look out at the man and his hands and smile, knowing he could never touch her.

———

On Friday night, though, her father didn't take her to the picture house. He led her to a laundromat on Leroy Street. "Spring's come early this year," he said to the bald man at the counter. The bald man waved them both around and through a curtain to a door that concealed a narrow staircase. Ruby could hear music and voices coming from below.

"Dad, is this a speakeasy?"

"How do you know about speakeasies?" he asked with a laugh. "Just like I said, you're grown up. Very grown up. Grown up enough to go to work, in fact. Help out."

"I do sewing," Ruby reminded him, but he didn't seem to hear her over the noise in the stairwell. The room below was smoky, like cigars and cigarettes, and smelled like turpentine and sweat.

Even before her father led her through the crowd, Ruby knew which man would be waiting for her in the room. "This is Mr. Crowder."

"We meet again!" the man from the theater said.

"Say hello, Ruby," said her father.

Ruby held out her hand mechanically. Mr. Crowder's palm was dry and warm, just like in the movie theater. When he touched her hand, her knee tingled.

"Mr. Crowder'd like to get to know you."

They sat down at a tiny table. Ruby stayed as close as possible to her father, as far as possible from Mr. Crowder, and politely refused his offer to buy her a drink. As the two men talked, she imagined she was in a movie. Not one of the talkies. The men's lips were moving, but the only sound came from the three musicians in the corner playing a sloppy version of "Fifty Million Frenchmen Can't Be Wrong."

Ruby stared past Mr. Crowder in his camel hair coat and imagined the color leaching out of the room, the brown wood table tops turning gray, the coffee mugs glowing pure white. *"When they go parley-vee and parley-vou, this for me, zat for you…"*

And just then, from behind a mustached man with shiny, slicked back hair, the Smiling Woman appeared, drifting towards the bar and glowing black and white like a firefly hovering lazily over the grass in the summer.

"Ruby?" her father was saying. "Isn't that nice of Mr. Crowder to want to take you to the pictures?"

"Yes." Ruby smiled, keeping her eyes on the glowing woman. "Yes, that would be nice."

————

Ruby stayed up late that night finishing up two pairs of socks. Early Saturday afternoon, she went to deliver them. "Don't be too long," her father muttered from his bed on her way out. Nothing got him up early on a Saturday. "Mr. Crowder will be by at six. He's got shares in a coal mine. Out in Pennsylvania..." He fell back to sleep.

Ruby shut the door behind her and hurried down the steps. Someone was singing with a radio somewhere in the building, and the scent of cabbage mingled with the usual cigar fog. The hallway was so dim she almost missed the baby sitting on the steps on the second floor.

Sunlight hit her like a punch when she got out to the street, knocked her back on her feet, but only for a moment. Then she was dodging people on the street, hurrying past the bank and a pushcart hung with sausages, catching bits of conversations along her way, mostly in Italian. Mrs. Minetti, the seamstress, was in such a good mood when Ruby delivered her work that she gave her half a *sfogliatella* along with her wages.

The nickel Ruby earned from the socks was meant to go straight into what her father called "the safe," a quickly emptied glass jar he hid under the floorboards for what he called expenses. But as she had nothing left to lose on this day, Ruby took the coin right to the theater for the matinée.

Ruby took a seat next to two girls in knit dresses. She wondered if they were friends or sisters, if they worked in a factory, and if they had mothers at home who curled their hair before bed, as she'd seen mothers do in movies.

On screen, the hero walked into the fancy party. Ruby sat up in her seat. She scanned the black and white figures in their tuxedos and evening gowns, the shiny finger-waves and long, black lashes. The Smiling Girl appeared almost immediately, lifting a glass of champagne off a waiter's tray and carrying it to the corner of the screen where she leaned against a pillar, waiting.

She looked at Ruby. Really looked at her, like it was the most natural thing in the world. As if Ruby was at the party too, and they were bored, and shouldn't they both go off and have some real fun?

Ruby felt herself nodding in her seat and tingling, as if her skin was lighting up from the inside. But how was she to get from where she was to where she needed to be? The Smiling Girl knew, and she was glad to tell her, not in words, but in pictures that played right in Ruby's head.

———

"You're fizzing like seltzer water!" Ruby's father said that evening as they waited for Mr. Crowder.

He was pleased at how excited she was for her evening out. A little guilty, maybe, Ruby imagined. Like maybe he ought to prepare her, so she'd know how to behave, but that might just make her nervous and besides, hadn't Crowder said he found her naivety quite charming?

Ruby was a little nauseous thinking about what was to happen, but if it was going to come anyway, she wanted it to be over with as soon as possible.

Mr. Crowder bought her dinner, and a big box of chocolate candy in a heart-shaped box. In no time, they were sitting side by side in the theater, and the hero was on his way to his fancy party one last time.

Mr. Crowder sat with his body angled toward Ruby, so much so that he was nearly sitting in her seat. He had to drape his arm over the back of the chair to keep himself up, and from there his hand dropped naturally onto her shoulder instead. Ruby fought the impulse to jump up and run to the lobby.

With her own sweaty hand, she reached inside her purse and pulled out her father's razor. It helped her stay calm to watch the way the light from the screen reflected off the blade, making it flash and flicker as Ruby herself would soon be doing. The big hand on her shoulder tugged her closer.

Ruby turned her head to look at Mr. Crowder's thick neck bulging over the starched collar of his shirt. The Smiling Girl had shown her just what to look for. A tiny jump under the skin. The pulse that would show her just where to cut.

Mr. Crowder planted a heavy kiss on her head. Ruby impulsively snuggled closer, as if she liked it. She turned towards him and stretched up, as if she meant to kiss him on the cheek, and flicked the razor just below his ear.

Mr. Crowder didn't even seem to feel anything at first. He shook himself, as if he'd been bitten. Put one hand to the side of his neck, then the other, the one he'd had on Ruby's shoulder.

Ruby watched in wonder at the dark liquid arcing over her, not red, but black, like the dark pomaded hair on the screen. Black like a tuxedo or a shadow on the wall. In seconds, Mr. Crowder was lying still, still bleeding, turning whiter by the second.

Ruby felt her own garish, colorful life draining out of her until she was glowing bright white. She looked up to the screen, where the Smiling Girl was finally beckoning her to join the flickering figures at the party.

———

She'd been there—she wasn't sure how long—enjoying her champagne, when she glanced across the room and saw a girl in distress. A hopeless-looking thing with a black eye and a wedding band, huddled in an aisle seat and gazing up at her with desperate longing.

Ruby looked right back at the poor girl, and she smiled.

————

Meg Belviso holds a BA in English from Smith College and an MFA from Columbia University. As Staff Editor for *Angels on Earth* magazine, Meg Belviso spends her days surrounded by heavenly creatures. But for as long as she can remember, she's been drawn to darker realms. She's written for various fiction and non-fiction properties, including *Looney Tunes* and *Dexter's Laboratory*. She's the author of several biographies in the *New York Times* best-selling *Who Was...?* series and is now also going in search of weirder subjects in the *What Do We Know About...?* series. She is a regular presenter at the Sirens fantasy conference, where she has presented on ghosts, hauntings, monsters, murder... and other subjects that often turn up in her fiction. She is determined to one day speak Russian fluently. To that end, she's working her way through all her favorite horror movies in the language.

Bluesky | Goodreads | Instagram | Amazon Author Page | megbelviso.com

SHADOW TRACER

F. MALANOCHE

AMADOR AND JUANA walked under the golden radiance of the Oriental Theatre's marquee, its glowing signage giving a pleasant tinge to Farwell Avenue. He held the door for Juana, hoping he was doing the right thing. He was a mess of nerves around her. Despite his name, he had little practice with dating. In fact, Juana was his first real date. He hoped she would be more than that.

While she admired the extravagant golden appointments along cutout silhouettes of lotus flowers over doorways, Amador took in her form. The fringe of her emerald satin dress flitted with her movements like some curious creature in nature. Her arm cradled her purse. She looked nearly unrecognizable from the starch-white nurse's outfit he typically saw her in at work. Amador stole glances, afraid to scare her off. He adjusted his tie to look a bit more orderly for her.

Juana said, "This place is so beautiful. All the gals in my wing are dying to get in. How did you ever get tickets?"

"Oh, it's nothing," Amador could feel heat rising to his cheeks as he grinned. "So, what title piques your interest more, *Metropolis* or *The Cat and the Canary*?"

"Whatever you want is fine." She smiled at him. Her white teeth contrasted with her crimson lipstick.

Based on the titles, Amador chose the latter of the two options, assuming it was about animals she might find cute. He purchased two tickets from the kid behind the counter.

"Can we get a snack?"

———

You sit perched on the metalwork of a blue canvas awning, staying out of light as much as possible, lest it burn you. Pangs of hunger take hold. It is your misfortune to have picked the one awning under a bank. It has been days since your last meal.

Clacking approaches. The sound of voices from a meal chirping to another. Nervousness seasons the tone of their conversation. The clacking belongs to a slender snack walking alongside a meatier fare. You drop from the safety of the awning into the opening of a handbag held by the slender snack. The contents of the bag rattle around. You hold tight, waiting for the ride to end in a dim area. Then, only then, can a meal be perfection.

———

Amador recalled the advice his brother Felipe gave him: *get her whatever she wants.*

"Sure," Amador said. They picked up a paper bag of salted popcorn and some new treat known as Raisinets from the concession stand before walking into the auditorium.

Red, ornate designs carpeted the aisles between rows of stained maple chairs. Statues of Buddha with green eyes sat in decorative bays all over the room. A blue, ornate design that looked like an iris decorated the proscenium arch.

"Que linda," Amador said, as he admired the beauty of the decor.

Juana turned to him, her cheeks flush, and said, "You're not so bad looking yourself, handsome." She straightened his tie and kissed him on the cheek.

The tenderness of her lips was so delicate, Amador wasn't sure if he imagined it. "Amador? I think people are trying to get by."

He noticed the people pouring in around him, but couldn't make sense of it. Juana hooked her arm around his, bringing him back to where he was. "Let's find a seat," she said. The rows were surprisingly empty for such a popular place. He walked her down to a few seats near the front, away from the majority of people.

———

The turbulent motion of the handbag is dizzying. A disk with floral-scented powder nudges your stomach. A new scent comes from a small bottle. You suck on the spritzer. Its alcohol-filled flavor whets your pallet. The desire to have a quenched appetite strengthens.

Sounds of the chow outside chattering become hushed. You feel your hiding place come down with a hard thump. Horns blare all around. Their harsh noise tells you to stay, to wait until the sound calms.

———

The lights dimmed. Trumpets blared the news reel to life. Grayscale images of men pointing at a designed wall appeared. An announcer, who sounded as if he was speaking in a tin can, explained the visuals.

"JANUARY, 1927. THE TOMB OF THE ANCIENT EGYPTIAN PHARAOH TUTANKHAMUN HAS BEEN OPENED UP FOR PUBLIC VIEWING. LET'S HOPE NOTHING WAKES UP. IN A STUNNING UPSET TO MANY, THE STANFORD INDIANS TIED THE ALABAMA CRIMSON TIDE, SEVEN TO SEVEN. AND THAT'S WHAT'S GOING ON IN YOUR WORLD."

Trumpets swelled again before dying down. The screen went dark. A third and final round of trumpets sounded a new song, showing an image of a mountain with stars hovering around it. The brass instrumentation gave way to strings as the mountain faded into dilapidated wooden shutters blowing idly in the breeze. Names hovered across the screen.

Amador savored the sweet Raisinets as he turned to Juana, watching her pop a kernel of popcorn in her mouth, and wondered how her lips would taste now. She returned his gaze. He offered her the Raisinets to cover up his faux pas, hoping she didn't notice him staring at her.

Felipe had said going to a show would be great for Amador's nerves because he wouldn't have to talk as much. Though Amador welcomed not having to struggle to ask questions, he loved hearing Juana talk. She'd spoken about her favorite author over dinner, giving premises and reviews of each books she had read. Her ideas excited him. In the theater, he had no idea what to do.

Shortly into the film, Amador was already uncertain as to who their characters were or whose will was being read. He looked around the room. Over his right shoulder, a gentleman toward the back wrapped a muscly arm around the dame next to him, pulling her close. The wet smacking of their kissing made Amador sick with want and desperation. He had no clue how to progress from where he was. Another man stretched as he yawned and lowered one arm around the woman next to him. Amador thought that seemed doable and considered when would be the best time to yawn.

———

The blaring horns have been replaced by the sound of potential meals tittering at one another. A minor blow to the bag tips it over. Through the opening, no direct light is visible. The exit looks safe. You slither out of the bag. The smooth concrete floor is cool to the touch. A black heel

sways into view. The exposed ankle looks delicate. The scent of this
amuse bouche *sends you reeling.*

You climb up the metal leg and wooden back of the chair to get a
good look at your dish. As you climb, their scent strengthens. One of
them smells like that alcohol you tasted before. The other has a smoky
scent. You perch on the back of the chair.

You lurch forward, covering them with your inky black flesh.

———

On screen, Bob Hope made his funny frightened faces as he
walked down the basement steps, tailed by Paulette Goddard,
who was asking him about reincarnation. Amador looked over
his shoulder once more. The couple that had been making out
had disappeared. He figured they must have left. Amador
feigned a yawn and raised his hands high in the air.

Paulette Goddard screeched as she fell into the shadows of
the basement. Amador was still mid-stretch when Juana jumped
and clutched his chest. The date had taken a pleasant turn.

———

A two course meal felt good. The smoky flavor paired with the boozy
glaze to make a complex flavor combination. Only your hunger isn't
gone. You look around. It is an expansive room shadowed in darkness—
apart from one light flashing images on a single wall. An oil painting of
a meal blinks. Another meal covered in a gingham pattern examines a
book. Her figure looks delicious, only she is bathed in light. It seems to
emanate from her. There would be no way to feast upon that meal.

You turn your attention to the wooden chairs all about. Fresh meals
sit in pairs all around. A veritable smorgasbord of tasty treats, both
meaty and delicate, savory and sweet. You inhale deeply and determine
which to dine on next.

———

Amador turned toward Juana. He sniffed her perfumed and curled hair. The smell put the image of pink flower petals blowing away in a late summer breeze. The scent was divine. He thought all women should smell that way. Her body felt warm under his arm. At that moment, more than anything, he wanted to kiss her long and good, but he didn't want to be too greedy. Didn't want to scare her away. He whispered in her ear, "How do you like the show?"

Juana nodded and whispered back, "It's good. Bob Hope is really funny."

A smile spread across his face. Amador looked over his left shoulder to discover an astonishing sight. Where he had previously observed a couple cuddling, now sat a solitary man with closed eyes, mouth agape, breathing hollowly. Amador puzzled over where the woman was. He held Juana tighter, hoping she wouldn't look over and assume the worst about what happens in the shadows.

————

You are halfway through another feast. Its companion tasted of nuts. This repast has taken on a certain oak flavor. It must have worked with wood. The flavor wasn't bad, just not as good as it could have been. Fortunately for you, the buffet of delights is only half complete.

————

The movie was making a bit more sense as it went on. Amador thought Paulette Goddard looked delightful, but she couldn't hold a candle to Juana. He was a bit hungry since they had run out of popcorn and Raisinets. His underarm was getting hot. He didn't want to sweat on her. Juana shifted as he did. The tips of their noses touched. Her breath felt hot. His eyes were drawn to her lower lip. He didn't notice her chestnut brown eyes staring into his, nor her hand moving toward his leg. Her breast heaved.

That quivering lip held his attention completely. He didn't notice how many people no longer surrounded them in the theater. His form sunk forward into his breath, into her breath. They kissed. It was long, and it was good. Nothing else mattered.

———

You make your way through the theater auditorium. The atmosphere of the theater grows on you. It is so much better than dropping onto an unsuspecting morsel in the dark of the night or, worse, in some snack's shadow in the breaking light of day, tracing their movements until there is somewhere safe. Here, the treats are organized like candies in a box.

Pains emerge again, no longer from hunger, but from fullness. Only two treats remain in the room. You catch a second wind as you eye your dessert. Inch by inch, you draw closer. Nobody will tell you not to play with your food. On your way underneath them, you can hear heavy breathing. A green heel sits in front of you. You crawl onto the toe of the shoe.

———

Amador's kisses, which began as tentative, progressed into full-blown passion. He clutched the small of her back. Then came the bright light. The two looked down and attempted to shield their eyes. Amador swore he saw a rat scurry from Juana's shoe.

The usher, donning an angular red jacket and matching velvet cap, lowered the light from their faces so they could see. He said, "Sir. Ma'am. I can't help but notice you two are rather, ahem, engaged. The Oriental Theatre does not condone such public obscenity. You are welcome to leave."

Blood rushed to Amador's cheeks. He felt he ruined everything. His eyes wandered over to Juana.

She was flush as well. She said, "That's fine. I'm sure we can find something else to do." Her red lips curled into a smirk.

Amador stood and offered her his hand. She took it and followed him out, giggling along the way.

On the screen, Paulette Goddard walked into a secret exit near a bed, silver pistol in hand. The secret passage she explored, hidden between rooms, was decorated by cobwebs and shadows. She failed to see a man dressed as a police officer in the shadows as she passed a darkened alcove. White silk clung to the form of the leading lady, making the usher dream dreams. He reached down and scratched an itch at his ankle.

———

You don't want to be annoyed at the intrusion of light. The larger dessert took off. Fortunately, a smaller, more manageable replacement treat arrived. It even looks like it has a velvet cherry on top. The little treat reached down toward its ankle for a scratch. You throw your inky form at the white gloved hand of this final dish. Dessert screams as you engulf its hand. You extend your mouth up its arm and over its mouth, muting its cries. It is soft and goes down smooth. You let loose a satisfying burp.

A light stroll is what the doctor ordered. You drag yourself across the cool concrete, but you just want to rest. You pull yourself into a familiar bag, pull it shut, and drift off with one blissful thought, "What a feast."

———

If you enjoyed this, check out F. Malanoche's other story in the Sinister Century *series. "Excommunicated," a dark story about an AI savior, can be found in* Lurk: A Disturb Ink Books Anthology.

———

F. Malanoche writes, under the cover of night, hoping to bring authentic and odd Latino stories into the world. He teaches English in the Midwest, has a wonderful wife, and a sweet vinyl collection. His writing has been published in *Demonic Workplaces* and *Darkness 101: Lessons Were Learned*.

Facebook | Goodreads | https://linktr.ee/F._Malanoche

DRESSED TO SEE

JANE DORING

HUMMING Hot Five's *Muskrat Ramble* under her breath, Ethel twisted the last of her sleek locks, then carefully pinned it just above her ear. "There." She smiled at her reflection, turned her head from side to side, assessing the product of her sleepless night with her hair in curlers. "Just like Mary Astor."

"Darling?" Frank popped his head into the room, his eyes sparkling from the two glasses of scotch he'd downed after dinner. "We are running late."

"Let me just—" Ethel chugged the rest of her gin rickey, only a lime wedge left at the bottom of the lead crystal glass.

Ethel swirled before the mirror, the beige beads streaming down from the corset of her dress clanking at each other in a most satisfying way. She side-eyed the door, but Frank was already gone, the sounds of his lacquered shoes hurrying toward the front door. Ethel rolled her eyes at her reflection in the mirror. Why did he insist on coming with if he was just going to ignore her anyway?

Ethel followed the trail of cigarette smoke, picked up her cream wool coat from the hanger, fished her tortoiseshell cigarette holder from her purse, and slammed the door shut. She caught up with Frank on the other side of the street. *Men and their obsession with being on time.*

The air stank of dying winter and—mostly—of New York. Only when they neared *Roxy*, did Frank offer Ethel his arm. He led her through the busy street, her heels getting stuck between the cobblestones time and time again. Each time, Frank urged her to be careful, as though her being careful would magically fix the gaps between the cobblestones.

The smell of popcorn and cotton candy dominated the long line that led from the grand entrance and all the way to 6th Avenue. Street vendors kept far enough from the entrance not to be asked to leave the area, yet close enough to make sales.

Ethel smirked at the ladies waiting in line. They shivered in the icy wind as their men talked business to one another, some shielding their women from the wind and some ignoring theirs entirely.

Frank escorted her past the line and handed his card to the valet, who had been waiting for them in his neat red uniform. Ethel soaked in the perfumed air of the well-lit vestibule of Roxy. Ladies and gentlemen in lavish dresses and suits smiled fake smiles at each other, wishing one another to have a great time at the premier.

Ethel rolled her eyes when Frank led her past a group of East-Sider wives. She did not care for them and their gossip, which was always served up at their bi-weekly meet-ups alongside their Bee's Knees and Tutti Frutti sandwiches.

The whole time they waited at the auditorium doors, Ethel fought the urge to meet the straying eyes of the East-Sider wives. Their hushed voices and sneaky glances were not as easy to simply brush off. Normally Ethel would have avoided it by simply arriving later.

"Ethel, darling," said Helen, one of the East-Sider wives, materializing from the crowd. "Oh and Frank is finally joining you." She batted her eyes, to which Frank cleared his throat, gave a curt nod and continued his conversation with a gentleman, whose name Ethel did not bother to remember.

"So nice to see you, Helen," Ethel said in the sweetest voice she managed to force out.

"You simply must come to Margaret's house this Wednesday and help us make sense of this movie. Surely with the expertise of a frequent theater-goer you can teach us a thing or two." She glanced at Frank, as though waiting for his reaction but he was far too involved in his own conversation.

"Perhaps," Ethel said. "I could also invite Samuel to help you make sense of it. He was the one who chose this movie after all.

"Samuel," Helen said, frowning. "You cannot mean Samuel Rothafel himself?"

There it is, Ethel thought.

"Why of course. Samuel invited us personally."

Helen's smile vanished. Who knew what her husband had to do to get her a ticket? His absence could only indicate that he'd only managed to get one.

"I'll consider your invitation, Helen." Ethel turned away from the woman and allowed herself the tiniest of smirks.

Finally, the doors opened and Ethel pulled Frank away from the crowd and into the auditorium, in search of their seats in the sixth row.

Once everyone was seated and the lights were dimmed, the sounds of the orchestra filled the auditorium and Ethel breathed out. She relaxed her face from the ever-annoying half smile, which was expected from a well-off, well-groomed, well-mannered woman of her age and status. She pushed Frank's hand off her knee, kicked her tight shoes off and crossed her legs, looking around the dark auditorium.

Mouths bearing a sweet stench of popcorn whispered to one another from all sides of the packed space. Hairdos sticky with perfumes turned from side to side, following the gazes of their owners as Mary Astor entered scene after scene. Her clothes, so lavish and so unlikely.

"Is this going to be your next go-to, darling?" Frank leaned in, and an acidic mix of alcohol and cologne brushed at the skin of her cheek. "Will you spend every night here? Rewatching the same movie over and over again?"

"Only if you promise not to join me," Ethel whispered, a clump of rage stuck in her throat. She focused on the image of the mob boss, surrounded by the members of his gang.

"What was that, darling?" Frank said, leaning in even closer. He fished out his flask from the inside pocket of his jacket and drank in full, daring her to answer.

Ethel did not bother to repeat herself. She shifted away from Frank and rested her elbow on the right armrest next to the stair aisle. Her favorite spot. Close enough to the center to say she had one of the best seats to *Dressed to Kill*; yet far enough that she did not actually need to see the movie.

Had Frank not tagged along tonight, Ethel would have slipped out by now, walked out into the side alley and smoked to her heart's content. She would, of course, slip back in to bid farewell to the East-Sider wives at the end of the film. Helen had surely briefed them in on their conversation earlier.

A childless lady of her status was expected to have a hobby, or better yet, a strange obsession. Hers was the cinema. Little did anyone know Ethel hated the cinema.

A bright flash beneath the moving screen, to the right of the orchestra, caught her mid-thought. The flash, having disappeared in a blink, left behind a strange feeling of unease. In that moment, the auditorium fell into complete silence. An icy shiver went down Ethel's spine.

The pumping of blood in her ears was the only sound Ethel could make out, as if she had been plunged underwater. Frank, together with the others around her, kept staring at the frozen shot of Mary Astor's big smile on the screen. Yet every movement, even the blinking of eyelashes, was much slower than what was natural.

Ethel poked Frank's shoulder apprehensively, expecting an annoyed reaction.

Nothing.

She waved her hand before his face.

No reaction.

Tap.

The sound, so delicate, so quiet, tore through the eerie silence of the auditorium. Ethel whirled her head, looking for the source of the tapping. Was this a joke? Would Frank turn to her now and laugh? Would the East-Sider wives appear from nowhere and point fingers at her stupidity? But Frank was not one for jokes. And the East-sider wives were either clutching to their men's elbows or focused on the screen. One of them, seated in front of Ethel, sat frozen in the act of an inaudible whisper, her red lipstick brushing at her husband's ear.

Tap.

Ethel dug her nails into the padded handrests.

I've been watching you, said a voice next to Ethel's ear. The hairs on the back of her neck stood up as the invisible lips blew at her skin. Ethel whipped her head around.

Behind her, a woman stared at the screen, an expression of interest melting into a slow yawn.

"What did you say?" Ethel said. She expected the woman to laugh, to yell at her, to get angry. Nothing. The woman's mouth was opening wider and wider, as her hand slowly raised to cover it. Right before her hand reached her mouth, however, for just a split second, Ethel thought she saw an eye blink inside of the woman's wide-opened mouth.

Ethel turned around and dove into her seat, getting as small as she could as she brought her knees to her chest and hugged them.

She closed her eyes and counted to ten.

This was not happening. She must have fallen asleep while watching the film.

When she opened her eyes, Ethel was still in the auditorium.

For a long moment, nothing happened.

Then, another quiet *tap* and Ethel caught a glimpse of a shadow moving ever so subtly at the corner of the large screen.

Ethel jumped to her feet, stumbling over her shoes. She left her shoes where they were and scrambled toward the exit, past the rows and rows of frozen faces.

Come to me, said the same voice, as close to her ear as the first time. Ethel yelped and scrambled up the steps, sharp pain spreading through her toes and her knees as she lost her balance. The beads on her dress dug into her flesh as she landed.

When Ethel raised her head toward the voice, she saw another member of the audience with his mouth open. An eye stared at her from between his teeth. Ethel pushed herself away from the horror until her back hit the cold wall.

"What's happening?" she yelled, terrified tears filling her vision.

Come, said the voice. This time, it echoed through the entire auditorium.

Ethel searched the space below the screen, where the orchestra kept playing their silent instruments.

Tap.

Ethel's heart sank when she noticed the microphone below the screen. She was finally able to place the tapping sound. A shadow appeared out of nowhere, taking shape behind the microphone. One hand gripped the microphone, the other stretched in her direction.

Come.

Ethel felt her body get up and walk toward the screen. She whimpered, unable to resist. All of the heads in the entire auditorium turned in her direction when she reached the microphone. All mouths opened, an eye staring her down from out of each mouth.

Ethel's hand reached out to the microphone. As soon as her fingers touched the slick steel, the shadow before her solidified: pale blue skin, long neck, thin white hair and misshapen burnt-out holes instead of eyes. Ethel's knees gave in when the creature's long claws dug into her shoulder, right above her heart.

It leaned in, blue skin touching Ethel's face.

You are mine now.

Ethel felt her mouth forced open before everything faded to black.

———

"Darling?" Frank tapped her on the shoulder, and Ethel jerked awake, fear turning into relief. She flattened her hands against her chest.

"Just a dream." Ethel looked around their bedroom, where the morning sun was cutting into the room from the openings between the curtains.

"You were mumbling," Frank said, turning away from her and getting comfortable to sleep again.

Ethel pushed away the blanket and headed for the bathroom.

"Ouch," Ethel said, studying the bead under her foot. She scanned the room: her dress, missing a few strings of the beads, lay on the floor.

She glanced at the bed, where Frank began snoring once more, his mouth wide open. Then, she rushed into the bathroom and stared at her reflection in the mirror—at the bruise on her left shoulder.

Ethel screamed and when she did, a black eye blinked at her from her open mouth.

———

Netherlands-based English teacher, **Jane Doring** often uses reading as a way to procrastinate on writing. She lives with her fiancé and an extensive collection of books. When she isn't traveling in the real world, she can be found exploring RPG fantasy or dystopian worlds. Fluent in four languages, Jane hopes to one day create her own, a world much like Tolkien's. Jane's story "Honey-Yellow Light" has appeared in the anthology *Orpheus + Eurydice Unbound* and her story "Rubble at Dawn" has appeared in *The Librarian* anthology, both from Air and Nothingness Press.

Facebook | Goodreads | Instagram

UNSCHEDULED INTERMISSION

CHERIE MITCHELL

IN THE SHADOWY recesses of one of the many auditoriums of the ambiguously named Upper Grand Theater, something dark and unseen subtly shifted position before falling back into a heavy, expectant silence. *Tonight was the night.*

Downstairs, the lobby was filling with this evening's quota of eager guests. The interior of the theater was richly opulent, a panorama of eye-popping grandeur from the cascades of crystal gems dripping from the looping gold chains of the numerous chandeliers all the way down to the plush red carpet spread luxuriously underfoot. The mouthwatering scent of hot butter and toasted corn hung in the air and mingled with a myriad of perfumes and colognes.

There was a sizable crowd here tonight, and the muted conversations and occasional bursts of laughter played out against a backdrop of classical music courtesy of the flamboyant pianist and the magnificent grand piano. Anyone who entered the Upper Grand Theater was left in no doubt they had shrugged off the everyday grime of the street and stepped into a brand-new world, a world where every sense was about to be cossetted, titillated, and enchanted.

Trixie concentrated on keeping her breathing steady and tried to act nonchalant and calm, as if she was a woman *au fait* with such splendor. She laid her gloved hand lightly on Robert's arm as they climbed the enormous staircase, attempting to take everything in without making it obvious that her gaze was everywhere at once.

This was her first date with Robert, a momentous occasion that she had been praying for ever since she first set eyes on him at a church supper several months earlier, and she wanted to make a good impression. No, she *had* to make a good impression. There were plenty of other young women in town who had set their caps at Robert Malone, especially pouting, bun-faced Betty Carson, who was just itching to take her place by his side. Betty's eyes had almost popped all the way out of her head when Trixie proudly told her that Robert had asked her to accompany him to the cinema this evening.

The uniformed usher at the top of the staircase checked Robert's tickets, and then smoothly guided them to one side, pointing the way with an officious wave of his hand. "You're in Theater Number Five."

Trixie blinked, tearing her eyes away from the woman in the shiny red court shoes and ermine stole who she'd been watching enviously as they climbed the stairs. The woman and her husband were following the rest of the crowd across the huge landing to where yet more people had gathered, waiting to buy food and drinks at the garishly lit refreshment stands or to enter other theater doors. Trixie gave Robert's arm a quick squeeze, worried they might miss some of the glamor. "Are we going in straight away?"

"Our movie is about to begin. We arrived later than I'd planned." There was a small but unmistakable note of censor in his tone.

Trixie felt her cheeks burn hot. She hurriedly dropped her eyes, feeling suitably reprimanded. She hadn't meant to keep Robert waiting when he called to collect her in his father's Model T Ford truck, but she'd wanted to make sure she looked perfect for their date. Pinning her hair into the latest fashionable bob and arranging her kiss curls had taken time—more time than she'd intended.

"I thought we could find our seats first, and then I'll come back out and buy us some snacks." Robert's moment of terseness had passed as quickly as it arrived. He grinned, the gesture making a deep dimple in his left cheek. Any protests Trixie might have had melted away like ice cubes dropped on a hot surface.

The usher stopped outside a lone door positioned at the far end of the landing and as far away from the other theater entrances and the bustle of the refreshment stands as it was possible to be. For some obscure reason, someone had placed a large potted palm in front of it, a ploy which disguised the door rather than highlighting its presence. Above the door hung a somewhat shabby gold "5," the painted coating lacking the glossy luster of the Upper Grand's other fittings.

The usher checked his watch and gave Robert a pointed look. "You should be aware that this showing doesn't have an inter-mission."

"Do you need to use the powder room?" Robert arched a solicitous eyebrow at Trixie.

"No, I'm fine." She didn't want to keep him waiting again, especially as her tardiness had clearly annoyed him. She looked again at the plain door, which gave no clue as to what was showing on the other side. "What is the film?" she asked politely.

"*Monster in the Auditorium*." Had Robert emphasized the first word or had she imagined it?

"Oh! I thought—" she stopped, biting her lip. In her excite-ment over Robert's offer of a date, she hadn't thought to ask him which film he had in mind. She had just vaguely assumed that it would be a drama, or perhaps even a light romance, something to quicken the pulse or raise a shared smile or laugh. Watching a scary horror movie on her very first date with the man of her dreams had never once crossed her mind.

Robert had noticed her hesitation. "Is that alright with you?"

"I'm happy to go along with whatever you choose." No man wanted a date who nagged or sulked. If she wanted to be asked out on a second date, she would need to curate her behavior and allow only her best side to be seen.

The usher yanked the door all the way open with a vigorous flap, creating a gust of air that stirred the potted palm leaves. "Come this way."

There was a small anteroom inside the door where Trixie and Robert waited as the usher took a lamp from the pedestal table by the wall. Using the lamp as guidance, he moved along the short passageway that would take them through to the theater and their seats. The busy noise of the landing had muted into nothingness. The warm, tantalizing scent of popcorn had also failed to penetrate this space, replaced here by dampness. The odor was suggestive of the type of mold that might encourage the speedy growth of toadstools.

The seating area now opened in front of them, but Trixie had only a moment to eye the rows of red velvet seats before they started up the shallow flight of steps. The usher's lamp bobbed on ahead. Robert seemed to have forgotten that he was supposed to be Trixie's escort. He trudged up the steps without stopping to take her arm or warn her to watch where she put her feet. Trixie grimly set her jaw and followed him. This was certain to be only a minor hiccup, a rare lapse of judgment on Robert's part.

She glanced briefly at the rows of seats as they passed, but it was difficult to make out anything more than the featureless shapes of the other patrons when she was concentrating so hard on not tripping up. Her shoes were new and a little big, which meant that slipping over and making a fool of herself was a very real possibility. She shuffled up the last few steps to where the bobbing lamp light had thankfully stopped and the two men waited for her at the end of a row. She gave Robert a tight smile before making her way down the narrow aisle, taking care not to bump her knees on the edges of the seats.

"What can I get for you?" Robert asked, his gentlemanly manners returning as she sat down in her allotted seat. He tossed his hat onto the chair beside her, but he hadn't yet taken a seat himself. He stooped, bending close, and the red lights in the domed ceiling high above glinted on the slick pomade that coated his hair. "Popcorn? A glass of soda?"

"Yes, please. Both would be lovely." She smiled up at him, adding a flutter of her eyelashes for good measure. However, her flirting was wasted as Robert had already moved away, perhaps unable to see her seductive expression in the dim light. She sighed as she watched him leave, picking his way back down the darkened steps to where the usher waited with his lamp. Seconds later, both men were gone, taking the lamp with them.

She leaned against the soft velvet seat back, taking care not to slouch. Now that she was alone, she could look around properly and sum up her surroundings. Unfortunately, the interior of Theater Number Five disappointed her when compared to the other extravagantly decorated halls and chambers of this building.

While the Upper Grand was renowned for its jaw-dropping architectural delights, this theater seemed to have avoided the designer's hand. Instead of intricately carved sconces decorated with whorls and vines, there were instead unlit indents on the walls, each one awash in deep shadows. The alcoves were the height of a man and the width of two men, but from where Trixie sat, their depth was unknown.

On top of everything else, the red lights in the ceiling combined with the thick carmine curtains that covered the screen and the red velvet fabric of the seats gave the entire space a distinctive scarlet tinge. The overall effect was eerie and strange. Cavernous, with multiple unexplained shadows and that odd red glow.

Womb-like.

She blushed in the darkness, mildly shocked by the unsummoned thought. She didn't often have conversations like this with herself, although she had listened with horrified awe when Betty and some of the other young women discussed such things. Betty had noticed her unease and given her a smug, knowing smile, but Trixie had haughtily pretended her interest was elsewhere.

Wrinkling her nose at the musty stuffiness that tickled her nostrils and made her want to sneeze, she shifted her attention from the periphery of the theater so she could study the other patrons. There weren't many people in here, and none of them appeared to be of the talkative kind. The theater was silent, although if she strained her ears and concentrated hard, she thought she could hear the faint tinkling of the grand piano. Her own row was empty, but there were a few people scattered along the rows in front. She turned her head to look behind and saw two anonymous pale ovals of faces in the last row, up near the lighted box of the projector room. Afraid they might catch her staring, she hurriedly turned away.

The clap of a closing door and the bobbing of the lamp light announced the return of Robert and the usher. Trixie's interest in the audience was swiftly forgotten. Robert bounced up the darkened steps without the aid of the usher's assistance and strode down the row to present her with a cold glass of soda. She had already removed her gloves in anticipation of the popcorn, and the beads of condensation on the glass soaked her fingers. Robert took his seat beside her and chivalrously offered her some popcorn from the bag. "I didn't know how hungry you were, so I got us the biggest one."

She decorously pressed her ankles and knees together and chewed on the popcorn. She *was* hungry—she had skipped dinner because she didn't want an unbecoming stomach bulge to distract from her appearance in her carefully selected outfit. Her entire future might hinge on the outcome of this evening, and she didn't want anything to go wrong.

As Robert righted himself, Trixie's traitorous, empty stomach let out a low, rumbling growl. She smothered her gasp and stared straight ahead, hoping her date hadn't heard it.

Robert frowned. "What was that?"

She glanced at him, prepared to ask what he meant, but he wasn't looking at her. Instead, he was looking past her into the shadows of the alcove at the end of their row.

"I didn't hear anything."

He continued to stare at the nothingness for so long that she began to feel uncomfortable. She couldn't see anything other than the thick black shadows. She uttered a ladylike sigh designed to draw his focus back onto her. "I haven't heard of this film. Will there be performances by any famous actors or actresses?"

"Huh?" Robert finally dragged his eyes away from the shadows to give her a blank, distracted look.

"The film. I don't know anything about it." A sudden exciting thought struck her. "Is it a talkie?" As soon as she asked, she felt giddy and foolish. There was no way this could be one of the new talking films that everyone was raving about. If that was the case, the theater would be packed from wall to wall and there would be a queue a mile long waiting outside.

Robert made a chortling, huffing sound. She hoped he wasn't laughing *at* her. "No, it's not a talkie, Trixie, but I think you'll enjoy it. The ending will surprise you."

She sipped delicately at her soda, deciding it might be best if she kept quiet and allowed him to lead the conversation. She hadn't engaged in too many one-to-one conversations with Robert until now—most of their interactions had been in the presence of others in the communal setting of the church or at church suppers.

Those weren't the type of places for private conversation, although they were the perfect environment for collecting enough threads of gossip to weave together an understanding of the newcomers, who had only recently moved to the city from somewhere in the hill country.

Robert, clearly educated as well as dashingly handsome, was working as a bookkeeping clerk somewhere downtown. There was no doubt that he was a good catch, which, of course, was the reason Betty was so envious of Robert's interest in her.

"The film's about to start," Robert said through a mouthful of popcorn. He had settled back into his seat now and was gazing avidly at the front of the theater.

Trixie took a few seconds to admire his profile before she, too, looked to the front. After starting with a halting, hiccupping jerk, the curtains drew all the way back to reveal the screen. So far, the evening hadn't panned out quite as well as she'd anticipated, but there was still plenty of time for it to correct itself. She would sit next to Robert and enjoy his closeness while they watched the film, and afterward, they would have something to talk about.

The projector up in the room above whirred to life, and the phonograph music started along with it. The curtains swished to a stop and the *Welcome to the Upper Grand Theater* greeting flickered onto the screen in a jittery display of black and white. Trixie held her glass of soda in her lap, clutching it with both hands. She hoped the movie wouldn't be too scary. She didn't like being given a fright, and she most definitely didn't want to watch anything that might give her nightmares.

"I'm looking forward to this," Robert whispered.

"Yes." The condensation from the glass was making her lap damp. She mentally crossed her fingers, hoping it wouldn't stain her dress. This was her special occasion dress, her first date dress, although if this evening went well, she might never have to wear a first date dress again.

The movie title wobbled onto the screen accompanied by a burst of ominous music. Beside her, Robert chuckled. Trixie took another sip of the soda. It tasted oddly bitter, but she wasn't about to complain. Nice girls, the type of girls who men chose as their brides, didn't complain nor make a fuss.

The film started sedately enough as the hero was introduced to the story. As was to be expected, each scene a short blurb or comment closed the episode and led the viewer into the next scene. Trixie had nearly finished her soda now, and yet she was having difficulty keeping her eyes open. She struggled valiantly, keeping her gaze fixed on the figures on the screen. The actors and actresses soon became indistinct and blurry, and the plot had escaped her completely, but that didn't matter. Keeping up appearances was imperative at this point.

A soft snoring sound alerted her to the mortifying fact she had fallen asleep. She blinked her eyes open wide, galled to have behaved so badly in this genteel public space. *What would Robert think of her now?!*

She jerked her head around so fast that she cricked her neck, but the brief stab of pain went unnoticed. Robert's seat was empty save for a lone kernel of popcorn lying near the crease at the back. She stared in disbelief at the vacant spot for several seconds as her brain frantically tried to reconnect the lost fragments.

How long had she been asleep? Had Robert been so embarrassed by her unladylike snoring that he'd gotten up and left her here alone? She whipped her head back in the other direction to scan the shadowy steps that had led them up to their seats. *Or had he simply gone to the bathroom or to get more snacks and, being the gentleman he was, hadn't wanted to wake her?*

At the front of the theater, the film played on while the rest of the audience stared steadfastly ahead. Trixie took some small comfort from the knowledge that her unplanned slumber appeared to have gone unnoticed by the other patrons.

She moved the empty soda glass from her lap and sat it on the seat on the other side of her before wiping her damp palms down her dress. She had time to compose herself before Robert returned. She refused to believe that he wouldn't come back. Once he was back in his seat, she would apologize profusely, and from there, the evening would continue. There was still a chance that it might end on a high note.

She surreptitiously rubbed the end of her nose. She felt stuffed up, bleary, not quite herself. Her stomach hurt too, a dull ache that reached all the way around to her kidneys. Maybe she shouldn't have skipped dinner.

The music from the phonograph changed in tempo, picking up pace to indicate to the audience that things were about to get messy. Trixie looked back at the screen. The current scene was taking place in what appeared to be a mad scientist's laboratory. She had no clue about what the story entailed, and she had no interest in trying to catch up with it.

Where was Robert?

Again, she looked over toward the entrance, but there was still no one there.

A hard thump on the back of her seat made her gasp. She spun around, prepared to direct a cross retort to whomever had kicked her chair, but the row directly behind her was empty. The damp, musty smell was stronger now, strong enough to penetrate the stuffiness in her nostrils and make her eyes itch. She ducked her head and sneezed into her hand before raising her head again, searching for the person who had kicked her seat.

Was it Robert? Did he think he was being funny? Had he sneaked along the row behind with the intention of scaring her? She would have liked to think he was too mature to play such a silly prank, but then you could never really tell with men.

After a quick glance around to ensure that she hadn't attracted any undue attention from the other patrons, she turned all the way around so she could kneel on the seat cushion. She gripped the seat back with both hands and peered down into the dusky gloom of the row behind her.

The brutal attack came from out of nowhere. She had less than half a second to comprehend the rushing onslaught of the bulky shape before it impacted with formidable force against the left side of her head. A bolt of agonizing pain surged through her left temple, her jaw clicked, and her teeth clamped down painfully on the outer edges of her tongue. She was flung sideways by the strike, landing on the armrest that lay between her seat and Robert's with a discernible

Oooofff.

Dazed and for the moment too winded to speak, she fought to draw in a breath and refill her starved and depleted lungs.

The small door of the hatch of the projector room slid all the way across with a rattling thud, abruptly shutting down the film mid-scene and removing most of the light from the theater.

The music faded to a low background hum, and for a few seconds all Trixie could hear was the sound of her own raspy breathing. She was shaking now, made weak by a combination of shock and pain. If Robert thought this was some kind of joke, it was time to inform him that the joke was well and truly over.

"Robert? ROBERT!" Her voice rose on the last syllable as a quick burst of anger overtook her shock.

She no longer cared if Robert thought she was unladylike or whether the other theater patrons thought she was acting like a madwoman possessed. It wasn't as if she was interrupting the film anyway, and it wasn't as if they had any reason to complain about her rudely disrupting their viewing pleasure.

She shoved herself upright, running her hand over her sore chest before gingerly touching her temple. It was only then that she realized none of the other people had voiced their concern over her antics or asked if she needed any assistance. In fact, the audience had remained deathly silent throughout her ordeal. Robert hadn't answered her shout either.

She slipped off the seat and stood up, squinting around the theater. That eerie red glow was now the only light, yet the shadowy audience remained focused on the blank screen. This wasn't right... none of this was right.

"Hello?" she said. "Can anyone hear me?"

Not one audience member moved, not one head turned toward her. The music suddenly increased in volume, the beat loud and pounding this time.

Abandoning any remaining sense of propriety, she hitched up her skirt and clambered over the seats in front, heading down the rows to get to her closest neighbor. She reached the aisle behind the row where her target sat and bent to say loudly in his ear, "Excuse me, but why has the film stopped? What's going on?"

The man didn't so much as flinch. She leaned in closer, staring hard at his face in the gloom before recoiling. "Oh!"

Bizarrely, the shape she had assumed to be a living, breathing person was, in fact, a wooden mannequin. Dressed in a smart suit, the mannequin was of the type used to display clothes in the window of Barney's Department Store. Trixie hastily checked the features of the mannequin's companion, only to discover that its face too was wooden and blank.

She ran along the row to where the next two shapes sat, bumping her knees against the seats as she ran. It didn't take more than an instant to determine that these were also mannequins. The entire theater was stuffed with an audience of lifeless wooden mannequins!

Another whack between the shoulder blades sent her tumbling forward. She lost her footing and fell over the seats into the row in front, dislodging a mannequin with her foot as she fell. She bounced off the red velvet seats and crashed to the floor with the stiff, unyielding mannequin falling on top of her.

Furious rather than frightened now, she shoved the mannequin to one side and jumped back onto her feet, ignoring the shoe that had fallen off in the scramble. She yelled up at the ascending rows, shouting at the faceless mannequins and the unknown person who had assaulted her. "STOP! Quit pushing me! I'm going home!"

The music cranked up another notch, the pumping beat reaching an ear-splitting crescendo that made her feel as if her head had been turned inside out. She took a couple of steps, preparing to race down the aisle to the shallow stairs and leave the theater.

This time, she saw her assailant coming, though that didn't leave enough time to brace herself for impact. Most horrifyingly of all, her attacker wasn't Robert or any other person.

What reared up above the seats and sent a long tentacle snaking toward her was a monstrous, dome-like, wart-covered entity. This ghastly apparition was the likes of which she had never in her life encountered, although once she had seen a drawing of an octopus that bore some resemblance to this *thing*.

The thought was knocked out of her head when the flailing tentacle hit her full in the face and sent her flying. She skidded backward and fell onto her bottom, landing awkwardly on the arm of the mannequin on the floor. The crack of splintering wood wasn't discernible over the cacophony of music, but she felt the arm break beneath her and the agony of the sharp shards as they pierced her tender skin.

She was screaming now, but the thumping music smothered the sound. Her nose, mouth, and chin were hot and wet, and she was sure the whack of the tentacle had broken her throbbing nose. The pain of her injuries melted into the background as a rush of adrenaline took over. Whatever that despicable thing was, it clearly had no intention of letting her escape from this nightmare in one piece.

Another tentacle snaked over the seats, and then another and another, until there were nine or ten of the waving monstrosities blocking her exit. She whirled around to run to the other end of the aisle. Two of the tentacles wrapped around her body, stopping and holding her in place while simultaneously squeezing tight. Trixie screamed again, but this time her scream was choked off when a third tentacle slid around her throat and pressed down hard against her windpipe. The tentacles wrapped around her chest and abdomen compressed, constricting her fragile human body beyond endurance.

Trixie's last awareness was of the squelching squish and plop of her intestines as they burst from her abdomen to decorate the red velvet seats, her guts laying across the seat cushions in curving loops that bore an uncanny resemblance to the gold chains of the lobby chandeliers. The music changed again, the beat now echoing the distinct notes of a funeral march.

Down in the passageway where he had enjoyed a view of all the action, Robert turned to the usher and said, "That should keep it satisfied for a while."

The usher nodded and trembled beneath the red glow of the theater lights. He held the lamp high as he backed away toward the theater entrance and the relative safety of the landing.

"Come on, let's get out here. We'll lock the door and leave it to its own devices," Robert said.

He grabbed the usher's free hand not holding the lamp and pressed a large wad of notes into his clammy palm. "Thank you, Eric. Split that with Jack in the projection room. You both know there's plenty more where that came from. We've been looking for a suitable location to house the critter ever since we moved into town, and this place is ideal."

———

Cherie Mitchell is based in the beautiful South Island of New Zealand, a rugged and relatively untouched area of the world that provides plenty of material for her writing projects. She enjoys creating plots that put the characters at the front and center, writing stories that dip and weave around these generally complex, complicated, but otherwise ordinary people. Creatures of various shapes, sizes, and temperaments often predominately feature in these books—they don't call it a creature feature for nothing! One of Cherie's most notable writing accolades was winning a whirlwind trip across the world to Portland, Oregon where she was presented with a glass trophy that now takes pride of place on her bookshelf. A selection of her most popular published books includes the *Lake Ness* series, the *Boulder Lake* series, and the *Survivor Atoll* series.

Facebook I Instagram I TikTok I Amazon Author Page I www.hotfromthepen.com

ARTHURS   HAWTHORNE   ZAPLE

CAPASSO   SHANNON

LISTEN

EDITED BY H DAIR BROWN

A DISTURB INK BOOKS ANTHOLOGY

LISTEN

EERIE RADIO | THE 1940S

DISTURB INK BOOKS

EDITED BY
H. DAIR BROWN

Published by Disturb Ink Books, an imprint of 79 Franklin Press, LLC.

www.79franklinpress.com

First North American ebook edition September 2024

ASIN (ebook): B0DDWN9DGY

Cover Image: Aden Lumbley

Designed by: H. Dair Brown

For those who listen for that creak on the floor in the dark of night

NOTES

Because we are fortunate enough in this collection to have writers from all over the world contributing to *Sinister Century*, you'll see a variation in the spelling of some words from story to story. The editor has chosen to respect the spelling of the country in which the author writes.

———

"Listen to many, speak to a few."

WILLIAM SHAKESPEARE | *HAMLET*

CHAPTER 1
I'LL NOT FORGET YOU, SWEETHEART

RACHEL M. SHANNON

SUNRISE TO SUNSET, the radio echoed through the empty rooms of the farmhouse and kept Marjorie Morris from drowning in loneliness. The comedy of Jack Benny and Bob Hope; the drama of *The Guiding Light*; news reports and Roosevelt's fireside chats; and music, music, music. Marjorie loved it all. She and Joe even sat and listened to thrillers on *Suspense* and *Lights Out* before he'd shipped off overseas, but she had no nerve for spooky tales when she had to endure the dark nights on her own.

She waddled from her chair and turned off the radio with a click of the knob. The day's chatter silenced, she could now hear a wrathful November wind howling against the house. She rubbed at the lump of appendage protruding from her rounded belly, seven months along and taut as a drum, then wrapped her sweater around it tightly and climbed the stairs to bed.

———

That night she dreamed of a picnic. An old woolen blanket was spread beneath the soft green tendrils of the willow tree at the edge of the pond, past their barn and opposite the fields. She lounged, eating an apple, and watched the baby no longer in her belly as it cooed on its back and watched the willow branches sway in the breeze. A voice carried in by that same wind called her name in the lightest of whispers.

Marjorie, Marjorie, Marjorie.

Joe's voice.

She looked around in the dream but could not see his face.

She opened her eyes to blackness, and a crackling reached her. A sound that, once she was free of the haze of sleep, she recognized as static from the radio in the sitting room. She was sure she'd turned it off before going to bed.

The hardwood floor, cold beneath Marjorie's feet, creaked as she descended the stairs. She held tight to the railing for balance, not trusting her pregnant gait to keep her upright so soon after waking from the smothering clouds of deep dreaming. Moonlight from the sitting room window transformed the sofa, armchairs, and tables into hulking demons crouching in wait. Marjorie's heart thudded. *Stop being such a silly girl*, she told herself as she entered the room and approached the radio in the corner.

The radio hissed and popped in nearly intelligible whispers. In her fretful imagination, Marjorie pictured the consciousness of souls long dead riding electromagnetic waves across the skies and into her home, spirits perhaps as lonely for someone to talk to as she was. The hairs on her arms stood at attention, and she reached for the knob to silence the static.

The tuning needle jumped on its own, and Marjorie flinched as the sudden volume of Vera Lynn's voice filled the room, crooning in a melancholy voice like slow-dripping honey how she'll meet her sweetheart again someday.

Her eyes flooded with tears as she remembered the last day she had spent with Joe. They'd shared a simple lunch of ham sandwiches at the small table in the kitchen, a tense silence between them with so much to say but neither of them finding the words. When this song came on, Joe stood and held out his hand and they'd danced to it in the kitchen, clinging to each other like they were drowning. That was May. They hadn't even known about the baby growing inside of her yet.

Through blurry tears, movement outside the window caught Marjorie's eye. The figure of a man sitting on the porch steps silhouetted by the moonlight. Shock mingled with delight flooded through her as she ran to the front door and yanked it open.

"Joseph!"

Marjorie flew through the screen door, and it banged shut behind her as Joe stood and faced her. He wore his dress uniform, and his seabag lay at his feet like an obedient dog. She embraced him as fiercely as she could with her large belly between them, firing questions at him through her tears while she breathed in the comforting tang of his shaving cream.

"What are you doing home? Why didn't you tell me you were coming? Are you well? I would have picked you up from the station. Why didn't you call? How long have you been sitting out here? Aren't you cold?"

Joe eased her out to arm's length and looked at her for a long moment. She felt a stab of dread as, at first, he almost seemed not to recognize her. She'd heard stories of men coming home from the war different: withdrawn, confused, sullen, angry, changed. Then his face broke into that charming Joe Morris grin that made her heart skip a beat every time. "You're beautiful," he said, almost in wonder.

She smiled back, smoothing hair that she was sure looked sleep-disheveled, and took his hand. "Come inside. You must be hungry."

He reached down and lifted his heavy seabag from the porch, deposited it inside the front door, and followed her to the kitchen. He sat at the table and watched her intently as she bustled about, fixing him two fried eggs and a slice of toast.

"I'm home," he told her.

She wrapped her arms around him where he sat and pulled

his head into her rounded torso. "I know, sugar. I missed you so."

————

The next morning Joe's side of the bed lay empty, and Marjorie feared the night before was only a dream. She slid her hand to his pillow. Still warm. She emerged from her cocoon of blankets, wrapped herself in her favorite sweater, and put on her slippers. A front must have blown through with that ferocious wind the night before. The house was freezing.

She searched the house, turning on her faithful friend the radio along the way, and discovered Joe out back. Beyond the autumn husks remaining in her victory garden was the barn where they currently kept a chicken coop but no other livestock. Marjorie hoped to raise goats one day, but so far, Joe had been resistant to the idea.

To the side of the barn was a wide stump Joe used to chop firewood. He sat on the stump, face turned to the faded blue and yellow strip of dawn to the east. Marjorie put the kettle on the stove to boil water for coffee. Deciding today was as special an occasion as any, she retrieved two cups from her cabinet of wedding china and rinsed dust from the rose-fringed vessels. By the time she carried the cups of coffee, aromatic and steaming, down the concrete back steps, the sunrise peeked over the horizon in a blinding flash of orange and gold.

The cold nipped at her bare legs, and her breath emerged as white smoke. Joe remained utterly still, hands on his thighs, taking in the sunrise. As she got closer, she cocked her head at an odd, tuneless hum that seemed to be coming from him.

"I thought you might like a coffee," she said.

Joe turned, and a sharp yelp escaped her.

His face was featureless. A blank. The space below his hairline looked like a melted blob of candle wax. No nose, no mouth. An eyeless oval searching for the source of her voice. Her arms dropped to her sides and coffee spilled from the cups, spritzing her legs with dots of heat. Her instinct was to run, but she found she couldn't move.

She gave a frightened squeak as he stood and reached for her, his blank face thrown into shadow by the light of the sunrise behind him. Then he touched her hand, and he was Joe again.

"Marjie, what happened? You look like you've seen a ghost." He stooped to pick up the coffee cups from the dirt at her feet.

Marjorie released a nervous chuckle and shook her head. *Silly girl, you've been on your own too long.*

"Nothing. Nothing. It was a strange trick of the light," she told him.

You had no face! she wanted to say but didn't. She presumed he had been through enough terror over the past months. He didn't need his skittish, pregnant wife making homecoming an unnerving experience.

"I thought I'd chop some wood, but I couldn't find the ax," he said, handing her the empty coffee cups.

"Wonderful," she said. "I've depleted the woodpile with this recent cold snap."

She led him into the barn and showed him where he usually kept it, hanging on a series of nails inside the door. "While you do that, I'll make a cherry pie to go with our lunch. To celebrate your return home."

"Do I like cherry pie?" he asked.

She measured her response. She'd met Joe at the county fair in 1937. Her cherry pie had won a blue ribbon that year, and Joe had been one of the judges. He'd escorted her down the midway that evening, making her laugh with his gentle jokes and winning her a stuffed bear by knocking over a tower of milk bottles with one pitch. Not long after, shortly into their courtship, he confessed to her that the moment he took a bite of her cherry pie, he knew he would propose to the woman who baked it, even if she ended up being a hunchbacked ogre with one eye. They were married the following year.

"Yes, you like cherry pie."

"Wonderful," he echoed.

She toddled toward the back porch and stopped when he called her name.

"Marjorie."

She pivoted. "Yes, sugar?"

"What happened to the corn?" He gestured past the barn to the field, now just five acres of loamy brown dirt, empty of crops. "I remember corn."

She frowned slightly. "We agreed to leave it fallow until you returned. I couldn't work the field on my own, and there isn't enough help to be had right now."

He paused. "Oh. Okay." He hefted the ax and split into the first log.

———

Marjorie hummed along with the radio as she rolled the pie crust dough. "Penny Serenade" bled into "Boogie Woogie Bugle Boy" bled into "A String of Pearls." She knew them all, and she loved working in the kitchen to the rhythm of a song. She put the filling mix on the stove to boil, and Bing Crosby's crooning abruptly turned to static. She wiped her hands on a tea towel and went to the sitting room to play with the dial. *Must be something with the weather.*

The static turned to whispers. It almost sounded like Joe's voice, reminding her of the times he'd breathed words of affection softly into her ear in the dark intimacy of their bedroom.

Marjorie, Marjorie, Marjorie.

Despite the discomfort of the baby weighing down her middle, she felt a hot blaze of desire fork through her. She wiggled the dial, searching for music.

Me the static whispered. *Marjorie, not me.* A burst of trombone, then more static. Then, *Careful. It's not me, not me.*

Joe reached from behind her and snapped the radio to OFF. Marjorie jumped. "Jesus, Joe, you startled me!"

He grinned boyishly. "I came in for a glass of water. Your cherries are bubbling."

She rushed to the stove, reduced the heat, and stirred, shaking her head at her fancy. The radio was not whispering to her. That kind of thing wasn't real. She had just been alone too long. Joe kissed her on the cheek and went back outside. He smelled of cold air and clean sweat. She watched as he crouched to pet one of the barn cats. The small black and white fur ball wound herself in and out between his ankles and arched up into his hand. Marjorie's heart swelled.

God, she had missed her husband.

———

That night in bed, he reached for her, and she responded by crawling over and straddling atop his hips. Her belly made things awkward at first, but soon they found a comfortable rhythm. His hands reached under her nightgown and coursed over her skin, and she rocked faster until she cried out his name. Seconds later, he was spent. They faced each other, limbs tangled, and held each other that way in the moonlight that spilled in from the window, hearts and breaths slowing after their lovemaking.

Joe twined his fingers in hers. His voice broke the silence hoarsely. "I don't... I can't...I'm having trouble remembering things, Marjorie. Some things I recognize, but then I have to think real hard to figure out their place and meaning."

She kissed him once, but stayed silent.

"I remember a cave. We were on this island, lush and green and hot. We had driven the enemy off the island, but they kept trying to take it back. Some days there was fighting, and some days there was nothing but waiting and tension and boredom and missing home. But on this one particular day, we came upon an enemy squad. I remember shooting, and screaming, and blood. Lots of blood. I got...separated from my unit. I think, I think I was shot, but I must not have been because I don't see anywhere on me now where a wound would have been."

At this, Marjorie kissed him and squeezed his hand tightly. She imagined with dizzy dread the devastation she would have felt if Joe had never come home to her.

"I thought I was shot, and I stumbled into this cave. I pulled myself into the cave as far as I could from its mouth, and I rested. Then I heard a noise deep in the dark. A rustling. And a figure came toward me. A man. I raised my weapon, and it came toward me. I couldn't see its face. It was almost as if it didn't have a face. It touched me, and there was pain, and a blinding light. And then it was like I was looking into a mirror at myself. I must have been dreaming. And then everything went black. And then there was nothing."

Joe paused for a long moment and swallowed hard.

"I remember the cave, and I remember sitting on the front porch. And I'm not sure what happened in between."

Marjorie rolled over, nuzzled her back into him, and pulled his arm over her belly. "We have time to figure it out. We have all the time in the world. Or, if you don't want to, you don't have to try to remember. You're here now, with me." She rubbed his hand over her belly, where she'd just felt the baby kick. "You're here now with us."

———

Marjorie dreamed that she was hanging sheets on the clothesline. She watched as Joe's silhouette approached from behind one of them. He walked all the way to a sheet, then leaned into it. His face, covered by the white sheet, was a blank, featureless mass. She watched in dismay as Joe's sheet-covered face opened in a scream.

She woke with a start and thought she heard static from the radio.

Careful. Careful. Marjorie. I'm not me. Not me. Not me.

She shook off the terror of her dream, curled into Joe's body, and drifted back to sleep.

———

The next morning, she again found Joe sitting on the chopping block watching the sunrise. She started the coffee, banishing thoughts of her husband turning to her with no face. She ignored the nagging thought that kept returning to her mind.

That is not your husband. That is not your husband.

Instead, she focused on how it felt to have his warmth next to her, his hands on her.

A knock at the door startled her out of her daydream.

The man on the porch wore a Western Union uniform. His face was secured in an expression of sympathetic determination as he handed her a telegram.

"This was to be delivered weeks ago, ma'am. I'm very sorry for the delay, and I am sorry for your loss." He spun on his heel and descended the porch steps.

Marjorie opened the telegram with shaking hands.

THE SECRETARY OF WAR DESIRES ME TO EXPRESS HIS DEEP REGRET THAT YOUR HUSBAND PFC MORRIS JOSEPH B WAS KILLED IN ACTION ON GUADALCANAL 24 OCT 42 CONFIRMING LETTER FOLLOWS

She folded the telegram and placed it in the pocket of her sweater. She walked in a numb daze through the house and out the back door. The ax was propped against the side of the barn. Marjorie picked it up and approached the chopping block, where the thing that was not her husband sat absorbing the bright light of the sunrise.

With preternatural calm, she lifted the ax. She imagined burying it into its skull. She considered ending the figure that was wearing her husband Joe like an uncanny costume, like a sick joke.

Then she imagined living alone. Tending this farm alone. Raising her baby alone.

She dropped the ax and put a hand on its shoulder.

"Come inside and get some coffee," she said. It stood and put its arm around her as she led it back to the house.

After all, many men come back from war changed, Marjorie reasoned. *I'm just thankful that some part of him came home at all.*

————

Rachel M. Shannon is a lover of storytelling who harbors a fascination with the spooky and macabre. She occasionally feels compelled to write fiction, and will take pen in hand to satisfy the Muse. She lives in South Texas with her husband, teen, and their cat Gigi.

Instagram

CHAPTER 2
CAN YOU SURVIVE THE NIGHT IN A HAUNTED TUBE STATION?

MASON HAWTHORNE

THE ADS APPEARED in several smaller papers distributed in London and ran on the radio between the serials.

Can you survive the night in a haunted tube station?

The patter of the copy was nothing unusual for that sort of thing, the wireless-borne descendent of the penny dreadful, but the prize money…well, fifty pounds is nothing to sniff at, even if ghost hunting is for fools with nothing better to do with their time.

"Mr. Griffiths—"

"Call me Blue."

"Blue…" the radio man smothers a grin, glancing across at the technician supervising the tapes. "You've volunteered to spend the night in a notoriously haunted tube station. Why don't you tell the people listening at home what inspired you to undertake such a terrifying ordeal?"

"Ad in the paper said fifty quid."

"It, uh, it certainly did, Mr. Gr—Blue. And you're not afraid at all of the ghostly visitations, the spirits which have been regularly reported emanating from this station?"

"Hm," Blue's eyes are blue, pale as old and well-washed denim, and they glitter as he looks over the radio man and the technician, "Can't say as I am. Seen a lotta things, haven't yet seen a ghost."

"Have you heard a ghost?" the radio man persists, "The dreadful moans, or the cries of the lost and wandering souls?"

"Can't say as I have."

"Surely you've heard of the tragedy in this station?" The radio man leans forward. "During the blitz, the station was used as a shelter, hundreds of people packed down there, lying like sardines as the bombs fell across London. One terrible day, there was a gas leak, and a shell landed in the street above, lit the gas, and the whole place went up, dozens killed, hundreds injured. A terrible day."

Blue sucks his teeth and shrugs. "Think I was in North Africa at that time. Didn't hear about it."

A couple of moments of dead air. It hardly matters, since this is a pre-recorded bit, ready to be slotted in when they air the full *Night in a Haunted Station* show. The radio man rallies, forcing heartiness into his voice.

"Your accent is interesting. You're Australian?"

"I am."

"Came over for the war, then?"

"I did."

"What made you stay in England? Did you meet a special someone?"

For the first time, Blue's expression changes. There's a quiver at the corner of his mouth, and he curls his hands together in his lap. "Yes."

"Where did you meet?" There's a genuine warmth in the radio man's voice, a gentle talent for wheedling which has carried him this far in his, admittedly, disappointing career.

"Hospital. After I was shot, they sent me back to convalesce. Met in the ward. Spent a few months there and...well," Blue smiles, broad and beaming, his sun-worn face suddenly showing the school-boy he must have been only a few harrowing years ago.

"Lovely. I'm sure she'll be very proud of you if you come through this experience with the same nerve as you showed during the war."

When he's managed to stretch the interview out to five minutes, the radio man signals the technician to wrap it up, and they start organising for the night's ordeal ahead. They'll just have to find a few minutes of extra audio to make up for the brevity of this portion.

———

With a wail, the gate to the old tube station is forced open under the combined strength of the radio man, the building superintendent, and Blue. Overhead the lights are flickering and yellowed, and everything has a fine coat of black soot over it, giving the place a grim atmosphere. Even the smell is of something burnt, though it is not overpowering.

"Now, you're not to go onto the tracks, or off the platform," the superintendent says quickly. "If you have any trouble, don't try to go through the tunnel. Trains do still use this line. Come back up the stairs to street level if you need to get out."

He proffers a bullseye lantern, round and squat with a bucket handle and a small partition that lets out only a circle of yellow light. "You'll want this."

Blue nods and takes it.

Blue is not as tall as he seems. He's slim and raw-boned and looks like a man who has shrunk a size or two all over. And though he couldn't be more than thirty, he is faded. The hair under his hat must once have been red, and his skin sun-burnished. Now he looks wan, like a picture left to bleach in the sun.

"This is where we leave you," the radio man intones. He has a portable microphone and recording deck, which he lugs along like a briefcase. "Under the terms of the ordeal, once you enter the station, you must remain down there alone until dawn, or you will forfeit the prize. This is your last opportunity to leave without facing the horrors below."

"I think I'll be alright," Blue lifts his swag onto his shoulder, and shakes the hand the radio man offers. "See you in the morning." His rangy figure disappears down the long flight of stairs, the yellow circle of lantern light bouncing around the stairwell ahead of him.

"Are you setting someone to watch the gate? In case he wants to get out?" the building superintendent asks, handing over the keys.

"Yes, not to worry, we'll be here," says the radio man and sighs.

———

The station platform looks much like any other. Some tiles have fallen away to reveal the bare bricks, and of course everything has its greasy coating of soot. There's a slight breeze through the tunnel, like hot breath gusting forth from the depths and it comes and goes in eddies carrying the smell of hot metal.

Blue settles himself on a bench, unrolls his swag and takes out the packed supper Reg put together for him. There's a thermos of tea, with a touch of brandy mixed in, and a parcel of bread with butter *and* jam.

"I'm being spoiled rotten," Blue says with a smile.

At the bottom of the brown bag, there's a box of cigarettes. Blue opens it, and a slip of paper uncoils. On it is a drawing of a steamship on curling waves, unmistakably by Reg's neat hand. Blue smiles, tucks the slip of paper into his shirt pocket, right over his heart, lights a cigarette, then pours himself a cup of the fortified tea.

He sits in quiet for a while, aside from the distant rumble of trains in the tunnels. It can't have been more than half an hour when a tinny, faint sound starts up, intermittent, like wind whipping around the eaves, or a dog howling.

"Time for a *reconnoitre*." Blue sets his cup down, flicks away the spent cigarette filter, and stands to pace back and forth across the platform. His steps are light and measured, and he turns his head as he goes, so that he can listen with his good ear for where the sound is coming from. It doesn't take him long to locate the speaker, attached to a wire and a little box contraption, and tucked away at the far edge of the platform.

Blue smiles, lights another cigarette, and retreats to drink his tea and eat his supper. And then, leaning against the back of the chair, he tilts his hat down to partially cover his eyes, and dozes.

———

It was Reg who saw the ad first. He scoffed at it as he leaned over Blue's shoulder to dish eggs and sausages onto his breakfast plate. "That station isn't haunted. It was shut down after a minor electrical fire."

Blue lifted the paper and folded it so he could get a good look at the ad. "Well, don't tell them that. There's prize money involved."

"Ghastly," Reg said, shaking his head as he put the frypan in the sink and returned to the table to tuck into his own breakfast. "And for what? Some dreadful radio programme?"

"Don't know about that," Blue said lightly, "but fifty quid would get you a nice weekend in Paris," he says it *Paree* in his out-West drawl.

Reg smiles, and his foot finds Blue's under the table, his stocking-clad toes skimming over Blue's bare ankle. "Well, now, you do have a strong case, don't you?"

"Hand me a piece of paper, would you? I'm going to write in."

Reg stands, his white shirt is crisp and clean, and his suit trousers sit snug at his narrow waist. Blue leans back in his chair and admires him turning in their narrow kitchen, light from the lace-curtained window painting him in sunshine shades. Together they write the application letter, speaking around mouthfuls of sausage and runny fried eggs.

"You know," Reg says later, up to his forearms in soapy dish-water, "I was thinking about that prize money."

"Mm-hm," Blue intones as he wields the dish-towel.

"Well, we could cover two tickets to Australia with it."

Blue pauses, teacup in his hand halfway to the cupboard. He clears his throat, finishes the movement, and closes the cupboard door. "You said you wanted to stay here."

"I've been thinking about it. The doctor says my father only has a few months left. And after that..." Reg's shoulders droop. Blue wraps his arms around him from behind, and tucks his chin against his shoulder.

"Well, after that," Reg leans back into the embrace, "there's nobody left. Here. I mean. We could move out to Mildura some-where. Near your sister."

Blue places a kiss on Reg's jaw and squeezes him tight. "We'll talk about it later, then. Your old man's a tough one. I wouldn't count him out too soon."

Reg sniffles and nods. On his way to the office that morning, he drops the entry into the post box, and doesn't think of it again until the reply arrives, weeks later.

———

"Do you have your costume?" The radio man has his head down, checking that the spools are properly clipped into place, and none of the wires have come loose.

"Do I really have to wear this?" The technician holds a crum-pled, somewhat dusty white sheet out in front of himself. "Ain't the scare noises enough? No one's going to see this."

"We said there'd be ghosts. We've got to have something," the radio man says impatiently. "Put it on. Hurry up. It's cold out there. You're lucky you get to wear that thing. At least you'll be a bit warmer."

"I'm happy to let you wear it."

"I have to do the recording. Stop arguing, we're running out of time. The noise reel only had two hours on it."

"Don't see why we gotta go through all this rigamarole. We could've faked it up in a studio, instead of being out at all hours playing silly beggars." The technician pulls the sheet over his head, moving it until he can peer out through the roughly cut eye-holes. "Stinks," he says, and then sneezes twice.

"Oh, pull yourself together."

They take a good ten minutes to make their way silently down the stairs to the platform. The technician hikes his sheet up like a Victorian lady holding her skirts.

Below, there's inky darkness, save for the still, faint streak of light from the partly shuttered lantern. Eerie sounds echo and multiply from the tiled walls, and a high, tremulous keen turns into a flock of mournful cries. The hairs on the nape of the radio man's neck bristle and the hand holding the handle of his recording machine grows damp with sweat. And he *knows* it's all fake!

There's a dark shape on the bench seat. It is very still.

The radio man stops a few feet away, and carefully sets down the recording equipment, wiping his palms on the legs of his trousers before he picks up the microphone, and then eases the switch on. They have timed their arrival very well. There's a last swell of creepy noises, and then it fades away to the background crackle of the speaker. The radio man gestures for the technician to move forward.

The technician raises his hands, making the sheet flare out around him, and he lets out the low, guttural moan that he'd been forced to practice dozens of times over the course of the evening's wait. He steps forward, and his shoe strikes the side of the lantern, with a sudden clatter of metal-on-tile, and a crazed play of light flashing as it topples over and rolls away, and then darkness. The aperture has snapped shut.

"Oh, bloody hell!" the technician yelps.

The radio man hisses sharply for quiet, but the technician isn't paying him any heed.

"Oh, Jesus, oh, bloody hell!" there's a fragile, quavering quality to his voice.

The radio man sets the microphone back onto its stand, and closes the space between them, fumbling along the ground for the lantern.

The technician yanks the sheet off and lets it crumple to the ground. He stares fixedly at the dark-on-dark shape on the bench seat. The radio man picks up the lantern and opens the aperture, so that a clear circle of yellow light spills out, illuminating the technician's chalky face.

They look together.

On the bench seat, with his swag spread out underneath him, Blue lies on his back, his head propped up at an awkward angle. His legs are bent at the knee, and one hand is flung out, as though he's reaching for his felt hat, which has fallen to the ground just out of his reach. His other hand is grasping at his collar, his fingers twisted into claws, one button torn loose. His face is the worst part. His mouth his stretched wide, like a terrible silent scream. Pain, or fear, is written into the weathered lines of his face.

The radio man turns the lantern aside and reaches for the technician. He grasps him by the shoulder and uses some force to turn him away from the bench.

"Run up and get to the phone box. Call for an ambulance." He grips his shirt front and gives him a shake when there is no answer. "Quickly, man! The ambulance!"

The technician moves at last, staggering at first, and then breaking into a run back up the stairs to street level. The radio man shivers and turns the lantern back to Blue's unmoving body. He wipes his hands on his trousers again and reaches out to feel along Blue's throat for a pulse.

But he feels only cold.

———

Mason Hawthorne studied creative writing at the University of Wollongong, and has been published in *Kaleidoscope: A Queer Anthology 2023, Unspeakable: a Queer Gothic Anthology*, and *The Monsters We Forgot Anthology*. His novelette, *Earworm*, is available now.

Goodreads | Kofi | Amazon Author Page | masonhawth0rne.tumblr.com

CHAPTER 3
ARTIE, CAN YOU HEAR ME?

SAMANTHA ARTHURS

ARTIE ROLLED down the windows of the old truck as it trundled along the rutted road, creaking and groaning with every roll of the tires. It was cool here in the woods, so much cooler than it had been in the city, and for that he was thankful. It was already hard enough to sleep at night without the sheets sticking to him and noise flooding in from the street below, and he felt hopeful that things would be better at the cabin. It had to be better, and he had to believe that. He was holding on by a thread, and this was a last-ditch effort.

Arthur "Artie" Campbell had come home from the war in February, shell-shocked with a jagged scar that ran from his left shoulder all the way down to his elbow. They had gotten out some of the shrapnel, but not all of it, and it still gave him trouble. He'd tried going right back to work at the docks, but he'd only made it a few weeks. The pain of his injury, coupled with the loud noises and often tight working conditions, was not a good fit. That was when he'd started drinking heavily and sleeping most of the day away. His parents had tried to support him, tried to help him fight his demons, but he was so tired of fighting.

He'd done enough of that in Europe, after all.

Eventually, winter gave way to spring, and then spring opened up into an absolutely hellish summer. Kids were out of school and running around the neighborhood, screaming and playing combat with sticks they found on the sidewalk. It was after he'd bloodied the nose of a twelve-year-old that he was finally seen by his doctor for his condition.

He needed time to recover, to regroup, and he needed to do so somewhere quiet. That was when his father had reached out to aunt Meg, who had gladly given him use of her lake house for as long as he needed. She was down south with her newest husband and wouldn't be making the trek back to New York anytime soon. So, he'd packed up his father's truck and gone, not looking back.

Already it felt better, just being in the quiet. He'd stopped twice—once for gas and once for groceries—and he had no intention of leaving again until he needed more provisions.

It took the better part of an afternoon to reach Provost Lake, a place he hadn't been since childhood, but when he finally arrived, he knew that this would be the place to heal him. There were very few other houses out here, the nearest neighbor a good hike away. It was only him, the small cabin, and the calm water. He breathed in deeply as he stepped out of the car, rolling his shoulders and rubbing the tender one gently as he walked past the small cabin to the edge of the water.

"I can get better," he said aloud to himself, closing his eyes. "I have to. I have to get on with my life, and this is the place where I'll do it."

There was no answer, of course, only the soft sounds of nature surrounding him. He felt his body relaxing for the first time in a long time, relishing the feeling of the tension falling from his muscles. Pulling himself out of his moment of meditation, Artie made his way back to the truck to unload.

The cabin was unlocked, just as Meg had promised it would be, and he lugged in bags of groceries, a rucksack filled with clothes and books, and a picnic basket his mother had made up for him to have for dinner. He busied himself with putting things away. He liked things tidy, finding spots for everything. Clothes went into drawers, food into the cupboards, and then he took the picnic basket outside to sit by the lake again.

After a dinner of cheese, fresh bread, and deli meats, Artie stripped to his skivvies and took a dip in the lake. The water was chilly, despite the summer heat, and it revived him. It felt a bit like being baptized, and he supposed starting over was starting over, whether it was renewing your soul or your sanity. He could use a bit of both after what he'd been through and what he had seen. He swam laps to get away from the thoughts.

Out of fifteen men in his unit, Artie was the only one who had come home on his own two legs and not in a pine box.

He hadn't talked about it with anyone—not his parents and not his doctor. And certainly not Emmie Lou, who'd been his sweetheart since high school all the way up until he'd frightened her to death during one of his episodes.

He didn't blame her for bailing on him. He'd left for the war a boy and had returned a shell. Nobody could love someone like that. Some of his old friends were still around the neighborhood, but he'd avoided them at all costs. There were things a man just couldn't talk about with anyone.

Once he'd taken a cold shower with water from the cistern, Artie settled down in the living room with a book. He flicked on the radio and managed to pick up a station broadcasting one of those serial shows that he never really cared much for. He left it on for the background noise, as the night was even quieter than the day around here. He read until his eyes grew heavy.

This quickly became his routine, and he enjoyed it. He took walks in the woods during the day, or swam in the lake. Once, he took out the old rowboat he found in the shed and caught himself a mess of fish. A week went by in a flash, and though he had a few shakes from the abrupt stoppage of drinking, he felt better than he had in ages. He still woke up at night with the odd nightmare, but even that was fading away.

Until day nine, when everything changed.

Artie settled in after dinner, as usual, with a book and a radio program. He read a couple of chapters and let himself grow drowsy. This time, he didn't make it to bed and fell sound asleep in the chair. The book lay open on his lap, one hand resting on the pages and the other against his stomach. His chest rose and fell peacefully, a soft snore escaping his nose as he shifted a little but didn't wake just yet. No, he didn't stir again until a voice, a familiar one, came through the radio. It sounded distant, like the signal was coming from very far away, tinny and echoing.

Art? Are you there, Art? It's Davey. Can you hear me? Am I coming through?

"Mmph," Art mumbled as his eyes cracked open, blinking sluggishly as he sat up. The book slid from his lap and onto the floor, the sound of it hitting the wood perking him up a little more. He looked at his watch, grunting as he reached to turn the radio off. He'd been dreaming again, or so he thought, though he snatched his hand back quickly as the voice came through again.

Arthur, come in. Come in, Arthur.

Staring at the radio in confusion, Artie's mouth went dry and his tongue felt sticky as he spoke. "Davey? Is that you? No, no. It can't be you, you're dead. You died. I was there." Rising to his feet, he started to pace the floor nervously. He wrung his hands together so hard it stung, palms sweating. "Now I'm hearing voices? Man, I must be even worse off than I thought."

You aren't imagining it, Artie. It's me, Davey. I'm pretty dead, I guess, if this is what dead is. Doesn't really feel like anything. Dark here, though, can't see a thing. Been trying to reach you for ages. We have questions, Artie. So many questions…

"What questions? For who?" Artie asked, the urge to turn the radio off even stronger now. He had to be dreaming this. This wasn't really happening. He was still asleep, and he needed to wake up right now!

For you. We're all here, Artie. Carny, Jones, Ora, all of us. We've just been wondering why us and not you? Why did you get to live?

They shipped me home to my family in pieces, Artie, but you got to walk away. Doesn't seem very fair now, does it?

Artie reached over and turned off the radio quickly, getting to his feet. His heart was pounding, his hands shaking, and his breathing was coming a little heavier now as his fear overtook him.

"No, no, no," he muttered, pacing back and forth. "You dreamed it, Arthur! You dreamed it or you just imagined it."

Kicking the book aside, Artie retreated into the small bedroom and collapsed into bed. "It's from quitting the booze cold turkey, that's all! Mom said this might happen, remember? This is probably just part of it." He repeated to himself as he fell asleep, "I'll be okay. I'll be fine. It's over, it stopped."

Still, he dreamed that night of all the horrible things that had happened to his friends over there. Poor Davey stepping on a German Teller mine. The fine mist of blood spraying all over those nearest to the scene. The pieces of Davey scattering in a nearby tree. His dog tags tangling up in a low branch, and Artie, fighting the urge to scream his lungs out from the sheer horror of it all, working for ten minutes to get them free so they could be sent home with what remained of Davey.

Blood slick on his fingers, growing tacky as it dries.

It was the same for all of them. Davey and the landmine. Carny and Ora being taken down by mortar rounds. Jones putting a bullet in his own head rather than suffering the agonizingly slow death of bleeding out from a wound in his side. And on and on with the rest of the men in their unit. They had all died and somehow, for some unknowable reason, Artie had gotten to live.

———

It was a new day, another chance to get his head clear, and he promised himself that he wouldn't dwell on it. He cut down some firewood for the cookstove and refilled the kindling box, then checked the cistern to make sure it was still holding up well. He propped himself up against a tree trunk and read through the afternoon and then took himself for a long walk to clear his head. He wanted to be nice and tired, to wear himself down so he didn't have a repeat of last night.

He made an early supper, and a storm rolled in from the west, darkening the skies. It was raining by the time he locked up, washing his face in the sink in lieu of a shower. Bypassing the radio, he grabbed his book and retreated into the bedroom, turning on the oil lamp beside the bed and settling in to enjoy the sound of rain on the tin roof until it lulled him to sleep a little earlier than usual.

Lightning lit up the sky and thunder cracked loudly, rumbling overhead. The storm was right on top of him. He didn't hear the radio dial clicking on, scanning through stations until it stopped. Through the static came a voice, just as familiar as Davey's, but with more of a southern sort of twang rarely heard in this part of the country.

Artie? Art? It's me, your old pal Jones. Did you already forget about me? I haven't forgotten about you. How could I? You were standing over me when I put that gun to my head. I begged you to do it for me, but you refused. Chickened out. All I wanted was for you to end my suffering, Art, but you couldn't even do that for me.

Artie felt as though his heart seized right in his chest, hands shaking so hard that the page he'd been in the middle of turning ripped in his fingers.

"Go away," he groaned, trying to sink himself even deeper into the mattress. "You're dead, Jones. You aren't here, you can't be here. I saw you die. Come on, man, don't do this to me."

Don't do this to you? What about me? My wife still cries herself to sleep every night. My kid, he doesn't have a dad anymore, but you... you just get to keep right on. It isn't fair, Artie. We all died except you. What made you so damn special, huh? We all had to go. Why not you? We just want to square up, Art. Make it fair. You know. Deep down, you know it isn't right.

"I'm sorry you died," Artie said, voice barely above a whisper. "I'm real damn sorry, but I ain't sorry that I'm still living. I'm not sorry for that, don't make me feel any more guilt! I feel guilty enough as it is!"

It's easy, Artie. Dying, I mean. It's so much easier than living. Living is the hard part. Just do it, man. Make it right, make it how it should have been. All of us together, the whole unit. Square up. Just do it.

Artie grabbed hold of his pillow and pulled it over his ears, blocking out the sounds of the storm and the voice from the radio. He cried, body heaving with sobs until he finally passed out from sheer exhaustion. This time he slept until late morning, unable to drag himself out of bed. When he did, he made a stop on his way into the kitchen to unplug the radio, before making himself some eggs that he could barely choke down.

That day he sat on the back porch, drinking cold coffee and rocking idly in the old rocking chair. Back and forth, back and forth, mind racing a mile a minute. *How was it right that he'd lived when the rest of the unit had died? Had he missed his turn? Had something gone wrong, an out of step sequence of events, that kept him here instead of sending him off with his brothers in arms?*

He'd catch himself considering what Jones had told him, how easy it would be.

He wondered what in the hell was wrong with him now—he'd gone from paranoia and struggling to fit back into the regular world again, to actually considering cutting short his own life. And for what? Because a ghost on the radio told him to?

More than anything, he wished for a drink, but he hadn't brought any, and the county he was in was dry. Not a single drop of alcohol to be found for purchase. He just drank more coffee and watched the day slip away.

That night, he parked himself in the chair again. This time, he flipped through an old magazine left by his aunt, giving up on the book for the time being. The radio was unplugged, the windows were open to let in the evening breeze, and he was not thinking about all the ways a man could dispatch himself in the middle of the woods.

You're struggling to fit back into the world, because you don't belong there, Art. You weren't ever supposed to make it back. You were supposed to go out with the rest of us. I think deep down that you know and understand that.

Carny's voice now, speaking in that low, calm voice, the type of man who had always been able to talk reason into everyone else around him. He had been among the oldest in their unit, in his mid-thirties, having spent his more formative years working for a traveling carnival. His real name had been Keith, but he didn't mind everyone calling him Carny, and had embraced the moniker. Hearing him on the radio startled Artie a bit less than the others had, despite the fact that the radio wasn't even plugged in, let alone turned on.

"I can't change what happened to any of you," Artie said, throwing the magazine to the floor beside his chair. "Why are you all doing this to me? We were brothers. We cared about each other. Can't you all be happy that at least one of us made it back alive?"

Something went wrong, Artie. It was supposed to be all of us. We aren't in your head, you know. We're here because we need you with us. Never leave a man behind, right? Things won't be right until you're here where you belong. You're never going to get back to how you were before. It will always feel wrong, it will always be off. You need to accept the message here, Artie. Please, brother, you know I'd never lie to you. Join us, it's the only way.

Artie was crying again now, leaning forward in his chair with his head in his hands. He had come to this cabin, to this isolated place, to work on himself. To sort out his demons, to get back on his feet. He wanted to be a productive member of society again, to shake off what the war had done, but what if his friends spoke the truth? What if there would never be normal for him anymore? What if he really was supposed to have joined them?

Getting to his feet, Artie gathered up a few things, the necessary things for a job like this, and then sat down on the floor in front of the old radio. He took in a deep breath and then wrapped his dog tags around his wrist, having kept them in his pocket since coming home.

"Alright, Carny," he whispered, closing his eyes. "Message received, brother. I'll be there with you all soon. Over and out."

————

If you or someone you know is struggling with suicidal thoughts, call or text 988 or visit https://988lifeline.org

————

Samantha Arthurs is the author of the Rag & Bone Trilogy, the Dreadful Seasons Series, and My First Exorcism. She is currently an active member of the HWA, and hosts the *Appalachian Spooky Hour Podcast*. She resides in Appalachia, and is living her best spooky life.

Facebook | Goodreads | Instagram | TikTok | Amazon Author Page | sarthurs.com

CHAPTER 4
OUR SPLENDID LOVES

R.C. CAPASSO

GINNY HURRIED INTO the small living room and turned on the radio. It would take a minute for the set to warm up before the 11:00 episode. She wasn't even sure she wanted to hear what was happening next in the story, but she couldn't bear not knowing.

She pushed aside the coffee table and set up the ironing board near the front window. There was no room in the kitchen. If she set up the board there, she'd have her back end jammed up against the cabinets or the sink. Someday, they would have a little house with a regular kitchen and maybe even a dinette, like the house she grew up in. She could plant flowers in the front yard and vegetables in the back. When Ron got steady work, they'd be able to do so much. He just had to get lucky. Too many men were looking for work now.

She wasn't complaining, of course. She loved her life. A married woman for almost a year now. She and Ron had their own apartment, because they wanted an independent life, not living with her parents or his, for goodness' sake. She loved keeping house. The neighborhood wasn't fancy, but it wasn't bad, and she still felt a thrill every time Ron came home to her after his day. A thrill of pleasure and even a little of nerves, if she had to be honest. She had dreamed about marriage for so long, but she probably should have prepared more, to be a better cook and housekeeper. A better manager with a budget. There was so much to think about, even in a little apartment where you could barely turn around.

That's why she loved her radio. It was so good to hear other voices while she spent the day alone. Her favorite radio program had been so much fun at first, with its beautiful, talented characters, all doctors and nurses living exciting lives and flirting among themselves. They enjoyed first one love, then another. Ginny didn't need all that romance; she had Ron. But it was fun to imagine going out with a sophisticated and darkly mysterious surgeon one night and a brash, honest intern full of life and laughter the next. Even the intrigues had been entertaining, melodramatic, almost comical in their intensity. It was just innocent fun, an escape.

Of course, she had to imagine all the settings, but somehow that made it better. Movies were wonderful, but with just the voices from the radio, it was easier to slip into the story. She could imagine herself as Lana, the surgical nurse, and Ron as the ex-Army doctor, Major Gary Masters. The actor even sounded like Ron. It was uncanny.

If only the program writers could have kept the story lines happier. You don't want to escape to a world that's too much like reality.

She pulled a damp shirt from the laundry basket and spread it out on the ironing board. She actually loved doing Ron's shirts. The faint hiss as the hot metal met the moist cloth. How the shirt looked so neat on its hanger, reminding her of his shoulders and his chest. This was something she could do well for him, just more proof that they belonged to each other.

The radio hummed, then a deep voice intoned, "Deluxe Soaps welcomes you to another episode of *Our Splendid Loves*. It is night as we return to a darkened hall in Mercy Hospital, where

Dr. Gary Masters draws Nurse Lana Reed aside for a chilling revelation."

Ginny stretched to turn up the volume so that the smooth, masculine voice filled the room.

"You can't say anything. Promise me."

Lana replied in a whisper. "But Gary, I don't understand. It was a simple mistake. They happen in surgery. The man's wounds were just too severe."

The doctor's voice dropped to a growl. "I could have saved him. You know I could."

"You have amazing skills, Gary. You're the best surgeon in the country. But the poor man's time had come."

Ginny imagined a face, handsome but etched with deep lines along the mouth. Marks left by a war that changed men.

"I decide a man's time."

Ginny caught her breath.

Lana's voice coaxed. "Darling, you can't blame yourself for this."

A heavy chord sounded in the background.

"Blame myself? Why should I do that? I'm quite proud of my decision."

Ginny nearly burned herself on the iron as she stood it up. The smell of hot cloth almost sickened her.

"Proud? Gary, I don't understand."

"Don't you, Lana? Don't you, really? Because I understand everything. I know you loved that man, the one lying dead on my operating table. Pete Kelley. A war profiteer. And your secret love. I know about treachery, Lana. And I know how to handle it!"

"Gary! No!"

An organ swelled, and Ginny rushed to cut off the sound. It was horrible. Why did they make that wonderful doctor a killer? The story was supposed to be sweet and romantic. It was all supposed to be lovely.

She stared at the white shirt, half pressed on the ironing

board. She made her fingers lift it up, positioning it so she could work on the sleeves. This story had to be a mistake. Tomorrow's episode would explain everything. Maybe the doctor was just testing Lana.

Heavy footsteps thudded up the stairs. Ron was back early today.

Ginny clutched at her apron for an instant, then touched her hair.

As Ron entered, one glance told her that he hadn't gotten that job, either.

———

"I think I might stop listening to *Our Splendid Loves*," Ginny said and took a sip from her cooling coffee.

Carole, her neighbor from across the landing, stared at her. "Why? I think it's wonderful! I can't wait to hear which intern Nurse Sinclair picks for her date on the boat trip. I'm betting on Jimmy, because he's such a laugh."

Ginny frowned as she laid down her cup. She didn't remember anything about a boat trip. "I don't like the story about Dr. Gary and the man who died during surgery."

"What man? I must have missed that. But you gotta love Dr. Gary. He has the most mellifluous voice. And look at him." Carole pulled a radio magazine out of her purse. "He's gorgeous! Not everyone on the radio looks like that."

Ginny risked a glance. She'd seen the actor before. "He looks like my Ron."

"He...what?" Carole choked on her coffee and took a minute to cough. "Wow, you are in love."

As Ginny looked up, hurt in her eyes, Carole muttered. "Well, same number of eyes and a nose and chin, I guess." She fingered her cup. "So, how is Ron doing, anyway?"

"Oh, he's fine. He's doing well. He's looking for work. He

goes out every day. Sometimes he gets something for a day or two, but....you know."

"Yeah, I know." Carole's man was older. He'd had a desk job in the Army and came back to a management position waiting for him. "Len tried to get him into the office, you know. It's just..."

"It wasn't the right fit for Ron." Ginny smiled, her voice light. Ron had aspirations, and she wasn't going to ask him to settle for just anything.

"That's exactly what Len said. It just wasn't the right fit. He said that Ron is plenty smart and, you know, always looks neat and presentable." She smiled and winked. "'Course, we both know how much a wife has to do with that, keeping his clothes just so."

"I don't do anything, really. Ron just has very high standards for himself." She traced a line on the tablecloth with her finger.

Carole tilted her head a bit as she placed her cup back in its saucer. "Yeah, high standards are good, of course. But then maybe if Ron tried to be a little more..."

Ginny's fingers stilled. "More what?"

Carole had the sense to blush slightly. "Well, less angry, I guess. Something went wrong one day, something little, and he called Len a few names." She fixed her eyes on Ginny. "He kinda flies off the handle. You know."

Ginny pushed back from the table. "No, I don't know. Ron is fine."

———

"Lana, you have to listen to me." Nurse Sinclair's normally high, giggling voice was suddenly sharp. "Dr. Masters is coming for you."

"For me? But why?"

"He says he knows about you and Len."

Ginny stood frozen, one hand clutching her apron. This was

ridiculous. The program wasn't fun anymore. It wasn't romantic. She didn't need to hear this, not with everything else she had to think about. But she let the voices run on. It was as if she *had* to listen to them, as if they were talking to her.

"Len? My neighbor? But he means nothing to me!"

"Tell that to the doc. He says you and Len have been cheating on him. He claims Len is a deserter, and that Len is going to report him for killing that man he operated on last week. He thinks Len is out to get the doc's medical license revoked. Masters says he's going to get you both."

"Get us?"

"Lana, he left surgery carrying a scalpel!"

Steps rang out along the echoing hall of the empty hospital as the last notes of the organ throbbed.

Ginny didn't even stop to switch off the sound. Slippered feet scuffing across the rug, she forced herself to turn toward the bedroom. Last night, Ron had taken down that box from the closet shelf. The one with the German gun he brought back from the war. He wouldn't have wanted her watching him, so she'd slipped away into the bathroom. Was the gun still in its box? Or did he want it for something?

As a sprightly, jangly commercial scratched across her nerves, steps plodded up the staircase outside. She'd have to check the box later.

Ron was coming back early again.

That was not a good sign. Her throat tightened as her eyes fastened on the door. She could only smooth her apron and brace herself to smile.

———

R .C. Capasso loves stories of hope and imagination. When not writing, R. C. travels, reads, and studies Italian. Short stories have appeared in *Bewildering Stories, Literally Stories, Zooscape, Teleport Magazine, Spaceports and Spidersilk,* and *Fiction on the Web, Flights of Fantasy (Iron Faerie Publishing),* as well as online and print anthologies.

Amazon Author Page

CHAPTER 5
RED ROVER, RED ROVER
TREVOR JAMES ZAPLE

ECHO ISLAND IS AN IMPORTANT OBSERVATION POST OF KOLI POINT. WE CANNOT ALLOW THE JAPANESE TO HAVE THIS POST. THIS BUNKER IS A KEY POINT IN THE LANDINGS.

———

JIMMY KOWALSKI'S biggest complaint about Echo Island was that all the channels on the radio sounded the same. Most of it was just howling snowstorm static. He hated that, especially when the rain was drumming like Gene Krupa on the cement roof over his head. The two combined themselves in a fashion that distressed him. If he let his mind wander, if he unspooled his ears and let himself really *listen*, would there be voices in the falling of the rain, as well? Kowalski thought there might be.

His grandmother would have forked the Evil Eye if she'd heard it, and told him that the words he thought he was hearing were the words of all the devils of Hell telling him to get saved or get lost. He wasn't entirely sure she would have been wrong.

Rolling the dial had been Peterson's job, but Peterson had left the bunker two days earlier, leaving Kowalski the last Marine.

He wasn't sure if Peterson had received his instructions or if he'd just had enough of the whole thing. He didn't blame the radio operator if it was the latter. Ever since they'd landed on the island twelve days ago, nothing had gone right. The whole mission was a circus.

If Lieutenant Ambrose hadn't been among the first to receive his instructions, maybe they could have maintained some semblance of control. *Maybe.* Kowalski could be honest now— who was left in the bunker to report him? It was pretty clear that Ambrose had been the son of somebody important and clever, rather than somebody clever himself. He could have just admitted that he didn't know why the brass had insisted on taking this little nothing spit of an island. They were all jarheads; he just had the commission. Sure, you could throw a rock and hit Guadalcanal, but surely a bomber run off the *Enterprise* could have dealt with it more effectively than sending forty Marines in.

There was nothing coming across the radio but that almost-speech, just as it'd been since the beginning. Peterson claimed the storm was the reason they couldn't raise home on the radio, but when the storm finally cleared up thirty-six hours later, they still couldn't call anybody.

Nothing but the static and the rain.

And the unprompted, incoming messages to "come on over."

————

Kowalski grabbed his bolt-action rifle and grabbed a wicked-looking knife off the provisions table. Several knives, the radio, and about twenty cans of food were all that had been there when they'd walked in. The food was mostly gone now. He thought there might be a couple meals in Corporal Miller's pack. Miller had left it when he ran out into the night when his call had come in.

Stepping out of the bunker, he was careful to examine each direction slowly and carefully, aiming down the rifle's iron sights and straining to see any movement, no matter how slight. He walked back into the bunker, his skin prickling. It was like something was watching him. There was nothing to watch him, though. There was nothing. There never *had* been anything.

Back when they first arrived, the patrols they had done confirmed to them that they were the only inhabitants of Echo Island. Several of them had been of the opinion that if Echo Island had only had some food, some private huts, and some girls, they could happily spend the rest of the war there. Kowalski had never believed it, still couldn't believe it. Clearly, there was something on the island. He wasn't just alone and paranoid. The others hadn't just walked into the ocean.

He walked down to the spot that overlooked the beach and stared out into the ocean. Black smoke rose out of the jungle cover that was his view of Guadalcanal. Nothing good was ever happening where that kind of coal-black smoke rose from.

He suddenly remembered standing in his grandfather's field when he was five. This was when they'd lived in Shelby, Montana, back when they'd still had land and a family business. They had awoken one morning to find a pall of black smoke rising from the north, up in Canada. He'd been fascinated with the way it billowed and spread, covering the deep endless blue of the sky, over the vicious golden coin of the sun. Later, eavesdropping on his father and mother, he learned that a small village near Medicine Hat had burned to the ground. Dozens of people had died. He'd imagined the blackened stumps of the town, the scorched corpses littering the streets. Had dreamed of it ever since.

In the sky came a roar, and he craned his neck up to watch a pair of Wildcats buzz over him. They flew out toward the main island, their fuselages glinting hard and blue in the beating hot sun. Halfway between Kowalski's position and the island, they veered off in different directions. Gunfire echoed down from above and Kowalski saw that a Japanese Zero was chasing down the Wildcat that had veered off to the right. The Wildcat pilot tried to bank suddenly, but the pilot of the Zero had the nerves and the reaction time, and a volley of gunfire slammed into the Wildcat's tail. Kowalski watched it spiral down into the island, near to where the black smoke was billowing up from. The Zero and the remaining Wildcat moved further down the coast of Guadalcanal, while Kowalski watched the spot where the victim had gone down. A few minutes later, another cloud of coal-black smoke formed from the general area of the crash.

Red Rover, Red Rover, he thought and shivered.

———

His friend Jackson had been the first to be called. Jackson was a rock for Kowalski. He was always positive, grinning his big wide smile and proclaiming that the faster they cleared up the Pacific, the faster he could get back to his real business—sleeping with Kowalski's mom. Jackson had been from Queens and had come up far differently than Kowalski. Still, they'd been friends since the first night on Parris Island. Kowalski remembered the moment Jackson was called over. Sometimes it was reenacted with eerie accuracy in his dreams.

They'd been huddled in the bunker, waiting for the rain to finally stop. Peterson was slowly circling through the radio dial, hoping to find a frequency he could use to call back home. Suddenly the howling stopped, and it took them all a moment to clue into that, even Peterson. He seemed shocked that he'd actually hit upon something active. The dead silence that followed was more unnerving than the endless static had been. Peterson picked up the hand receiver and spoke into it.

"This is Echo Platoon, over."

"Red Rover, Red Rover," a calm, flat voice replied. "We call Private Jackson over."

None of the jarheads gathered in the bunker made a sound. The absurdity of the reply seemed horribly funny to Kowalski, and he had to bite his lip to prevent a peal of crazy-sounding laughter.

"Come again?" Peterson said.

"Coordinates H8, Echo Platoon," the voice replied. Kowalski thought it sounded like the voice a dog would use if it were given the power of speech—like something unused to speaking. Peterson flapped open his lips to respond, but the static returned, louder. More than a few Marines shouted in surprise when it did.

Lieutenant Ambrose had formed a squad to investigate H8 on the map. That had turned out to be the circular clearing, sending Corporal Baker, with a couple other privates, and Jackson, who had volunteered immediately. Jackson had been so excited, like he'd won the lottery. Kowalski would normally have volunteered alongside Jackson, but it was as though a little voice had spoken somewhere deep in his stomach and told him that he'd be a fool to do it. He'd held himself back, and when the squad had failed to return after twelve hours, he'd balanced equal weights of satisfaction and guilt within himself.

Ambrose and the remaining corporals had whispered furiously to each other throughout the night, once everyone realized that Miller and Jackson and the rest weren't coming back. Kowalski hadn't been able to sleep, and he'd listened to them argue when they thought they couldn't be heard. The corporals wanted to mount a raid on the H8 position, claiming it was either an artillery position the scouts had missed or it was one of those dug-in tunnel systems he'd heard the Japanese had riddled all their islands with. They were convinced that Miller and Jackson's disappearance meant there was something the Japanese were protecting out there. Ambrose had refused all night, claiming they needed to wait for reinforcements that even Kowalski knew weren't showing up anytime soon.

Around dawn, the radio crackled. Everyone woke up. No one had been sleeping that deeply.

"Red Rover, Red Rover," the flat, oddly disjointed voice said again. "We call Lieutenant Ambrose over."

No one spoke for ten minutes. The Lieutenant and the corporals spent some time staring at each other and finally Sergeant Williams cleared his throat. If the Lieutenant wasn't going to answer the call, perhaps he could. Ambrose, the coward, had agreed.

Williams took Mason and five privates out to scout the location. The rest of the platoon huddled down around their packs and waited for them to return. Rain blew through off and on. They tried to talk about what they thought was happening on Guadalcanal as they sat there on their hands, but the topic grew boring at first and then, as the hours stretched and Williams and company remained out, it became dreadful.

Ambrose went out to take a leak in the night. When the light of dawn flooded into the bunker, he was nowhere to be found.

———

Kowalski saw the message on the wall as he approached the bunker door. It wasn't something he tried to look at—he actively attempted to ignore it, in fact—but it was ostentatious and written in smeared red. *We called you over.* He tried not to think about whose life had been given to write that message.

Back inside the bunker, he took inventory of the foodstuffs. It passed the time. He figured, with some rough calculations in his head, that he had about a week's worth of food. Surely, someone would come looking for them before that week was over. It was "a vital observation post for the invasion," after all. Corporal Mason had said so often enough.

He went back out to the beach several times that day, staring out at Guadalcanal with binoculars. He saw no movement but the smoke. The first source had dissipated into a sullen smear in the sky. The second was still puffing upward, although with less force as the hours wore on. He heard more airplane engines, far off and out of sight.

In the late afternoon he blinked and for a lingering moment in time he thought himself back on that hard, sun-dried plain near the Canadian border, watching a village burn at a distance. Then he was back at the edge of a Pacific jungle, staring out at the rippling blue ocean and another jungle in the distance.

———

There had been twenty-eight men left after Corporal Baker's team, then Williams team, then Ambrose went missing. Between the night that Ambrose had disappeared, and the moment Peterson had bolted out the door a couple of days ago, the radio had crackled and spoken twenty-one more times. It had always said the same thing:

Red Rover, Red Rover.

They had all known better than to answer that call, had spoken quietly amongst themselves about it and then, closer to the end, out loud to the platoon. It was death to answer that call. They would stay in the bunker and defend it until reinforcements showed up. There had always been something in their faces, though. Kowalski, who had never received his instructions, watched them all carefully and saw the twitching, the muscle tics in their cheeks and the grinding of their teeth.

Obeying orders was what they did, after all. You could question them privately, but you could never simply disobey them. One by one, they had slipped out once their instructions came through on the radio:

Come on over.

None of them knew what was waiting for them, but all of them had gone. Most had gone by themselves, but some—men who had been solid friends, men who had ensured each other's survival in previous campaigns, in different jungles—went together.

———

He'd played the game before, of course. They all had, on school yards, that, for all their wildly different surroundings, had been more or less the same. You formed two lines, and one side called a name over. That person then broke ranks and ran for the enemy line, feet flying over asphalt or beaten grass. The goal was to break through the linked arms of the enemy, driving with such force that interlaced fingers came apart and arm strength failed.

Come on over.

He ate self-consciously from the dwindling supplies, his shoulders tense. Twenty minutes later, it began to rain again.

Some time in the night, he opened his eyes into a blackness so complete it seemed as though it had always been. The rain thrummed against the concrete overhead in waves and then in little spurts, driven by wild winds into a mockery of Morse code. He lay on his back in a worn, uncomfortable cot, listening to the rain. After a while, the words form, and then he can't unhear them, can't fathom how he didn't always understand them. The rain told him the secret names for God, each one less pronounceable than the last. He stared into the darkness in rapture, repeating each one silently, his lips forming each syllable with careful love.

When the rain falls silent, the radio crackles.

"*Red Rover, Red Rover,*" the uncanny voice said again, "*We call Jimmy Kowalski over.*"

Kowalski closed his eyes, but it made no difference.

He lay still on his cot, trying to breathe shallowly, quietly. The orders were stupid. It was a child's game. He clenched his hands into fists and burrowed them into his sides, letting the unpleasant sensation cover for the shaking fear that was filling him. Orders. You heard, and you obeyed. His knuckles dug deeper into the bottom of his rib cage, the organs carefully arranged in the area protesting at the unnecessary treatment.

We called you over. Four words smeared in dripping blood on the weathered concrete above the bunker door.

We called you over.

"Echo Island is an important observation post of Koli Point."

"We call Jimmy on over. Come test our might and despair. You, too, can be smoke rising from the quiet sun-soaked jungle, a whole town burning in you, Jimmy. Come now, because we call you over."

He moved faster than thought, scrambling for his flashlight and then gathering up his Springfield rifle and his pack. The bunker door squealed loudly as he opened it, and he nearly bolted for the beach. It was only by carefully corralling his fraying nerves that he made his feet move one by one into the dense black jungle night.

The wet ground caused his steps to make unwholesome sucking sounds. Rainwater dripped steadily from the trees he walked under, spattering onto his helmet like tricky tapping fingers. There were no bird calls or animal noises of any kind. The surrounding jungle held its breath as he walked through it, watching. Waiting.

He stopped often to consult the map. In the darkness, he had to make his best guess as to where he was, but kept going anyway. He had already broken the ranks. Even if he was the last, the very last jarhead on Echo Island. He was on course, speeding towards those interlocked hands, those muscular arms bound together stronger than steel.

Out of nowhere, the trees let up, and there was nothing. He skidded to a halt and shone his flashlight here and there, but it was just smooth, flat dirt. He stopped, knelt, and affixed the bayonet to the barrel of the rifle. The flashlight went into the bracket on his pack, and the rifle was clutched white-knuckled in both hands. He followed the empty clearing around and found that it formed a perfect circle.

"I'm here," he whispered. "I've come."

The ground erupted in thick black smoke, like a coal field caught ablaze. Kowalski choked and sputtered, moving toward the edge of the clearing. If he made it back to the bunker, he would be safe. It was the only clear directive in his head.

At the edge of the clearing, he found bodies standing upright, their arms strung together with barbed wire. These guardians were clearly dead. To his right was Corporal Miller, missing half his head, the other half oozing out a thick, clotted black slime. Further down the line to his left was Peterson, his lower jaw missing and his tongue lolling down out of his throat like a dog trying to beat the damning August heat. They were all there. This is where they'd all gone to. The harsh glare of the flashlight illuminated a cacophony of death surrounding him. The light whipped back and forth, a sentry sure of intrusion, the strobe-like flash of movement searing panic inside of him.

He spun and ran. On the other end of his path was Lieutenant Ambrose, his mouth slack and lifeless. His eyes had been gouged out and replaced with leaves stuffed into the sockets. Black blood oozed out of them, collecting on the ends of the leaves and then dripping down his face in thin black dribbles. Kowalski approached him cautiously and the officer's face came to a hideous half-life, the seeping eyes tracking and locking onto his face.

"I came on over, eventually," Ambrose said. His voice had been reduced to a whisper, like sand blown over eroded stone. "We all do. You'll be part of this, Kowalski."

Kowalski ran again and found Jackson at the end of his path this time. His friend's face was whole, but there was a jagged, gaping hole punched through his chest. The light of Kowalski's flashlight shone through it into the dark jungle beyond.

"Come on over, Jimmy," he croaked. It reminded Kowalski of the calls of lizards he'd heard since shipping off to the Pacific: low, ragged, inhuman.

"We call Jimmy over."

He ran from point to point and found no gaps in the line. The entire platoon was there, tied arm in arm with glinting barbed wire, flesh torn and oozing where the barbs cut into them. He fled finally to the center and crouched in the sterile brown dirt. Smoke billowed around him, smelling of charred wood and melting glass and the mouth-watering temptation of cooked pork. It choked him. He knew he had to do something soon or it would overcome him entirely. He looked up at the bayonet gleaming in the artificial light.

"Red Rover, Red Rover," he whispered. His fellow Marines moaned and chittered in the dark around him.

He rose to his feet, hefting the Springfield rifle before him. It was time to follow his orders.

We called you over.

With a war cry that shredded his throat raw, he charged into the line; the bayonet held out before him as any primitive spear would by any man sent to engage the enemy.

———

He came to on the beach in the glimmering light of a new dawn. A man in amphibious landing gear crouched over him. Kowalski opened his eyes just as the soldier was slapping him.

"Wake up, buddy," the man said.

"Stop," Kowalski moaned. "I am awake. I've been awake—"

He sat up, staring around. A landing craft stood beached on the shore, two or three squadrons of Marines standing around it talking and pointing up at the bunker. He shivered and fought back laughter. He thought they might put him out of his misery altogether, hearing what laughter might issue from his screaming throat.

"Where's the rest of the platoon, Private?" the man asked. He had a corporal's insignia on his arm. Kowalski shook his head, and the movement made his stomach hurt. He concentrated on that and then, whoops, there it was: a little bit of that mad laughter leaked out before he could clamp his lips down.

The corporal gave him an odd look and tilted Kowalski's chin back with two fingers.

"Where's the rest of the platoon?" he asked again, gently this time. Kowalski shook his head and more of that laughter came out, a peal now, enough that the jarheads standing by the landing craft looked over with wary expressions.

"They received their orders," he said, trying to fight down the laughter and failing. It was impossible, like stopping an orgasm once it had started. The peals of laughter spurted out even through his pressed lips.

"They got their orders on the radio, and they went over. I'm the last one, the very last one."

The corporal stood up and considered the vacant concrete bunker above them, his eyes thoughtful. On the gritty island sand, Kowalski continued to laugh, abandoning all pretense of keeping it locked down.

If you enjoyed this, check out Trevor James Zaple's other story in the Sinister Century *series. Jimmy Kowalski's story continues in "Sorry Girls, He's Married" in* Watch: A Disturb Ink Books Anthology.

Trevor James Zaple is a web developer with a youth-focused educational non-profit. His work has most recently appeared in *The Brazenhead Review, Bleed Error,* and *Quill & Crow's Bleak Midwinter.* He lives in the other London with his wife and daughters.

Facebook | Goodreads | Instagram | Threads | Amazon Author Page | trevorzaple.com

GRAY   RYAN   ZAPLE

WATCH

EDITED BY H. DAIR BROWN

A DISTURB INK BOOKS ANTHOLOGY

WATCH

TERRIFYING TV | THE 1960S

DISTURB INK BOOKS

EDITED BY
H. DAIR BROWN

Published by Disturb Ink Books, an imprint of 79 Franklin Press, LLC.

www.79franklinpress.com

First North American ebook edition September 2024

ASIN (ebook): B0DF6SLWBV

Cover Image: Aden Lumbley

Designed by: H. Dair Brown

Proofread by: Jon T. Macy

❀ Created with Vellum

*For fans of the kinds of scary stories that you have to read (or watch!)
while peeking between your fingers*

NOTES

Because we are fortunate enough in this collection to have writers from all over the world contributing to *Sinister Century*, you'll see a variation in the spelling of some words from story to story. The editor has chosen to respect the spelling of the country in which the author writes.

———

CHAPTER 1
A QUERY FOR THE QUARRY

RUSSELL GRAY

GREG WATERS SMILED as he escorted his client through the hotel lobby toward the front parking. The woman was in full glow mode after the wrap meeting, her cheeks flushed beneath a light amount of makeup.

"Holding these meetings at a hotel was brilliant," the woman said. "I never knew you could *rent* a ballroom. It beat sitting in a generic conference room each day, that's for sure. The food was amazing—you were amazing. There's no way I could've written ten articles in a single month without you."

Greg chuckled, "I appreciate the thought, but I'm merely a translator of your thoughts on their way to the page. You're the creative force behind the project."

She swatted at his arm and pursed her lips in a wry smile. "Always so humble."

"My wife trained me well."

"Oh, do tell Betty hello for me. I swear, her show taught me more about cooking than my own mother."

"She'll be thrilled to hear that." He held the lobby door for her and then reached for a business handshake. He accepted a full hug in its place.

"I'll call you when I decide on my next project!" She climbed into her car with a small wave.

Another job finished, another satisfied client. Greg adjusted his tie and basked in the late afternoon sun. It was time to celebrate.

———

Greg breathed deeply, enjoying the rich smell of the quarry waters. The moon was full, making it a perfect night to navigate the surrounding woods and treacherous, rocky footing at the quarry's edge. The quarry was no longer mined for limestone, but it had become a popular date spot for young folk to make out and skinny dip. Over the past five years, it also served as a dumping ground for victims of the Quarryman Killer.

At this moment, the Quarryman was enjoying a night out at the theater, surrounded by alibis. In his place, Greg had acquired a girl with appropriately pale skin and dark hair, strangled her, removed her clothing and her eyes, then sank the body into the quarry depths.

As usual, Greg was only the workhorse for the project. The Quarryman was the creative force, but the artistry of it transfixed Greg. The pale skin sinking beneath inky black water, framed by cold and gray rock. He wondered if the Quarryman felt the same way. Or did all great artists eventually find their projects mundane?

Voices drifted and echoed across the quarry. Some giggles. Greg enjoyed one last moment under the moon and then faded away into the trees.

———

Greg leaned against his kitchen counter and watched the portable television. His wife's cooking and variety show aired in the morning's local programming block. She was walking the audience through the finishing touches of making an omelet. Truly, an artist in her own way.

He sipped his coffee and savored the texture and earthy notes of the blend in his mouth for a few seconds before swallowing. The aftertaste spread pleasantly across the back of his throat. Of course, he'd followed his wife's simple pour-over brewing method. Greg imagined her narrating his process for the show. "Three magic ingredients," she'd say. "Water...fresh and carefully measured. Coffee...the proper grind, and carefully measured. And time...carefully measured. A simple recipe for perfect coffee." It was only through the TV, but Greg felt like they spent breakfast together.

The show ended and moved into a news segment, so Greg turned the set off. He stared into his coffee mug. Inky black liquid framed by white ceramic. He added a sugar cube and watched it gradually sink to the depths. Pictured dark hair billowing in the water and empty sockets staring back at him. He took a deep sip and savored it. Enjoying these peaceful moments between jobs was vital. There was a never-ending demand for Greg's various services.

The wall phone began ringing, and Greg sighed. After answering the line, he heard his wife's voice on the other end and smiled.

"Good morning, Mrs. Waters... Mm-hmm, it *was* a late night last night. Sorry I missed you this morning. You could have woken me up, you know... Mm-hmm... Oh, you enjoy my sleeping face? I see how it is... Yes, I did. You were fantastic, as always. I'm sure even I could make a perfect omelet now... Oh? Okay. Guess I'm not the only busy one... I'll take care of that this afternoon... Okay... Love you too, Bets. Bye-bye."

Greg ended the call and reached for his coffee. He was mid-sip when the phone rang again. Greg chuckled and pulled it from the cradle. His wife probably remembered something else for the To-Do list.

"Did you forget—"

"I know what you did."

The words spilled from the receiver, heavy with anger. Greg waited a moment, but no follow-up came. Just a slight rumbling in the background of the phone line.

"I believe you might have the wrong—"

"Don't play dumb, Greg Waters. I know what you did. I even have pictures."

Greg had long wondered how he would react to getting caught. He was surprisingly calm.

"I'm afraid I still don't know what you're referring to, Mr....?"

The voice on the line chuckled darkly. "You don't know? I'm referring to what you did yesterday. It was brazen. Practically in plain sight. It's like you wanted to get caught."

Greg slid into a nearby chair. This might be a problem.

But why was this man calling him instead of going to the police? Something didn't add up. How clear could a picture taken in the woods be, even on a moonlit night? No, the pictures didn't matter. Even eyewitness testimony would cause problems. Back to the other question: why call him and not the police?

This man wanted something.

"What do you want?"

"Heh, good. We're on the same page. Honestly, I don't even blame you. You're no different from me, no better than me, thinkin' you can get away with it. A sickness. That's what it is. You're sick, Greg. But that's okay. I may not be a doctor, but I believe in medical privacy...for a price."

Greg frowned. This was going in a strange direction. Maybe a client from his second job gave out his info, and this was an interview or vetting process. But good business is based on trust, and this wasn't getting off on the right foot. What was that rumbling sound in the background?

"And what's the price for maintaining my privacy?"

"Not much. Not much at all in the grand scheme of things. Especially for a guy like you, what with your celebrity wife and all. Probably just pocket money for a guy like you. 10K. Cash. In a bag."

What the hell? Run-of-the-mill extortion? Disappointing. He had expected someone trying to milk a *pro bono* contract for a preliminary job. But just money? And why mention his wife? Intimidation? Something was missing. He heard a bell chime twice over the line. Was the guy calling from a service station?

"This whole situation must be a shock, I know. And I'm a caring guy, so I'll give you two days to get your head right and round up the money. Two days, and I'll tell you where to deliver the bag. See you soon, buddy boy."

The call ended, leaving Greg to consider his options. The longer the conversation lasted, the more the voice on the line changed, the anger giving way to arrogance and self-satisfaction. This payment would only be the first of many. How did it end? Did the guy think Greg would make payments for the rest of his life? Risky play to extort a killer.

'No different than me. No better than me.' The other man had to be a killer as well. Had to be. And was just lining his pockets while making his move. That's why the police weren't involved. Wouldn't be involved. Was the Quarryman setting him up to take the fall? The alibi wasn't enough?

Greg remained still with the phone in his hand. That rumbling in the background. Combined with the bell. He smiled when it finally clicked. It looked like Greg's To-Do list had grown longer.

———

Greg pulled into the Shell service station and eased into the spot alongside a pump, smiling as his tires rolled over the ground cable and caused a bell to chime twice. A young man in a pump jockey uniform jogged over.

"Afternoon, Mr. Waters. What can I do for ya today?"

"Just the usual, Jimmy."

The boy gave a tip of his hat and began pumping fuel. Greg looked past him to where the railroad tracks cut through town.

"Still training your private eye skills, Jimmy?"

The boy flashed a crooked grin. "You bet, sir. Gonna be just like Dick Tracy in a few more years."

"Here's a quick quiz for you, then. How many people have used that payphone over there today?"

The boy looked up at his brow line for a second and counted to himself. "Eleven, so far."

"That's good. You have to stay observant. You never know what little detail might be the connection you need. Here's a harder question: What can you tell me about the man who used that phone this morning a little after 7:30, right when the train was passing by?"

Jimmy finished pumping and hung the nozzle up. "Ah, the silver Chevy. Sounded like it needed a tune-up. The plate was 12A3434. The guy was wearing a black suit but with a brown tie. Had a creepy smile on his face while talking on the phone. I wondered if he was callin' his mistress or something."

Greg raised an eyebrow.

The boy's eyes grew wide, and his face reddened. "Uh, I mean, I'm sure he was an okay fella. Don't mean to speak poorly of any customer."

Greg laughed. "Don't worry about it, Jimmy. I'm sure the guy was a right pervert if you say he was. I trust your memory." He handed the boy a $5 bill. "Keep the change. Start saving up for when you open your detective agency."

Jimmy took the money with a smile and tipped his hat again before jogging back into the station. Dick Tracy might have a fancy watch and other gadgets, but Jimmy had a photographic memory. Mr. Silver Chevy picked the wrong pay phone. As Lefty Gomez always said, "I'd rather be lucky than good." Unfortunately for Mr. Silver Chevy, Greg was both.

———

The sun touched the horizon as Greg pulled into a typical suburban neighborhood and parked along the curb. He sat and watched for a few minutes. There was just enough pedestrian traffic to cover the comings and goings of a person any day or time of the week, but not enough to hinder any late-night adventures. It was an ideal neighborhood for a killer to live in. It answered a few of Greg's questions, but too many remained.

A little over a block away was a modest ranch-style house belonging to a man named Morris Cummings. A silver Chevy Corsair, license plate 12A3434, also belonging to Morris Cummings, sat in the driveway.

Greg had helped a detective named Michaels with his memoirs some years ago. While working on the book and over the years after, they talked about quite a few things that never made it onto the pages. Things like how much more comprehensive an insurance company's database was compared to law enforcement's for identifying people and how easy it was to develop relationships with certain people at an insurance company. The detective had joked that insurance agents led to more arrests than call relay tracing ever did. Discretion being a cornerstone of his business, Michaels was always great about helping Greg without asking too many questions.

Greg left his car and went for a stroll, relishing the smell of fresh-cut lawns while smiling and waving at the occasional pedestrian walking their dog. Most residents were in for the night, likely tuning in to their favorite show after dinner. He eventually circled to the side of Morris's house. Minimal outdoor lighting. No security mirrors angled toward the front door. No prickly bushes to keep peepers from the windows. Greg had to be missing something. Peeking through a window revealed a living room dimly lit by a pole lamp and the flickering glow of a television. A man smoked in a recliner. The man's face was average, nondescript. The kind of guy that wouldn't look out of place in most settings with appropriate attire. Ideal for a killer.

Greg navigated the backyard quietly, peeking through

windows as he went. Nobody in the back bedroom. Basic double-hung window. No dowel in the track for added security. He looked over the yard one last time. No water dish or dog house. Still, there might be one indoors.

The back door was a simple design with a standard lock. He picked it quickly and eased the door open an inch. No hint of squeaking from the hinges. The man was practically inviting people into his home. The back door led into a kitchen with minimal food smells, mostly from the trash. Store-bought Salisbury steak dinner. No skittering sound of nails or paws on the hardwood floors, nothing but the TV's faint droning.

Greg slipped inside and closed the door. Relocked it and crept deeper into the house. The soft leather of his shoes made no sound, but he remembered a handyman a few years ago who said you could never have enough nails in a subfloor. He tested the floor with every step, wary of sticky linoleum and creaky boards. The house had an open layout, with the kitchen spilling directly into the living room. Floral print wallpaper adorned otherwise bare walls. No mirrors. Almost too easy.

Morris was facing away from the kitchen, toward the television on the far side of the room. He extended an arm to tap some ashes into a tray on a side table. The cigarette was almost finished, and an open pack of Marlboros sat beside the tray. Greg recognized a routine when he saw one. One last drag and Morris stubbed his smoke, then reached for a new one, causing his body to lean forward over the arm of the recliner.

Greg double-checked the room's corners for surprises, found none, and closed in. He slipped an arm under Morris's chin and pulled up and back, blocking the flow of blood to the man's brain. Morris's first impulse was to throw his arms out to the sides as he felt himself going backward. This wasted a precious second he could have used to fight the choke or weaponize the ashtray. He was unconscious moments later.

Greg frowned at how easy it was and had a fleeting urge to adjust his grip and slowly grind his forearm across the windpipe until it crushed like a damp branch. *No. Purpose now, pleasure later.* Questions needed answers. He closed the curtains and turned down the TV volume before pulling Morris into the back bedroom and onto the bed, tying his wrists and ankles to the four corners. Satisfied everything was secure, he took a longer look around the room. A work desk with multiple stacks of photo albums. Lots of posters. All women. He didn't recognize any of them as missing or killed.

On the bed, Morris regained consciousness, gradually at first, and then with confusion and attempted flailing. Greg wondered whether Morris was confused by a brief dream he had or the fact he was tied to his bed.

"Wha-what the hell!?"

"No, you're not dreaming."

The man jerked his head, and his eyes widened. "You! What do you think you're doing? You won't get away with this. Forget I have pictures? You sonofabitch!"

Greg smiled. "That's exactly why I'm here. I would *love* to see these pictures. And I'd like to know who put you up to this."

"Heh, you're in deep trouble, buddy boy." He jerked his head toward the desk. "Take a look over there."

Greg walked over to the desk and flipped one of the albums open. It contained pictures of a stout but shapely woman undressing before a shower, taken from outside a window. He recognized her as one of the local news personalities.

"Not that one. Christsake! The red one."

Greg pulled another album across the desk and began flipping pages. Dozens of photos, awkward angles of various restaurants and storefronts. They all had something in common: his wife, Betty. He frowned. A few pages deeper and he saw some wide shots of a hotel from across a street. The door opening. A man holding it open for a woman. The couple hugging. The man watching as the woman's car pulled away from the curb. Then, a focused shot of the man's face: Greg's face.

Morris laughed hysterically. "See!? I got your cheating ass!

What's your wife gonna think about this? What will people think?" He quit laughing, and his eyes narrowed above a Cheshire grin. "She's playing Julia Child homemaker while her hubby is out banging broads in broad daylight! No better than me. All fake."

Greg just stared at him as the last pieces fell into place. There was no killer here. *Jimmy was right. Morris Cummings is just your run-of-the-mill dirtbag.*

Eventually, a giggle slipped out, which unsettled Morris enough to make his smile fade.

"What's so funny?"

Greg ignored him and walked over to the closet. Rooting around inside, he was pleased to find a large suitcase, which he brought out and placed at the end of the bed. Morris watched in confused silence.

Greg smiled.

"This is rather embarrassing, but it seems we've misunderstood each other. You see, I'm a ghostwriter. You know what that is, don't you? Well, I write things for other people. And that hotel is where I prefer to meet my clients. The food is great there, by the way. And that woman in your photo...one of my clients, not my mistress."

Morris blinked rapidly, his mind evidently reeling. "Then what the hell is going on?"

"I enjoy ghostwriting, Morris. It pays the bills, but I have another job. Another passion. I guess you could say I'm a 'ghostkiller.' This whole time, I thought you had taken pictures of my *other* job that day."

Morris's mouth gaped open and closed a couple of times, like a fish out of water, but no words came.

Greg kneeled until only his eyes peeked over the suitcase. He thumbed the latches with a satisfying snap, causing Morris to flinch.

"To think I doubted the Quarryman."

Morris's face had become pale. Beads of sweat gathered on his forehead, and he feebly kicked against the bindings.

"You look like you could use a little sun, Morris. There's a regular train that goes all the way to San Francisco. The overhead luggage racks are quite spacious."

Greg stood and gestured to the suitcase. "You know the amazing thing about a suitcase like this one, Morris? I've done work for a gentleman who showed me how to fit an average-sized person inside one of these cases. All you have to do is dislocate the appropriate joints and break a few things here and there. Truly, the man is a savant."

Greg cracked his knuckles as he approached the bed. "I haven't taken a job from the Traveler in a while, so maybe I'll give him this one for free. He'll appreciate the extra publicity. Just think, Morris, when they open your suitcase, you might get to be on TV. A dream come true, right?"

By this point, Morris was moaning and had clenched his eyes shut.

"Have you ever been to a chiropractor, Morris? Get an adjustment? The first few pops might be a bit rough, but by the end, all you feel is relief."

———

Russell Gray was born in the Midwest and raised on a steady diet of horror, fantasy, and science fiction, interspersed with episodes of *In Living Color*. A lifelong fan of stories and storytelling, he spends most of his free time reading. Occasionally, he tells a story of his own.

Goodreads

CHAPTER 2
UNSETTLED

JOHN JOSEPH RYAN

ELBERT SAT in his unreclined La-Z-Boy, his feet tapping arrhythmically. Around him moved various family members, immediate and in-law. Because of the laryngectomy, he could not smoke, but his eldest son, Billy, sat at his right hand and exhaled Elbert's way. The humidifier, whose purpose was to help keep his stoma moist to prevent crusting around its margins and thus impede respiration, sat to his left. The machine pushed out fine water vapor that swirled and merged with his son's cigarette smoke, giving Elbert a Mephistophelean aspect. His black eyes lay submerged beneath the hooded shrouds of their lids.

In the kitchen, the trash can overflowed with paper plates stained with baked bean sauce and potato salad residue and barbecue grease. Two flies sparred in rapid swirls above those contentious spoils. Aunt Bernice returned to the front room from the kitchen, having loaded more ribs on her well-used plate.

"Where's my beer at?" called Billy, her brother.

"You didn't ask for one," she responded without looking at him.

"I'm asking now," he said, not smiling.

Bernice frowned at him, but at Elbert's solemn nod to her, she huffed and turned back to the kitchen. The flies went to their corners at her indignant jostling of the trash can after she flung open the door to the fridge.

Back in the front room, little Jeanine, toddling, stumbled into a Fisher-Price toy, a carousel, causing it to ding. She sat down as though pushed backwards by it, her legs jutting straight in front of her on the scratchy Berber carpet. She grimaced at the toy, then tried to pick it up. Unable to, she batted it, and it hit one of Elbert's restless legs. Her mother, Sue, one of Elbert's in-laws, chastised Jeanine, but Elbert's admonishing right hand stopped her incipient harangue. The egg-shaped toy, about the size of a distended soccer ball, was weighted in such a way that it could not be toppled over. No matter how it was spun or tossed, it always landed upright, its three little rocking horses see-sawing in place on their fixed axes. Jeanine began trying to pull the horses off.

Bernice returned with Billy's beer and tossed it at him. He caught it, glared at her, and tapped the can's sealed opening before pulling the pop top off and flicking it at her. Elbert leaned his chin against his chest and appeared to bulge like a bullfrog. The hooded eyelids seemed to peel back, disclosing red and watery whites.

Angenette, the youngest of Elbert's children, had recently arrived back in town. She sat in a camp chair just to the left of the TV throughout the meal and paid scant attention to the doings of the rest of the family. She looked in that instant from the TV to Elbert.

"Oh, my, oh look-it, Dad, oh man!"

Bernice and Billy disengaged from their contest of wills to regard Elbert, who thrust his chin up and, controlling a mouthful of air in his throat using esophageal breathing, expelled the few words he could articulate.

"Cut. the. shit."

Elbert's family had by now grown so used to reading his nonverbal cues and commands that his unexpected vocalization chilled the room. Bernice plopped down on the edge of a pleather ottoman and settled in to the task of pulling rib meat off bones. Billy held his freshly opened can up to his father to offer him the first sip, but Elbert just scowled at the cap of foam that covered the top. Seeing it, Billy sucked the foam off, then held the can out again to his father. Elbert knocked the knuckles of his right hand against it and returned his hand to the armrest. The backside of it exposed the illegible legend of blue homemade tattoos.

Angenette leaned back in her aluminum folding chair. Bernice chewed her ribs. The humidifier sighed and bubbled audibly once or twice. Out back, the chained hound bayed and went still. Billy sipped at his beer and smoked.

Sue walked over to the TV, where Walter Cronkite was on the screen, addressing someone off-camera, the volume too low for anyone but Angenette to hear. Sue turned the volume knob up. Her presence disturbed the reception, causing Bernice to protest, so she twizzled the antennae a few times. Cronkite did a couple of vertical turns across the screen, then settled with a zap of static.

Sue sat back down on a loveseat next to her husband Billy's chair. The family gathered as though dispersed unevenly around an invisible ovoid table, Elbert on the squashed side diametrically opposed to Walter Cronkite. In between them, little Jeanine continued to fiddle with the carousel toy.

"Wow," said Angenette.

"What is it?" Sue asked.

"Well, it's just—I don't know, maybe you had to hear it. Hang on, listen."

"—it possible that a part would be left out? I mean, he's looking for an L-bracket. Is it possible that back on—?" Cronkite was asking.

"Ah, it's just more technical bullshit," Billy proclaimed.

"Yeah, but before that—" Bernice began.

"Shhh!" Angenette interjected angrily, straining to listen.

The camera cut from Cronkite to another fixed on correspondent Harry Reasoner in the New York studio, seated with Gloria Steinem and a Brown University student activist.

"*Miss Steinem, is there something to you in this day's events that leaves your pleasure mixed?*" Reasoner asked.

"Booooo!" Billy called out.

"Shut up!" Bernice scolded.

"Bra-burning bitch," Billy replied.

"Fuck you!"

"*—been trying very hard to get enthusiastic about this day's events,*" Steinem was saying. "*Perhaps it's the kind of stories I've been covering lately, which have been migrant workers and welfare recipients—*"

Billy, about to get to his feet, felt his arm restrained by Elbert, his grip strong and absolute.

"*We're discovering a new world, but I wonder if we don't have our own Inquisition going on in Vietnam in the name of that great religion of anti-communism—*"

"Blah, blah, blah," Billy continued, looking directly at his sister, goading her. Bernice ignored him and concentrated on the screen beyond her fingers, holding one last rib bone. "Hey, pop, when you were a kid and first saw an airplane fly overhead, what'd you see, hunh? A woman?"

Elbert stared at the screen.

"Naw," Billy said. "And how about who flew across the ocean first?"

"*Miss Steinem,*" Reasoner went on, "*even assuming that most of what we're doing overseas is awful, isn't it still better to do something like this, which is not napalming anyone or injuring anyone and is advancing human knowledge? Isn't it a good thing to do?*"

"Fuckin' A right," said Billy.

"*—not saying that I would not do it if I were suddenly, magically, given the decision about priorities,*" Steinem continued. "*It just seems that we could go a little more slowly. It seems there's been a big change from 1961 when President Kennedy initiated this program—*"

"That's right," Billy jumped in again, still hoping to get

another rise out of Bernice. "It was a *man* who flew over the ocean. And who was at the controls when we dropped the big one on the Japs, hunh? And one more thing, who's up there *now*—"

He never had a chance to finish. Elbert surged to his feet and, in two moves, grabbed his son's hair in his right fist and began hammering the side of his head with his left one. Billy's half-drunk beer spilled into his lap as he tried to cover his face.

"Dad!" Bernice yelled, rising to her feet, dropping her paper plate.

"Elbert, Elbert," Sue exclaimed, coming over to him more out of concern for her father-in-law's heart than her husband's beating.

The two women reached Elbert simultaneously. Bernice hugged her father from behind, pinning his upper arms. Sue got in front of him, a plea in her face, her palms upraised in conciliation. Elbert's left hand fell back to his flank. His right still clutched Billy's hair. For an eighty-year-old man, Elbert still had remarkable strength when doling out violence.

As Bernice put her size into the effort of restraint, Elbert tipped back against her and his right hand pulled his son's head along with him. Billy knocked into Sue's behind. As Sue fell against Elbert, front to front, Elbert released his son's hair. Angenette, exasperated with another eruption in the familiar cycle, stood and cranked the volume knob of the TV all the way up.

"*Are they going to sink in the moon dust, or are they going to, with their one-sixth gravity, sort of bound across it?*" Cronkite seemed to shout.

"Genette! What the hell!" Bernice yelled at her sister, holding their father in her arms.

"I can't hear what's going on!" Angenette yelled back.

"*Ten minutes to the touchdown. Oh, boy!*" Cronkite shouted. "*Ten minutes to a landing on the moon!*"

Billy sat back in his chair, and Sue extricated herself from

Elbert to check on him. The left side of his face was puffy, but Elbert had drawn no blood. Billy raked his fingers back and forth through his thick hair down to the scalp.

The toddler, Jeanine, sat still, her hands covering her ears. She stared at her grandfather. Bernice helped him turn around and held his forearms as he sat back down. She could have been a good nurse's aide assisting a geriatric in an old folks' home.

"Should I get your oxygen, El?" Sue asked, looking into his strained eyes darting from family member to family member above his reddened face.

"Yeah, go get it," Bernice instructed. "Turn that down!" she yelled at Angenette.

Jeanine found one of Bernice's rib bones on the floor and used it to strike the carousel toy.

"Pop, just relax. Pop, we're getting it," Bernice said.

"*5200 feet. Less than a mile from the moon's surface.*" Cronkite's voice boomed.

Jeanine thrust the bone in her mouth and sucked on it like a pacifier.

"'Genette! Jesus!" Bernice yelled.

Angenette, frowning, got up and turned the volume back to a reasonable level. Jeanine, the bone fixed in her mouth like an unlit cigar, stood up and, wavering, teetered forward. Angenette, nearly tripping over Jeanine on her way back to the camp chair, scooped her up and brought her onto her lap as she sat. She cuddled her and began whispering in her ear. Jeanine popped the bone out of her mouth. Angenette, seeing it, grabbed it away from her fist and tossed it onto the ottoman.

Sue returned with the oxygen tank and equipment. She set it down as Bernice removed the filter from Elbert's stoma. Bernice attached the hose to the component fitted into the stoma while Sue opened up the tank. Billy took his Camel hard pack out of his damp shirt front pocket and, sneering at his father, lit it.

"Not around the oxygen!" Bernice scolded.

"I'm goin' outside!" Billy yelled back. He strode into the

kitchen, grabbed another can of beer from the refrigerator, and thrust open the back door. He didn't close it after storming out. The hound howled and stopped abruptly with a grunt and then a whimper.

"We've been talking about what these fellows were going to say when they landed," Cronkite began, "and they were talking away. They had their things to report, their job to do. But...my mouth and my throat...."

His correspondent, Eric Sevareid, responded, "Sometimes silence is the most eloquent thing on earth. Silence."

Cronkite said something in return, though only Angenette heard it—and Jeanine, too, perhaps, though she was too young to understand. She stared hard at the carousel across the room. Sue and Bernice concentrated on the flow of oxygen into Elbert's stoma and the color of his face. The red blush had faded, and his color looked almost normal. His black eyes moved from theirs to the TV screen to theirs and then came to rest on Jeanine, sitting quietly on Angenette's lap. Then the hooded shrouds of his lids descended. And there they stayed.

———

John Joseph Ryan's work has appeared in River Styx, McSweeney's, and The Dark City (U.S.), and in international publications such as Mystery Magazine (Canada), Samjoko (Republic of Korea), Grievous Bodily Harm (Australia), and A-Z of Horror (U.K.). John is co-author of the noir short, "Hothouse by the River" (University of Iowa Center for the Book), and he is also the author of a crime novel, A Bullet Apiece (Amphorae Publishing Group, 2015). As a passion project, John hosted the YouTube series, Creepy Poem of the Day. John lives in St. Louis, Missouri.

Facebook | Goodreads | Instagram | YouTube | Amazon Author Page | Author Website

CHAPTER 3
SORRY GIRLS, HE'S MARRIED

TREVOR JAMES ZAPLE

ALICE KOWALSKI CHOPPED the onions and told herself that the tears welling in her eyes were just a defense mechanism. Surely she wasn't the one who was causing her crying jag. She was stoic, remained calm under pressure, and was a Mother, capital letter intended, the stuff of legends. A Good Christian Woman, as the pastor would say. Even if her husband and his no-account brother had been off drinking all afternoon and most of the evening, that didn't change anything. Their dinner still needed to be made.

Snow blatted against the kitchen window, followed by the howling of the wind. It was like the cries of dogs in screaming pain. She tried to put that idea out of her head. It had only been a few days. It was perfectly normal that she would still feel distressed about it, but the sound put her on the very knife's edge. The storm screamed and her skin crawled and a peculiar sensation ran along her long brown hair, from the scalp down to the tips.

In the living room, she heard commercials on the television. One good thing about Harry's farming acumen was that he could afford things like a television. Alice was deeply unsure what she would have done most nights otherwise. The farm was a long way out of the way, even of Havre, and that town was merely the largest settlement in their part of Montana. It wasn't all that big on its own.

You could only scrounge up so many books in the area, and the habits of the other ladies in the area seemed as dull as worn rocks. She had no talent for crocheting and sewing, and any desire she might have had to put together social events was put to rest by her husband's taciturn behavior. The television prevented her from walking out into the lethal wind that drove the temperature far below zero. She would be dead in minutes out there. She dumped the onions into the macaroni salad and chuckled brokenly, small sobs poking through here and there. She should be on CBS. "The *Judy Garland Show* saved my life!"

June and Mark were in there, waiting for *The Ed Sullivan Show* to come on. They had been talking about it all week, or rather, June had been talking, and Mark had been listening. Alice had seen the commercials featuring some group of English boys with identical haircuts and similar dopey expressions on their faces. June obviously thought they were cute, but Alice couldn't see what was so special about them. Tonight was the night, though, and June had gotten Mark excited about it as well.

She had been worried all week that Harry would spoil their fun all week. She kept picturing her sullen husband clomping in and demanding to watch what he wanted to watch on the television. According to him, it was his, after all. "It's my TV, and I'll watch what I want to watch." Then he would demand beer and question her about when dinner was supposed to be ready.

He and his brother Jimmy were drinking out in the barn now, though, bone-chilling weather be damned. Let them stay out there.

She had fed the kids three hours ago, while Harry and Jimmy were down in Havre. Their oldest, Maryanne and her friend Margaret, were up in her room, but they would be down soon enough. Although they pretended to consider June's excitement over the show "baby stuff," at seventeen, Maryanne, at least, was not immune to the charm of cute boys.

With any luck, Harry and Jimmy wouldn't come in until the show ended. Alice would have to keep the ham foiled for longer than she'd like, but it probably didn't matter. They'd both be too soused to taste it anyway.

Alice was a good woman and had to allow room in her heart for kin, even if they were bastards, even if Jimmy did equal—or exceed—Harry's vicious tongue. The things that came out of Jimmy's mouth shocked even Harry sometimes. He would never admit it, but she saw the way his eyes popped when Jimmy would say disturbing things, mostly about the experiences he'd had in the war. He'd been on tours throughout the Pacific and had earned a Purple Heart in Guadalcanal, so Alice was willing to at least countenance his presence in her home. And, of course, Harry hadn't given her much of a choice.

There was brassy fanfare from the TV in the living room, rising boldly over the howl of the storm that was really the only thing Alice could hear in the kitchen while she cooked. Curious, she walked out into the living room. The potatoes were in the water, waiting to be boiled up whenever Jimmy and Harry came in. She had plenty of time to take in what her children were watching.

She walked in just as Ed was talking to the crowd. He was performing in his usual style, where he staggered and mugged for the camera. The kids found it quite funny, but it had always reminded Alice a little too much of Harry when he was starting in on drinking. Ed was telling everyone that Colonel Parker and Elvis had sent a telegram of support for these "Beatles" to be successful in the United States.

That was nice. Unlike a lot of people at church, she had always had a soft spot for the King of Rock 'n' Roll. Of course Harry thought he was worthless. He always called him slurs and talked about how Johnny Cash and Buck Owens didn't have to sound Black to sell records. God knew what he would make of this Beatles group. She didn't know what they sounded like, but they had the support of Elvis, and they didn't look like they'd just stepped out of a cloud of exhaust and cigarette smoke in Bakersfield, California.

It went to commercial, and she took the opportunity to get back to the kitchen and check the ham in the oven, to make sure it wasn't getting too dried out, even on low heat. She heard creaks in the floorboards overhead. Maryanne was stirring, finally. *Good*. They'd been cooped up in her room all evening, doing who knows what.

Alice shook her head as she shut the oven door. The girl had slept over at Margaret Munroe's house, and now it was their turn to have Margaret over. Alice was not fond of the Munroe girl and even less fond of her parents. Maryanne had been clever enough to ask her father first. Alice couldn't very well contradict her husband in front of their children and expect to escape unscathed.

The Munroe girl was an odd duck. She looked as normal as anyone else in their sleepy little snatch of the country, but she had unwholesomely bright eyes. Her parents weren't farmers, despite the rambling old farmhouse they lived in. She'd asked around, and no one could really pinpoint what it was they did for a living. There was something off about them, especially Margaret. It felt to Alice as though Maryanne had started keeping secrets after becoming friends with her.

The living room erupted in a cloud of screaming girls, and Alice returned to the set and her children. The four members of the Beatles—all of them wearing the same suits—were playing a song with a catchy melody as the camera lingered on each of them. She supposed they were handsome enough. The one in the back playing the drums looked like he'd be worth a laugh or two, with an expression that went back and forth between goofy and soulful. The three guitarists up front ran the gamut: the one on the right looked serious and a little broody, the one on the left earnest and sincere, and the one in the middle a mixture of these two.

The song was okay. Back before she'd gotten married and started raising a family, she'd worn bobby socks and screamed for Frank Sinatra. From what she could tell, the girls that the camera kept panning to were doing much the same. The faces were young and fresh, but she recognized all the expressions. June was just following in her footsteps. Maryanne would have been too, and not that long ago. Margaret seemed apart from the usual adolescent pursuits, and Maryanne had gone that way as well.

"Oooh, aren't they all so handsome?" June cooed.

Alice thought they were all a little too fresh-faced to be handsome, but kept her thoughts to herself. She sat on the couch and watched. She wanted to understand what was making the girls scream, what the link between her blue-eyed youth and these mop-topped Brits was.

They were much more rock 'n' roll than they were crooners, but there was a bit of both in the mix as far as Alice could tell. It was like they had taken Elvis and sanded down the edges to make it safer for girls like June to listen to. Less objectionable for the parents. Alice might not have minded a little less sanding-down—the song they were playing felt a bit treacly for her—but it was both catchy and, as far as she could tell, inoffensive, and as such she supported June's adolescent infatuation with them.

They launched into another song, similar to the first, and now there were names showing up under them as they played. Here were the introductions. The goofy-sweet drummer was Ringo, which Alice felt had to be made up. The earnest and sincere one was Paul; the handsome middle one was George; the broody one on the end was John. Underneath John's name was another line: "Sorry girls, he's married."

She blinked away a snap flood of tears with the back of her hand. She couldn't blame this on the onions. *Sorry girls, he's married? Like it was any special thing to be married. Like it would prevent him from doing whatever he wanted.*

The room seemed dimmer, and she rose and practically lurched back to the kitchen. She entered it just as Harry and Jimmy were coming in from the outside. They shook snow off their boots onto the floor, and she grimaced.

"Dinner isn't ready?" Harry asked. He sounded disgusted. "What have you been doing"

"I've been waiting on you to decide to come in" she said before she could put a clamp on her temper. She scraped a match across the box and lit the gas under the pot of potatoes.

Harry bristled, but Jimmy stepped between them. "Think I'll go see what the fuss in the living room is all about," Jimmy muttered.

Harry grunted, sat down heavily in a kitchen chair, and kicked his boots off all the way. "Is that lazy girl out of her room yet?"

Alice shrugged. "She was moving around but she hasn't come down yet."

"I better go get her then," he said. "Wouldn't want her to get lazy like her mother, who can't even get dinner on the table at a proper time."

Alice glared at his back but kept her lips sealed. She didn't need the trouble. She wiped away more tears.

Sorry girls, he's married.

Like it was any great thing. She wondered who the broody young Englishman with the good looks was married to, and she pitied her, though she did not know her. She'd discover it soon enough, maybe when they started having kids and facing what her husband was really like.

Alice heard a series of knocks from upstairs, and then a heavy thump on the floor directly above her. She stared at the ceiling. From the living room, the sounds of the Beatles playing their lively little songs continued. Creaks came from overhead, and then a long, heavy sound, like something being dragged roughly across the floor.

She went out to the living room and glanced up the stairs. There was no further noise, and no one appeared at the top of the stairs. On the TV, the Beatles were talking to Ed Sullivan. There was something wrong with the reception; every once in a while, the picture would roll, and there were snaps and snarls of static.

"How have you found America so far?" Ed asked.

"Well, we followed the trail of blood," George said. The audience laughed and howled.

What did he just say?

"Did you hear something from upstairs?" she asked, one foot resting on the bottom step, one hand gripping the railing. The kids remained glued to the television screen, but Jimmy turned to look at her, his expression bleary.

"Sounded like a shelf fell over or something upstairs," he drawled out. "Should probably go check it out." Alice ignored him and continued to stare up the staircase.

"Harry?" she called up. There was no answer.

"Would you say that Ringo is the best drummer in the world?" Ed asked on the television, in between snaps of static.

"He's not even the best drummer in the deep," George quipped. The audience laughed hard at this. George turned to look directly into the camera. "Drums in the deep," he said. "You cannot get out."

Alice glanced over at the children. June still seemed rapt, but Mark looked confused. Jimmy, for his part, seemed bored with the whole thing.

"Well, if Maryanne shows up, send her into the kitchen," she said, backing away from the stairs. No one responded to her.

"Paul, are you getting married?" Ed asked as she turned to head back to the kitchen.

"I don't know," Paul demurred, blushing a little.

"Are you getting married to Susan Atkins?" Ed continued.

"Well, when you get to the bottom," Paul said, "You go back to the top of the slide."

What did that mean? Was that some new slang?

She needed to check the potatoes. The last thing she needed was for them to boil over. She was in the middle of draining the boiling water when Harry came into the kitchen. She ignored him at first, intent on seeing dinner through to the end. He hovered near the door, not moving. When she finally looked over at him in irritation, she realized that something was very wrong with him.

He was grinning widely, to the very limits of his face. It wasn't a jovial smile, or even the mean, sullen grin he put on when he started verbally laying into her. It was an awful smile, sly and knowing. His eyes were calculating on top of that tilted half-moon smile, and shadowed, as though something utterly and finally wrong lurked behind a veil in there. They were not her husband's eyes. She was unsure that they were even the eyes of a human.

"I'm so hungry, Alice," he said. His voice cooed, as though he were desperate to fill some bottomless void that he found darkly hilarious. "Where's dinner?"

She shivered. It was cold in the kitchen, as though the door had swung open, and the blizzard had flown in. What was this thing, standing in her house? Her skin pimpled. It was too difficult to move. She forced herself to smile.

"Any minute now, darling," she said. Her smile felt frozen on her face. She glanced around and saw her long kitchen knife sitting out on the counter.

Harry crossed the kitchen with shocking speed. He was practically in her face before her paralysis broke and she finally lunged for the knife. As she grasped the handle of the knife, he grabbed her hair and yanked her head back. She saw, mercifully briefly, the rubberband tense cut of his smile looming next to her skin.

Her arm jerked, her wrist twisted, the blade of the knife

found purchase in the tight flesh of her husband's neck. Blood washed over her hand, and she cringed back from it. Harry's grasp on her hair did not loosen, and he slammed her against the counter. Pain radiated out from her ribs, and she struck out wildly with the knife. She felt it cut into him several times. He didn't flinch back from the cut of the blade once.

His feet slipped on the blood on the floor, and he had to adjust his stance. This caused him to loosen his grasp on her hair just enough for her to lunge forward and escape his grip. Even so, a handful of her hair ripped out of her scalp, and she yelped from the pain.

His face was slathered in blood, but he still had that creepy wide grin plastered on his face, and his eyes still had that flat, calculating stare. Something lurked in them. She couldn't see it so much as she could sense it: unbridled glee, even seeing the knife gripped tightly in her fist. It was the look she imagined a hawk would give its prey right before striking.

Outside, the wind blew snow against the house. It splattered along the length of the outside wall and sounded like a series of hands slapping against the siding. Her mind flashed an image of hundreds of small children standing in the storm, their wan little hands hitting the door, slapping the window, demanding to be let in. Then Harry was moving again, slower this time. Now his expression said that this was all fine, that he was going to take his time. He was going to enjoy it.

He stopped to open a drawer. From out of it he drew, with loving, liquid grace, the cleaver that her mother had given her as a housewarming gift. She kept it wickedly sharp. He hefted it, admiring the edge of the blade, and then turned that ferocious, infernal grin on her.

"We're going to have some fun with this," he said. "First, I'm going to carve off each one of your fing—"

The door to the kitchen opened, and Alice saw Jimmy standing in the doorway. He looked shocked and unsure. She wanted to scream at him to help her, or to run and take the kids somewhere safe, but the paralysis had crept over her again. She always pictured herself as a lioness, swift and vicious, ready to save her children at any time, but she realized too late that when reality came knocking, she would simply swallow and open the door.

"Harry?" Jimmy said. Harry turned that devil smile on him, and he simply backed out of the doorway and let the door swing shut. From the living room, she could hear the Beatles playing another song, jaunty and quick, at odds with the way the entire world seemed to have slowed down for her. She tasted something sour and coppery, fear and shame and disappointment warring on her tongue.

Harry turned back to her, and waves of pure cold ran up her legs. He approached her with the cleaver, and in her mind's eye it was already descending with terrible speed, cutting fingers off joints, carving her up as ruthlessly as a butcher dressing a hog.

Then an explosion, and her husband's head burst apart with a pop like a balloon breaking. He collapsed with a heavy thump at her feet, and she scrambled backward until her back was at the cabinets. She kept trying to move further, as though she could melt right through the cupboard door, her fingers trying to find a grip on the floor tiles.

Sorry girls, he's married.

She moved in and out of focused consciousness. Someone was dragging her. Small cries on the periphery of her hearing. An audience roaring with laughter, only it didn't sound like they were finding anything funny. A crisp-looking English boy in black and white looking mournfully at her. Then a sharp slap and the cold, stinging rush of water in her face. She sat up and found herself on the living room floor. Jimmy squatted beside her with a wet, empty glass. June and Mark held each other on the couch, their faces contorted in fear.

Alice opened her mouth, but Jimmy put a finger to her lips and then pointed outside. He didn't seem drunk anymore.

"What's the great truth of the universe?" Ed asked on the

television. He looked thin and unhealthy, like he'd become suddenly ill while taping the show.

"Having to shoot your brother will sober you up in a real hurry," John said. The audience laughed or screamed. Alice could no longer tell.

"What?" she asked. Jimmy tightened his lips and pointed forcefully upstairs. As though on cue, a heavy slithering sound came from the second floor.

"Do you think they have a chance?" Ed asked. The words came out of his mouth in a funny little moan, as though it both pained and pleased him to say them.

"I think that Maryanne and her new friend will make sure that they don't," George said, leering at the camera. "It's always nice when your kids bring their new friends home to meet the parents."

"It's always interesting what can happen when girls start mimicking the things they see their parents do, isn't it?" Paul asked.

"Except when you need to follow strict rules to make sure nothing escapes," John replied. "Then things might go wrong."

"Drums," Ringo said, "in the deep." His face looked slack, like the skin was drooping off. The reception rolled nauseatingly, and then his skin really was falling off, hanging precariously off his skull.

Motion to her right broke the fascination she'd developed with the television screen. Jimmy waved at her, and once he caught her attention, he pointed forcefully out the front door. The wind screamed against it, and she just blinked. They couldn't go out there. There was no way they were getting down the laneway, let alone out down the rough road.

"There's no way out," Ringo groaned on the television. The audience roared and cheered. One of the top stairs creaked, and then another, further down. Jimmy pointed a big rifle up the stairs. It looked like one that he might have carried in the war, but she wasn't a good enough judge of guns to know. The children were sobbing while they hurriedly threw their boots and coats on.

"Get out to the truck," Jimmy shouted. He threw something at her, and it wasn't until she caught it that she realized it was the keys. "Get it started. I'll be out in two seconds." There was another creak on the stairs, and then Jimmy fired the rifle. A scream came from the stairs, and then once the ringing from that faded, Alice heard a low, throaty chuckle.

Her own coat went on without thinking, and she was halfway out to the truck with Mark and June before she realized she was still wearing her house slippers. There was no chance to turn around now. She heard another rifle blast from inside the house. June clamored into the tiny back seat of the truck's cab, and Alice had to lift and practically throw Mark to get him in. She rushed into the driver's seat and started the engine. Her feet were numb but throbbing, a bad sign. Frostbite was easy enough to get in this kind of weather, especially out here where the wind would blow through unimpeded.

She hunched over the steering wheel and turned the heater on. The cold inside the cab was oppressive, and it was hard to draw in a full breath. She stared intently at the house. Nothing moved at the door. Inside, at the edge of what she could see, the television screen rolled and snapped. When it stabilized, she saw what looked like a man standing over another and beating down on him with a drumstick. She thought it might be Ringo over Ed.

The silence was shattered with another rifle blast from inside the house. A moment later Jimmy came tearing out of the house, the gun held upright, his arms pumping. As he came closer to the truck, Alice saw with dismay that he was also in his socks.

"We have to go now," he shouted. "Get us out of here!"

Alice leaned over and grabbed Jimmy's chin. She yanked his face closer and stared into his eyes.

"Alice, we have to go," he said.

She held on to his chin, which made his words stilted and

malformed. She watched his eyes carefully, looking for that shadow. Was there an awful thing lurking in there, too? Something peeking furtively from around his pupils?

Something loped out the door and through the snow. Alice let go of Jimmy's face and threw the truck into reverse. The tires skidded on the snow, and for a moment Alice thought they would be stuck. But then they were rolling backward, and in the headlights she saw something—

blink

She froze. Jimmy was stretched across her, his hands on the wheel in a death grip, adjusting it this way and that. She realized that her foot, now screaming in pain, pressed the gas pedal right to the floor. They were flying backwards up the lane, the engine revving loudly.

She took her foot off the pedal. Still, they swerved wildly to the right. Jimmy steered into it, and they came to a stop in a pile of snow. In the backseat, the children screamed.

"No!" Jimmy shouted. "Back on the gas, Alice!"

She looked over at him. There was nothing horrible lurking in what she could see. Just sweat, fear, and a mournful expression, like that George boy from the television.

"Where are we going?" she asked firmly. "What is that?"

Jimmy remained silent. The children's screaming died off into whimpers.

"I saw things in the war," he said finally. "Men, mostly, men and the horrible things they can do to each other. Worse, though, once or twice. The men on the other side, you can understand it after a while. You might do the same thing, if you had the advantage. If it was your life on the line. It's when it's your own, that's when it gets evil. When the ones you've come to trust are the ones with their hands around your throat, you know things have gone deeply wrong."

He smiled, and it was bloodless in the glow from the headlights.

"I guess we're all lucky that I've seen something like it before. We'd all be dead otherwise."

The radio crackled to life, offering a burst of static that faded out into some far-off DJ's thin voice.

"...was voted down in the Senate. In lighter news, England's famous Beatles made their television debut tonight, sealing the pact with the Exiled Ones for all time. We interviewed a local girl, Maryanne, about her thoughts on the matter."

Another burst of static, and then:

"Maryanne, what would you say to listeners about your experience with the Beatles tonight?"

"I would say I'm so hungry."

Alice recoiled. It was Maryanne's voice, but it was strange and draggy, like it was coming from underwater.

"I want to know when dinner is. I'm coming up the lane right now, and I've got *such* a hunger on. I'm coming to eat."

The wind screamed against the truck. Alice began to sob, but it quickly broke into jagged laughter, as she remembered the *useless* potatoes, still in the sink. They were cold now, beyond repair. *It figured.*

Snow spattered against the windshield, and she felt Jimmy stir beside her. The children were breathing quietly in the back. She could feel their misery, coming off them in waves.

She pressed the gas pedal down once more. The wheels spun fruitlessly in the deepening snow.

If she didn't figure something out soon, her daughter's dinner would be served up straight out of this tin can.

———

If you enjoyed this, check out Trevor James Zaple's other story in the Sinister Century *series. Find out what happened to Jimmy Kowalski* before *the events of "Sorry Girls, He's Married." Join him during his service on Echo Island during WWII in "Red Rover, Red Rover," featured in* Listen: A Disturb Ink Books Anthology.

―――

Trevor James Zaple is a web developer with a youth-focused educational non-profit. His work has most recently appeared in *The Brazenhead Review, Bleed Error,* and *Quill & Crow's Bleak Midwinter*. He lives in the other London with his wife and daughters.

Facebook I Goodreads I Instagram I Threads I Amazon Author Page I trevorzaple.com

Capture

DEBRAAL   GAYDON   LAU   SMITH

EDITED BY H DAIR BROWN
A DISTURB INK BOOKS ANTHOLOGY

VICIOUS VIDEOS | THE 1980S

DISTURB INK BOOKS

EDITED BY
H. DAIR BROWN

Published by Disturb Ink Books, an imprint of 79 Franklin Press, LLC.
www.79franklinpress.com

First North American ebook edition September 2024

ASIN (ebook): B0DF69H57X

Designed by: H. Dair Brown

For the horror writers who capture our imaginations and then torture them the exact right amount

NOTES

Because we are fortunate enough in this collection to have writers from all over the world contributing to *Sinister Century*, you'll see a variation in the spelling of some words from story to story. The editor has chosen to respect the spelling of the country in which the author writes.

———

"To capture the essence of life itself, one must first capture the heart."

LEONARDO DA VINCI

CHAPTER 1
TAPED

RICHARD LAU

YOU SHUFFLE through the endless shelves of the videotape rental store like a denim-and-flannel-clad Pac-Man gliding smoothly through his neon blue maze.

However, instead of gobbling delicious cookie-shaped dots, you're simply restocking the rental returns.

Still, there are things to avoid. Pac-Man has his nemeses—ghosts named Inky, Blinky, Pinky, and Clyde—each one with its own personality and pattern. You have customers and coworkers who serve that purpose and have named them Nervy, Pervy, Topsy-Turvy, and Dougie. They, too, have their distinctive traits.

Nervy has a pushy attitude, saying things like, "You know, you really shouldn't be carrying this movie" and "You really ought to carry more copies of..."

Pervy will usually stop you and ask "Is <enter actress name here> really nude in this movie? And for how long?"

Topsy-Turvy is just clueless, usually asking where the Children's Section is while standing in the middle of the Children's Section, blind to the brightly colored Disney covers.

And Dougie is your manager, who fancies himself a dead ringer for Rick Springfield on the soap opera *General Hospital*. You think he bears more of a resemblance to Sheriff Rosco P.

Coltrane from *The Dukes of Hazzard*, both in appearance and competence.

It is to Dougie that you ask if you can leave now that your shift is over.

"Right after you take out the trash," he says, spitting a wad of gum into the plastic bin, just to add to your burden. "Oh, and take this." He hands you an unlabeled video tape.

"What's this?" you ask.

"Someone dumped a home tape in the return slot by mistake." He looks at his Swatch to both indicate that you are officially on your own time and that you're wasting his. "It's been back here in the Lost and Found for months. No one's asked for it, so you might as well throw it out."

You empty the trash in the rusting metal dumpster behind the store and return the bin behind the counter with the tape still tucked under your arm.

On the bus ride home, you wonder what could be on the tape. Scenes from a family vacation? A graduation or prom? Amateur porn? Probably just a pirated copy of an official Hollywood release. Still, curiosity keeps gnawing away at you like a hungry dog, and you can't wait to get home to satisfy its desire for an unknown and unexpected treat.

Home is a simple studio apartment in the "shady" side of town. Ever since you graduated high school and moved out of your grandparents' home, money has been tight. But home is where the miracle device resides along with you: the VCR, the all-seeing, all-knowing videocassette recorder (just add cassette).

When you were in high school, the families of all your friends were getting one. But you were living with your grandparents who grew up during the Great Depression. Who needed this new-fangled VCR when a *black-and-white* TV worked just fine for *Lawrence Welk* reruns?

When one of your friends had mentioned the color-change in *The Wizard of Oz*, you had naively asked, "What color change?" So, she had gotten you a copy of the movie... on VHS tape, of course. Not having a device to play the tape on, you spent hours staring at the colorful cover and using your imagination.

It was never that you didn't like movies—quite the opposite. You *loved* movies. All kinds of movies. And, of course, that led to the desire for you to build your own collection.

Long before the VCR came on the market, you had been recording the movies broadcasted on television onto audio cassette tape. Sure, this turned the visual media into an audio-only experience, essentially radio shows. The situation wasn't ideal. There was the loss of content when you had to flip over the tape at the 30-minute or 45-minute mark or put in a new one. Plus, along with the movie audio, the recording caught various ambient sounds, as well. Why is there a dog barking at Jimmy Stewart in *Vertigo*? Because the tape recorder picked up the sound of your next-door neighbor's dog having its own dizzy spell about a *femme fatale* cat on the backyard fence.

You still cringe at the sound of your grandfather loudly yawning during the dramatic three-way showdown in *The Good, The Bad, and the Ugly*. That yawn is forever burned into your memory as part of the Ennio Morricone soundtrack.

Even so, you had captured at least part of the movie magic. And you could play it again and again whenever you wanted.

Before you had even moved out, you already had a particular model on layaway, a special TV-VCR combo. All other expenses circled around it, like planets around a star. A place that was affordable enough on a monthly basis, but in a safe enough neighborhood so that the VCR wouldn't be stolen. You also needed money for the electricity to power it.

Video rental stores were popping up all over the place, and their presence provided a dream job of money for rent and bills, free tapes, and even "liberated food" in the form of Raisinets, Junior Mints, and red licorice from the check-out counter. Once, you had picked up a package of instant popcorn before realizing that you didn't have a microwave. It went back on the store's concessions shelf the very next day.

Except for the cube of the VCR/TV combo against one wall, the only other piece of furnishing is a sofa cushion you brought from your grandparents' house. How did your grandmother miss one crocheted pillow out of so many? But she had.

The apartment is far from empty. Along all four walls are three-foot-high stacks of plastic cases and loose videocassettes. You have no interest in decorating with movie posters. Why waste money on still photos or painted portrayals when you can have the real moving image?

You close the apartment door, making sure to lock it and turn the deadbolt. This is your time. You will not be disturbed and will not be answering any knocks, though you don't expect any or normally receive any visitors. Your eyes struggle to adjust to the fading daylight bleeding through the curtain-less window. You own no lamps, preferring to see by the multi-purpose glow of the TV set.

You kneel before the altar of the latest version of the Magic Lantern with your offering. You press the power button and the soft hum of your prayers being answered reaches your ears. You feed the unlabeled tape into the hungry god's slotted mouth.

Quickly curling up with the sofa pillow, you watch the screen as brown magnetic tape feeds onto the VCR's play heads. For several moments, there is only a black-and-white particle snow-storm and the sound of static.

Then, without the preamble of credits or previews, the first scene flickers onto the screen. It appears to be security footage from the viewpoint of a camera mounted high in the corner of the ceiling. The location is a video store. For a moment, you aren't certain, but as you scoot closer on the floor, you realize it is the store where you work.

Had Dougie given you a store security tape by mistake?

Then the scene changes to a view of a street at twilight. In the distance, a bus pulls over to the curb, and you see someone board it.

You have a sneaky suspicion you know who the passenger is.

However, because all the employees at the video store wear the same uniform to work every day, you are uncertain if it really is you or what day the scene was recorded. But the bus stop is certainly the same one you use.

You feel some bile angrily rise in your throat. Is one of your co-workers being creepy, stalking you? For a moment, you consider bringing the tape back to the store and turning it over to Dougie. But what if it's Dougie who's the stalker?

The screen goes back to static for a moment, but then things clear up again and you see a series of dim horizontal lines. It is only when the lines bend outward that you realize they are the wooden slats on your hallway closet door.

The closet next to the front door.

Right behind you.

The camera slowly, almost painfully, moves out of the closet, momentarily focusing on the closed and bolted front door. The image conveys the silent message of "no hope for a quick escape here."

That settles it. With breaking into your apartment, a line has been crossed. It's no longer childish and creepy. Now it's criminal. Forget about taking the tape to Dougie. You're going to the police!

But what you see next paralyzes your body and mind with fear.

The camera pans across the room to a silhouette of someone sitting in front of a television set. As the frame zooms out, you see a shadow on the wall next to the TV set on the screen. The figure is humanoid, except for the blocky rectangular head resting on its shoulders.

Your eyes climb up the wall behind your own TV. The figure is there, too. But much larger, much clearer. This is a hundred times more horrid. Unlike its tiny doppelgänger on the screen, the shadow on your wall is lifelike and life-sized. You now see that it isn't actually block-headed. It has no head, but instead simply a VHS video camera resting on one shoulder.

You know that the streetlight outside your apartment window must have turned on. You know it is shining its light into your apartment through the window. But something has moved between the window and the wall, casting the shadow you are seeing.

You panic at the presence of something in the room with you.

Wait! How can a prerecorded tape played on a VCR show what is currently happening live? As the commercial asks, "Is it live or is it Memorex?" Is this somehow... both?

Past and present welcome the future onto the tape.

Though you sit motionless, the person on the screen slowly turns, and stares into the camera, breaking the fourth wall.

It is your face. And you look horrified.

Succumbing to irresistible temptation, you slowly turn to see what fate has prerecorded for you.

You hear the sharp click of the video tape reaching its end as you experience your last fade to black.

———

Richard Lau is an award-winning writer who is published in magazines, newspapers, and anthologies, as well as in the high-tech industry and online. His stories have recently appeared in *Sci Phi Journal*, *The Last Line Journal*, and *Carpe Noctem* (Tyche Books). His dark holiday story "The Winterclaus Tree" appears in *Still of Winter*, an anthology published by Inky Bones Press.

CHAPTER 2
THE PARADE

DAWN DEBRAAL

OPAL HATCH HELD the heavy camcorder on her shoulder. It was the latest invention, and all the good parents had one. The large RCA camera held a full-size VHS tape, so there was no diddling around. The moment was recorded directly onto the tape, and the video could be played immediately through the camera or on a VCR.

She stood at the edge of the crowd of the Thanksgiving Day Parade, feeling like a professional videographer as she swept the camera along the road, catching the faces of the children sitting on a blanket folded on the sidewalk. An adorable four-year-old in pigtails jumped up and down in excitement. Each float that came by would toss candy to the clamoring children holding empty bags to gather the sweet treats to save for later.

She videoed her sister's three young children panning up to their mother, Garnet, who shook her head and waved Opal away.

"Save the video for the parade, Opal," Garnet told her. They could hear a marching band in the distance.

Opal stood on the parade route, capturing each float, then zoomed in on her nieces and nephew, scrambling for the candy.

People clapped, appreciating all the work done on the parade entries.

Then the strangest looking clown on high stilts with flowing robes passed them. He stooped down, handing candy to the little children walking by them. He was mesmerizing, and Opal followed him with the camera until he faded out of view. A woman across the street screamed, "Cara!"

Opal swung the camera in that direction.

People quieted, facing the frantic mother.

"My little girl Cara is missing! She's wearing a red sweater and a pink bow in her hair."

People ran around looking for her. Had she wandered off? Been taken? Soon, an officer approached the mother and led her over to the police cars. Another officer asked if anyone had any information to please come forward. He passed out his business cards to everyone in the immediate area.

Garnet grabbed her children.

"Mom, the parade is not over yet," her children whined.

"Don't worry, kids, I'll video it and drop it off." The disappointed children followed their mother back to the car. The tone of the crowd had changed.

Where had the little girl gone off to?

Opal caught the rest of the parade and hauled the heavy camera back to the car. She would call Garnet later and tell her she'd bring the recording over. For now, she was hungry and wanted to get something to eat.

Once home, Opal grabbed a sandwich, slipped the video into the VCR, and pushed play. Her nieces and nephew were goofing around and having a great time while candy rained down on them. The camera panned across the street with the little brunette, about four years old, wearing a red sweater and a pink ribbon in her hair. Opal stopped the video and stared at the blurred picture. Was someone behind her or off to the side, ready to kidnap her? She shuddered, thinking how close her family had been to the incident.

She let the film run forward. In between floats, the camera still picked up on the little girl. When the weird clown on stilts and flowing robe walked by, she followed the brightly colored clown long after he passed her. The camera went back to its previous angle.

The little girl was gone.

Opal stopped and rewound. The weird clown flinging his arms while his clothes flapped like a flag on a clothesline caught everyone's attention. And then the little girl was gone.

"What happened here?" she whispered and made a copy of the video. She called the police and told them what she had.

"Could you come down with the video? It could help us find the little girl."

"Of course." Opal stuffed the video in her bag and raced to the police station.

"Mrs. Hatch? I'm Detective Bordon. Please, come in." The man held the door for her and pointed to a seat at the front of his desk.

"Please take a seat." Opal sat down on the hard folding chair.

"Mrs. Hatch, you said you have a video of the missing girl."

"It's Miss Hatch, and yes, I do. I was standing directly across the street from her with my sister and her kids during the parade. I focused on a clown on stilts, and when I got back to the parade, I noticed the little girl had disappeared. I don't know if someone around her grabbed her while everyone was distracted by the weird clown or if he was the one who stole her."

"Interesting. I'd like to see this for myself." Detective Bordon said.

Opal handed the video to the officer, who pushed the cassette into the machine and watched the television set sitting on a roll-away cart.

"I'm sorry. This is after her disappearance. I forgot to rewind it before coming in." The detective pushed the rewind button, and the tape rewound to the beginning, resetting itself.

First, there were Opal's nieces and nephew sitting on a

blanket next to the road. Then there was just Opal and a shot of the mother and her daughter across the street.

"See, there she is." Opal pointed to the television set. The officer nodded and continued to keep his eye glued to the event. Twenty minutes into the parade, the clown appeared bright and big. The children loved and clamored up to him, touching his clothing and running alongside him as he handed out suckers. He was flamboyant as he moved his hand hypnotically, drawing your eye on him. The video follows the strange man down the street and then resumes the old angle, and the little girl is missing.

"See. Something happened right there. The little girl is in the group when he is coming, and she's gone after he goes by."

"I'd like to keep this video," the officer told her.

"Of course."

"Thank you for coming forward, Miss Hatch. We'll be in touch."

Opal was still shaking when she left the police station. The idea of a missing child and that she could have caught the incident on video was disturbing, let alone how close her nieces and nephew were to a kidnapper.

She answered her sister's call when she returned to the apartment.

"Hi, Garnet. I just got back from the police station. Do you realize that we were standing *directly* across the street from that little girl who was kidnapped? I took a copy of the video and gave it to the police. It's scary. One minute she's there, and the next, she's missing."

"That's terrifying. I hope they find her."

"I kept a copy. I can still bring it over for the kids to see the end of the parade. They won't notice when she goes missing. You have to know what you're looking for."

"That would be great."

"I'm going to watch it a few more times to see if I missed something."

"I hope you find another clue. I can't imagine what that mother is going through," Garnet said.

Opal hung up and sat down, pushing the VHS tape into the machine. With the remote in hand, she watched carefully.

The little girl was sitting on the blanket on the curb across the street. When the clown moved past her, his clothes flowed about him. He was high in the air, on stilts, as he swirled around. The children rose from their seats and flocked toward him. This time, his face stared into the camera and came closer.

Opal shrieked and pulled back on the couch, smashing the pause button.

That wasn't on the other tape. How could this one be different?

She'd given an *exact* copy to the police and watched it with Detective Bordon. How could the clown's face now be dead center in the camera, staring at her? His feral smile exposed razor-sharp teeth, with saliva dripping down. He came in for an extreme Norma Desmond/*Sunset Boulevard* close-up and laughed before closing his mouth around the lens.

That didn't happen.

How was the video changing every time she played it?

She rewound the video and rewatched it. She waited for the little girl to jump up as the creepy clown came along. She disappeared behind his flowing clothes, like usual, but this time, the clown seemed to look right at Opal as she sat on the couch. His mouth hung open, the sharp teeth dripping, and, once again, he closed on the camera. Then the clown pulled away, winked at her, and danced down the street. When she refocused the camera, the little girl was gone.

"Something is *very* wrong with this video," she whispered. "None of that happened."

It was as if the creature knew she was going after him to find the little girl in the video. It was trying to scare her into silence. She turned off the VCR. Was the version she'd given to the cops still the same? Were the videos really morphing? What kind of control did this tall clown have over her imagination?

In her dreams that night, she saw the evil clown flouncing from side to side of the street, giving suckers to the children.

Opal awoke and wondered, *Is that when he took the little girl?*

Opal felt the pull of the recording and rewound the video, pushing play again.

Her nieces and nephew scrambled for candy thrown from the floats. The little girl with the red sweater and pink ribbon got up after the float passed and grabbed the candy. She felt tense knowing the next parade entry was the evil clown on stilts. She could see him dancing as he ran along the parade route, throwing candy with a baton in his hand like he was leading a marching band, laughing evilly. The little girl stood excitedly when the clown came by. She was gone an instant later.

The clown stops and turns to Opal. He knows she has captured his kidnapping, and his mouth is again open, sharp teeth dripping with saliva. Opal's heart is beating wildly. She can't catch her breath. The clown raises his scepter and runs it through her.

Opal sits on both the sidewalk and on the couch in her living room. Time merges. This scenario didn't happen, but she feels her life's blood running down the sewer drain, anyway. She falls sideways on the couch.

———

Garnet calls her sister several times before dropping off the kids at school. Afterwards, she goes by to see why Opal hadn't answered.

"Opal?" Garnet knocks a few times before using the key her sister gave her for emergencies. Entering the apartment, she sees the television playing the parade and notices the clown coming closer to the screen. His baton rises and falls while he keeps time to an imaginary band. Garnett scowls, confused.

I don't remember the clown having a baton.

She's horrified when she sees the little girl sitting across the street, the one who went missing, and even more so when the clown stops and seems to recognize her. She steps forward, only then seeing Opal's vacant stare as she lies dead on the couch. On the TV, the clown turns around, opening his mouth, his teeth coming toward Garnet and her dead sister with dripping saliva. "Please be kind, rewind," the clown says and Garnet jumps, turning back toward the television.

Then the VCR stops and rewinds itself.

The parade starts at the beginning, and Garnet's children scramble for candy. She hears a scream, and it doesn't register that she is the one screaming.

————

Dawn DeBraal lives in rural Wisconsin with her husband, Red, a dorky rescue dog, and a stray cat. She has published over 600 short stories, drabbles, and poems in online magazines and published anthologies. She also co-wrote a novel, *what the hell happened to joan?* with author Copper Rose under the pen name of Garrison McKnight.

BookBub | Facebook | Goodreads | https://linktr.ee/dawnde braal

CHAPTER 3
WHAT ANGIE WANTS

BETH GAYDON

PATTY STARED at the phone as if that might somehow change the news she'd just received. Angie couldn't be dead. She couldn't. They'd seen each other only a few days ago, at Hal's New Year's Party, all of them thrilled to dance the night away as 1988 became 1989. But according to Hal, Angie would never see 1990.

After far too long, Patty plucked the phone back off its receiver and dialed the number to their mutual friend, Ed. Ed was a cop. He'd know the truth. Maybe Angie was just injured, or gravely ill. Even if she had been murdered, maybe Ed would have proof that Angie's husband Michael hadn't done it. They'd only been married for three years. They'd been talking about babies, for goodness' sake.

"Hello?"

"Ed? It's Patty."

"Patty, hi," Ed said. His voice sounded hollow, and Patty felt cruel for calling him. He'd probably been fielding calls like this all morning, since the news had broken. "It's true, chica."

"All of it? Oh, Ed, it can't be. We just saw her."

"I know, Pats. I can barely believe it myself. But they're saying he stabbed her fourteen times. Strangers don't kill like that, trust me. They're bringing Michael in later today. We expect to get a confession."

"But why would he do that? They were in love. They were happy."

"You can't ever see inside someone else's life, though, can you? What we saw could have been for show. Maybe Michael didn't want kids. Or he did, and Angie refused. One of them might have been cheating. We have to hope Michael gives a confession in full. Because unfortunately, it's impossible to get the other side."

Patty clutched the table below. "So she's gone. She's really gone."

"It's heavy, I know. Listen, a lot of disturbing details are going to come out about her death. Just don't follow the news too much, okay? We'll get Michael prosecuted and get her justice, I promise. You don't have to torture yourself."

"Okay. Thanks, Ed." She hung up the phone and tried to imagine something more disturbing than a husband stabbing his wife fourteen times, but couldn't do it. Then, because she'd never been a good listener when it came to taking care of herself, she curled into a ball and flipped the TV on, hoping to catch more information about her friend's death despite the world seeming to spin around her.

———

As the bright green numbers of her wall clock shifted to 5:00 P.M., Patty returned to the TV. The morning news had been too early to catch the details, but after dozens of calls between their friend group, she'd learned the police arrested Michael and reporters had met him at the courthouse. It would be on the evening news, and she didn't want to miss it.

Sure enough, the local reporters led with the tale of Angie Nelson's murder. They plastered a picture of the twenty-five-year-old brunette on the screen, one of Angie's better ones. Her smile was bright, and she had impeccably styled her hair, some-thing she rarely did, saying she didn't have time for the hair products the rest of them blew half their paychecks on. They showed the outside of the Nelson home before flipping over to the courthouse, where officers led Michael upstairs in handcuffs.

"Michael, Michael! Why'd you do it? Why'd you kill your wife?" reporters called.

Patty leaned in, wanting to hear this. The police officers holding him tried to push him forward, but Michael stopped walking and turned back to glare at the camera. "I didn't do it," he said. "I love my wife. Everyone knows I love her. I'm inno-cent! I would never hurt a hair on her head!"

Michael got more belligerent as the reporters egged him on, but he admitted to nothing, swearing he hadn't killed Angie. Patty thought he looked devastated. Not like what you'd expect of a killer trying to hide his crimes, but a truly distraught husband who'd lost his wife. She wished the news would zoom in on his face, but as quick as the report had started, it stopped, moving on to the upcoming state fair. Patty would have to set up her VCR for the next time. Though Ed had told her not to pay too much attention, she felt like she'd need to replay every single clip if she was ever going to truly accept Angie's death.

The VCR brought back a detail Patty had forgotten: the camcorder on New Year's Eve. Viv and Frank, the only couple in attendance with both kids and money, had splurged on the camera to tape all of little Tiffany's dance recitals. They'd brought it with them and filmed everything. Patty needed to get her hands on that tape, to watch Angie and Michael together. How could they all have missed the signs? Patty was willing to bet if she watched it, everything would make more sense.

Patty called up Viv and asked to borrow the video, telling Viv she wanted to see their friend alive and happy again. Viv, who sounded frazzled with both kids' screams piercing the phone line, told her no problem, but she'd have to come pick it up. Then she asked what Patty was planning to wear to the funeral, and the two of them spent another twenty minutes trying to determine what was tasteful and appropriate for a murder victim's last goodbye.

————

Visiting Viv took another two hours—now that the kids were quiet, they had to gossip about everything that'd gone on, and whether they believed Michael did it—so by the time Patty got home, exhaustion hit her hard, and she wasn't sure she'd be sharp enough to watch the tape. Still, she pushed it into the VCR slot, and lay on the couch with a box of tissues, certain no matter what she saw, she would cry.

Would their group ever be happy again? Or would 1989 be the year that crushed all their hopes and dreams forever?

Angie wasn't in much of the video at first. Frank had the camera, and he was filming the boys doing shots in the kitchen. Patty didn't remember that part of the party, but they looked like they were having fun. Michael was there wearing a silly grin, along with Ed, and it was strange remembering they now stood on opposite sides of a very serious crime. They clinked their shot glasses together again, and then Frank moved on, though he still stuck to the guys in the group.

Angie passed by in the background once, her face pinched, but it wasn't until halfway through the video that Frank focused on her and the other women. Patty saw herself looking a bit buzzed, embarrassingly enough. She and Angie clasped on to one another for a stirring round of Auld Lang Syne. After that, Angie and Viv started doing their best *Footloose* dances, until Frank put the camera down and told Viv he'd catch her for the *Dirty Dancing* dance instead. Frank hadn't filmed that part, which was for the best—Patty vividly remembered him dropping Viv and both of them falling on the floor.

The video held many more fun memories, but only showed Michael and Angie together twice. Frank caught their midnight kiss, which looked sincere in Angie's opinion. At a later point in the night, they danced together and held one another so tightly that it seemed impossible one of them killed the other only a few short days later.

When the film ended and the screen turned to gray fuzz, Patty rewound it, unable to help herself. Something compelled her to watch it again, to catch some sign that Michael would soon turn murderous. Flirting with another woman, perhaps, or secretly scowling at Angie. Patty let the tape spin back to the beginning, through the shots, through Angie walking behind everyone, through—

Patty paused the tape. Angie had been in the background the first time, Patty was certain, but she'd been further back, appearing out of the hallway near the bathroom. Now she was closer—barely—but closer. Patty hit rewind again, watching the people scurry backwards until just before Angie appeared. She pressed play.

Angie stared at her from the screen. Not at Frank holding the camera, but at Patty herself. She stood even closer now, another few steps. Patty shivered as goosebumps popped up on her arms, and she yanked a blanket down from the couch. It couldn't be. She'd lost her mind in her grief—that had to be the only explanation. She clicked the TV off, wrapping herself up like a child scared of the bogeyman, and tried to sleep.

———

Patty slept all night on the couch, never quite comfortable enough to enter her room, although that made no logical sense. It wasn't like she wasn't used to it. Patty had lived alone for two years, since her last roommate got married. There was only one door leading out of the apartment. If someone broke in and spotted her on the couch, she had little chance of escape. Still, her bedroom had seemed too lonely, especially when she pictured Angie, stabbed to death in her own bed.

After blinking the sleep away from her eyes, Patty stretched and opened the blinds. In the light of day, she was sure she'd be less crazy, better able to study the video. But first, she wanted coffee. She could use all the help she could get in freeing her from the unfortunate funk surrounding her. She dawdled around the kitchen, pawing through yesterday's mail, before turning back to the living room. As she passed through the doorway, the TV lit up.

Patty froze. The remote control was visible from where she stood, exactly as she'd left it on the coffee table. She tried to pretend she'd imagined it, but no, there was the blue screen, the small number three up in the corner indicating she had the right channel to play a video. Patty sucked in a breath. What was happening to her?

She could have called someone. A few neighbors down the hall liked to chat and have coffee. They'd at least give her company, even if she didn't share her fears. But Patty suspected she was already in good company—just not the living kind.

"Angie?" she whispered.

Nothing.

Patty forced herself back to the couch, sat down, and hit play again. The moment she wanted had already passed, so she rewound it a couple of seconds. She watched as Angie crept even closer to the screen. Angie still seemed flustered, but she directed it at Patty now.

Patty rewound it.

Angie, a bit closer, looking even more disconcerted. Rewind again. Angie, almost in the foreground now, staring at Patty.

Rewind.

This time, Angie marched right up to the TV's curved glass and then turned left. She stared over her shoulder before turning back to lock eyes with Patty.

"What are you showing me, Angie?" Patty whispered, chills tingling her entire body. She reversed the video to Angie's first entrance, and things were somehow back to normal. Angie exited the hallway, her face once more unsettled, before leaving the hallway for off-screen shenanigans.

But this time, Patty paid little attention to Angie. It was the left side of the screen she needed to examine. A few seconds after Angie moved, someone else stepped out of the hallway, likely a man, but Frank was already spinning the camera before the person's face materialized.

Patty pressed pause and cradled her face in her hands, now rocking back and forth. "What am I doing, Angie? Am I going mental? Or are you telling me something?"

She viewed the clip three more times, grabbing the TV Guide and a pen from the end table and scribbling out a few notes. Then she started the whole video over and watched again, looking for a man wearing jeans, white sneakers, and a bright blue and white striped shirt. She found him towards the end. Patty studied the video. He seemed to be arguing with someone off camera. Though the man's dispute partner only showed arms flailing about, they looked feminine.

Angie? Patty thought so, but it was difficult to be sure. None of the women had worn long sleeves, other than Sheila, who was always overdressed and had chosen her best puffy-sleeved black cocktail attire. So it wasn't Sheila, and it wasn't Patty, obviously, but that didn't make it Angie.

But, now that Patty had a better view, she thought she had pinned the man's identity. Though Patty didn't know every single person at Hal's party—Hal had a wide circle of friends—she had met most of them at least briefly. Patty searched her memory. The arguing man was named… Ross? No, Russ!

When they'd been introduced, Hal had said that Russ hadn't been around in ages. Years ago, he'd worked with both Hal and Angie back before they'd all gotten professional jobs. Back when they were all still stuck in mind-numbing retail. Patty didn't miss those days she spent folding shirt after shirt at Sears, while getting screamed at by random ladies for the smallest thing.

"Russ, right, Ange?" Patty asked the air. "Is that who did this?"

But only silence greeted her.

————

Though Patty believed Michael could help her, it was impossible to talk to him immediately following Angie's murder. There were an awful lot of steps in arresting, charging, and bonding out a suspect. Eventually, a judge denied Michael's bail, leaving him in jail awaiting trial, and Patty was able to schedule a visitation. Even that wasn't simple, requiring her to call out of work for the day to make the jail's visiting hours. Michael accepting her visit almost surprised her. Surely, he must have assumed she was coming to berate him.

The body search she was subjected to unnerved her. The other inmates leering at her didn't help, either. Why did they even look in her direction when they had visitors of their own? But Patty was determined to help Angie, so she stayed and waited for Michael, her body tense and tight as she waited.

When they brought Michael out in handcuffs a few minutes later, he looked gaunt, though he'd only been in jail a week. Patty wondered if he was eating. He sat down across the table from her and slumped back against his seat. "What do you want, Patty?"

Michael was so wary, Patty didn't bother with any pleasantries. "What do you know about Russ?" she asked, studying his face to gauge his reaction.

Michael's brows furrowed. "Russ? The guy Angie used to work with? Not much. Why?"

"Angie didn't mention anything about them fighting? Arguing?"

Now Michael leaned forward, folding his hands together on the table, the cuffs clinking against the wood. "What are you talking about? Do you know something? Something to help me?"

Patty shook her head. "No, I don't know anything for certain. But there's a video from the New Year's Party. He's fighting with someone, a woman, and I think it might be Angie." She paused. She couldn't mention Angie coming to the front of the screen without sounding crazy, and one little fight didn't seem like much evidence. "Ugh... I don't know, Michael. I just want to believe you're innocent."

"I am." Michael slouched back again and tilted his head to the sky. "I loved that woman more than anything in the world. But to go around accusing people, to put them through this hell..." He gestured around the room, his eyes lingering on the tiny rectangular window at the top of the wall, and shook his head.

"Russ may have flirted with her that night," Michael said. "But if so, I didn't see it. I know that they went on a few dates back before we met. They'd all lost touch, as far as I know. At least, until Hal ran into him again." Michael leaned forward and rubbed his eyes. When he opened them again, Patty saw how dark the circles under his eyes were. "Angie would have mentioned any problems to me, wouldn't she?"

Patty didn't know what to say. Her foot began bouncing under the table. "Any chance you have his address?"

Michael blinked. "Why would I have that?? Wait, Patty, you think this guy might have killed Angie, and you want to, what, go visit him?"

"I didn't say he killed Angie. I just asked if they were arguing."

"But you must think something more than that. You wouldn't come to the jail to ask about some random tiff."

Patty shifted in her seat. "It's not my video. It's Viv's. But if I were you, I'd ask her for it. There's two parts. One, when Angie exits the hallway. She looks upset. Someone follows her. Based on the clothes, it's Russ. Later, there's the argument. I can't be positive it's Angie, but if it is... Like I said. Ask Viv for the VHS."

Michael sat still, holding his breath for a moment`, and then he nodded. "I'll do that. You believe me, Patty? Really?"

"I think I do," Patty said, picturing Angie's face on that video.

———

After that, Michael's defense was up to him. Patty returned the VHS to Viv and attempted to restart her regular life while still grieving her friend. Sometimes she laughed and felt guilty for laughing, but more and more able to turn her thoughts to something else each day. She assumed that was what Angie would have wanted—for her friends to go on with their lives.

But one evening, after a long day of work, Patty stood in her kitchen, still wearing her uniform, spooning soup out of the Campbell's can and trying to remember if Andy Warhol had died last year or the year before. She was in the middle of wondering why the entire country had gone so mad over soup portraits, when the TV came on. Patty heard the click first, then the sound of static, followed by voices. She froze, soup can in one hand and spoon in the other.

"Angie?" she whispered.

"The trial of Michael Nelson, accused murderer of his wife Angela Nelson, has been set for early next year. Michael, once a popular—"

The TV switched off. Patty shook the ice out of her veins and put her dinner down, then wandered over to her couch. She clicked the TV back on, but the news report was already over. "What do you expect me to do?" Patty asked the empty air. "I told Michael about the video."

Her dead friend didn't offer any insight, but Patty understood well enough. The video hadn't been enough. It wouldn't be enough. She had to get more evidence. She hadn't seen Russ once since the New Year's Party. How could she possibly worm her way into his life now?

She grabbed her address book, lifted the phone off the receiver, and tapped out Hal's number. "Hal? Hi, it's Patty. I was wondering, is your friend Russ seeing anyone? No? Well, then, how about doing this gal a favor?"

———

Russ showed up at Patty's house to pick her up right on time. Patty pretended not to be ready on the pretense of getting him inside. Her new camcorder sat in the back of the room, the little red light hidden by a dark piece of tape.

"I'll be just a minute," she said. "Would you care for a drink?"

"Sure. What have you got?"

"There's some coffee on the pot. Or water or beer. Oh, and there's a few cold Cokes in the fridge."

"A beer would be great. But don't trouble yourself. I'll get it. You want one, too?" Russ called, already moseying his way into Patty's kitchen.

"That'd be great, thanks!" Patty called back. Now she wouldn't need to pretend she wasn't ready. She would suggest they finish their drinks before leaving instead. She ran back to her bedroom anyway, slipping on shoes and taking in a deep breath. "This is for you, Angie."

Russ was sitting at her tiny kitchen table when she reached the kitchen. He pointed at a full beer across from him and took a sip of his own. "Not many women in my world drink beer," he commented.

"They must not be sophisticated like me," Patty replied, offering him a smile.

Russ laughed and leaned back in the chair. "I have to admit, when Hal called me, I didn't quite remember you."

"No one remembers me when Angie's around," Patty said,

not adding that she wouldn't have remembered him either if their dead friend hadn't pointed him out in a video. "You knew her through work, right?"

"Right. Real shame, what happened to her."

"Yes. A real shame." Patty sipped her beer, crossing and uncrossing her ankles as nerves took over. What was she doing? She should have tipped off the police. "She said you two dated a few times, I think. Is that right?"

Russ studied her before answering, taking a long sip. His eyes narrowed. "A few times, yes. Didn't work out. She wasn't my type."

"Oh no? She said the opposite." Now it was Patty's turn to study *him*. For a second, Russ's mask dropped, and his face twisted.

"I might be misremembering," she said.

That seemed to placate Russ a little. "What difference does it make, anyway? She's dead. Sorry. Not to be brash, but women like Angie, they're all teases. Make you think they want you, when they really want some rich guy who'll take care of them. You're not a tease, are you, Patty?"

Patty's hands grew clammy. "I'm not after anyone's money, if that's what you're asking. But I don't take men to bed on the first date, either. So don't get any ideas."

Russ grinned. "I can respect that. Most definitely. But I bet some men could change your mind."

"They haven't yet," Patty replied. She didn't smile, not liking where the conversation was going. She took another long swig and set the bottle down. "Well. Should we get going?"

Russ waved his hand. "Take a chill pill, Pats. We're getting to know each other. Dinner can wait."

The overly familiar nickname did little to appease her, but Patty needed more on video, anyway. "Should we move to the living room? It's more comfortable." *And closer to the door, should escape become necessary.*

"Righteous." Russ gave her a cocky grin as he stood.

Patty scrambled up and reached the couch first, hoping she didn't look too crazy, sitting herself nearer the door. Even if Russ hadn't killed Angie, he gave off a creepy vibe. After he sat on the other side, Patty glanced between him and the door. Nothing blocked her way. If it came to a race, she would win.

"Oh, hey, that reminds me. The night of the New Year's Party at Hal's—what was it you and Angie were fighting about?"

Russ's body tensed, and he rotated toward her with a raised eyebrow. "You ask a lot about Angie."

"She was my friend, and the one sure thing you and I have in common. And I guess I just miss her." Patty had already prepared that answer. She fully expected him to get weirded out by the questioning, even if he was innocent.

"Well, I don't like thinking about her." Russ turned to the TV. "Should we put something on?"

"Sure." Patty handed him the remote, thinking it would give her a little time to recalibrate her questions. Her head started to swim. She put her finger to her eyebrow. "Wow. One beer is really doing me in."

"Chicks. You're all lightweights." Russ shook his head, but Patty caught him smirking.

"Oh my god," she said, jumping up even though it made her wobble. "You drugged me. You put something in my drink."

Russ scoffed. "Right. Like I'd need to drug you. Look at me and look at you."

Looking was impossible for Patty, whose vision was blurred. She blinked, but her eyes felt heavy. She struggled to her feet, but swayed in her spot. Russ watched her, leering, and then stood up. Patty tried to step back, but her legs were too wobbly. Russ put his hands on her arms.

"That's alright, Pats. I'll take good care of you. And we'll keep this between us, won't we? I'd hate for your reputation to take a hit."

"You killed Angie," she said.

"What if I did?" Russ asked. "Stupid woman acted like we

weren't perfect together. But you won't remember this, Pats. I don't know how you figured it out, anyway. Weird, since the cops didn't. Did she tell you? She must have. She rejected me. Like she cared about that stupid husband of hers. She'd been leading me on all night. Told you I *hate* a tease."

Patty didn't comprehend most of what he was saying. Her head was spinning too hard, and she was blacking out. She knew that Russ was pushing her onto the couch, and then—

Then she burst up, full of a strength that made little sense. She didn't feel like her body was her own anymore, like someone else had possessed her. Her arms pushed Russ away, and her hands found the vase on the end table. They lifted it high over her head, but it wasn't her doing it.

"You bastard," Patty heard Angie say as she smashed the vase over Russ's head. "You bastard." She smashed it twice more, but then it shattered and fell on the floor, and Russ fell next to it. "I wanted it to be fourteen times. Three is far less than you deserve."

Angie had given her strength, but Patty could feel it waning.

"Thank you, Patty," Angie's voice said. Then she let out one long cry, a cry for help, and then Patty was falling, falling.

———

Darkness. Patty tugged her eyelid muscles, but they felt heavy. She moaned and pushed herself up, certain Russ had drugged her. She needed to call for help—

"Whoa there. Sit back, dear. You need your rest. There you go. Good girl."

Patty got one eye open and saw a nurse standing next to her.

"What happened?" she said, her voice hoarse. "How did I get here?"

"Your neighbors brought you. You did a real number on your date, but I say he deserved it. Drugging a sweet little thing like you. But I've never heard of someone drugged fighting back so hard. You must be some kind of miracle."

"I didn't fight anyone. Angie did."

"Pretty sure they said you were the only two people in the room. You almost killed him, they say. The police will want to question you, but I've already told them you'd be too out of it to give a coherent statement. You just rest now."

Patty closed her eyes. Would they charge her with an assault she didn't remember while Russ got away with Angie's murder? It was too much. She let herself drift back to sleep.

———

The next day, the hospital discharged Patty, but not Russ. She hadn't met yet with the police yet—had snuck out, actually, not wanting to oppose Russ's version of things when she had no counterclaim. When she got home, she ran to her camcorder, praying it would tell her the truth about what happened. It was dead, of course it was dead, but she was able to get the tape out anyway and she shoved it into the VCR.

"I'd hate for your reputation to take a hit," Russ said when Patty hit play.

"Thank you, God." Patty closed her eyes and let out a long sigh of relief. It was all right there, on tape.

She let it play a little longer, her eyes widening at Russ's confession, and then, to her utter disbelief, Patty watched as Angie appeared on screen and entered her body. Starting there, Patty spoke with Angie's voice.

Patty hadn't gained extraordinary strength while drugged— she'd been possessed—a gift from Angie for tracking down her killer. Afterwards, the screen went fuzzy. Patty stared at it, and a second later Angie walked onto the screen. She stared at Patty for a long time, smiled, and walked away.

She watched the tape again, though this time Angie wasn't visible, and Patty only heard her own voice as events unfolded.

"Goodbye, Angie," Patty whispered, pressing her palm to the screen. She took the VHS out, ready for that chat with the police.

———

Beth Gaydon is an internet analyst living in Tennessee with her kids, dogs, and a husband who made her get rid of her VCR. Her most recent publications include stories in online magazines such as *The Sirens Call* and *The First Line* and in several anthologies, including *Transform the World* (Other Worlds Ink) and *Ill Winds and Wild Weather* (Smoking Pen Press).

Fable I Goodreads I Amazon Author Page

CHAPTER 4
PLAY

C.R.J. SMITH

"YOU GUYS DON'T HAVE A VCR?" said David.

"A what?" said Marie.

"A VCR? For watching video cassettes?"

"Oh, a video box," said Marie. "No, we haven't got one, but we can rent one from the video shop sometimes. We got one the other week and watched *Ghostbusters*. It was mad. Have you seen it?"

"I saw it in the theater about two years ago."

"The theater?" said Marie's little brother, Jimmy.

"Yeah, a movie theater," said David.

"Here in Ireland, we call it a cinema, David," said Marie.

"This town has one, right?"

"It does, yeah."

"Well, that's something, I guess."

"It burned down a few years ago, though," said Marie. "We're waiting for them to fix it up. The closest cinema's in Navan, but Dad doesn't like going there, so we don't go much. He might bring you though, since you're on your holidays and that."

"Great," said David, and walked out of the room.

Marie called out after him, "Me and Jimmy are headin' out to play in the field if you wanna come with us."

"Maybe another time," said David from the hallway. "I don't know if I could handle the excitement of a field on my first day." He went into his room, lay on the bed and said, "It's gonna be a long month."

———

Marie and Jimmy played tag in the field next to their house until Jimmy fell down, exhausted.

"Come on, Jim."

"Can't. Need a minute." He lay out.

Marie sat down beside him and let him catch his breath, then asked, "What do you think of David?"

"I don't know. He seems a bit." He furrowed his brow as he searched for the right word.

"Pompous," said Marie.

"What does that mean?"

"Thinks he's better than us."

"Yeah, that."

"It's gonna be a long month."

"Maybe he'll be alright when he gets used to it."

"Nah, I heard Mam and Dad talking about Auntie Bridget before and how she got all highfalutin after she moved to America. He seems to be like that, too."

"Marie?"

She rolled her eyes and said, "It means she got all fancy and started having notions."

"Oh, okay. High…"

"Falutin."

"High falutin."

"Don't leave a gap. It's all one word."

"Okay. What if we just play out here all the time? If he doesn't wanna come out with us, then that's not our fault."

"Mam won't let us. She'll want us hangin' round with him so he can't go back and tell Auntie Bridget that he was ignored."

"Jimmy," their mother's voice called out. "Marie."

They both instinctively ducked down further in the long grass. Their mother called their names again.

"What should we do?" said Jimmy.

"I don't know. I'm fairly hungry."

"Me too."

They got up and made their way back towards the house.

"Will you read to me tonight?" said Jimmy.

"I thought you were bored with me reading to you."

"Yeah, well, I changed my mind."

Marie smiled. "Of course," she said, and put her arm around his shoulder.

————

After dinner and bath time, it was time for bed. Jimmy jumped on to Marie's bed and she searched around underneath it. Eventually she popped up holding a book—Stephen King's *The Shining*.

"Okay, I haven't started this one yet, but it's meant to be a bit scary. Is that okay?"

Jimmy frowned. "How scary is it?"

"I don't know. A girl in my class said it was really scary, but she gets scared at thunder and lightning, so…"

"I get scared at thunder and lightning."

"Yeah, but you're six, that's okay. We'll start this and if it's too much, we'll stop, okay?"

"Okay."

Just as she opened the book, the bedroom door opened. David walked in, holding a camcorder to his head.

"Here we have my Irish cousins, Jimmy and Marie. Say 'hi,' guys."

"What are you doing?" said Marie.

"Making a little documentary of my trip. I wanna be able to show my friends back home how primitive folk live."

"Why do you have to be such an arse?" said Marie.

David ignored her and continued his narration. "Although it's hard to tell, they actually are speaking English."

"Get out of me room," said Marie. She stood up and pushed him back out the door.

"I seem to have gotten too close. I'll retreat and observe from a safe distance."

"I'm tellin' Mam about this."

Marie slammed her door shut and could hear David laughing as he went down the hallway. She hadn't even got back to her bed when her mother burst into the room.

"Who slammed that door?"

"It was…"

"I thought the house was falling down."

"No, but David…"

"Auld Mrs. Reilly up the road probably heard it."

"I had to…"

"And are you gonna buy a new one if this one breaks? Doors don't grow on trees, you know."

"But I…"

"And I don't need David telling his mother we are slamming doors in the middle of the night."

"It's half nine…"

"Now, into bed, the two of you."

With that, she left the room, closing the door very carefully. Marie couldn't hear him, but she knew David was laughing his head off in his room.

"I don't like David," said Jimmy.

"No, me neither," said Marie. "Anyway, let's get going at this." She opened the book and started reading, "Chapter One, job interview. Jack Torrence thought, 'officious little prick.'"

"Eh, Marie?"

She rolled her eyes. "It means…"

———

The next day, Marie and Jimmy wolfed down their breakfasts and tried to slip out the back door unnoticed.

"Where are you two off to?"

"Just going out to play."

"Take your cousin with you."

"Ah, Mam, do we have to?"

"Yes."

"But…"

"No buts. You're not leaving this house without him."

Marie fought back the urge to argue. "Fine." She went and knocked on his door and there was no answer. She knocked again. "He's not up, Mam," she shouted. "He's probably jet-lagged."

"Alright, leave him for now, then."

"Does that mean we can go out?"

"Go on."

Marie said nothing, ran to the back door, Grabbed Jimmy by the arm, and dragged him out.

"Don't go further than the field," their mother shouted after them.

"Ah, Mam, why not?"

"Because I don't want to be searching for you when your cousin wakes up."

"Ah for fu—"

"Marie Ann Finnegan," said her mother in a voice that chilled her blood, "What was that?"

"Nothing, Mam," said Marie as she pushed Jimmy away from the house. When they were out of earshot, she said, "Let's go and call for Catherine."

"But Mam said to not leave the field."

"Yeah, but I want Catherine to come to the field to play with us, but for that to happen, we have to leave the field to get her and bring her back."

"I don't know."

"She got one of those *Ghostbusters* backpack things for her birthday and she might let you play with it."

"Really?"

"Yep."

"Okay then." They walked on a bit, then Jimmy said, "It's a proton pack."

"What?"

"The *Ghostbusters* thing, it's a proton pack, not a backpack." He followed this with an exaggerated eye-roll. Marie gave him an evil eye and laughed.

"You're a cheeky little sod," she said.

They arrived at Catherine's house and knocked on the door. Catherine answered, looking annoyed, and said, "What do you want?"

"Do you wanna come out?" said Marie.

"No, we rented a video box, and we just put the first film on."

"Really?" said Jimmy, excitedly.

"Can we come in and watch it too?" said Marie.

"What?" said Catherine, looking horrified. "No, my dad said—"

"Ah, it'll be grand," said Marie, pushing past her. "We'll be quiet. Ya won't even know we're here. Jimmy, behave yourself, alright?"

Catherine stood at the open door for a moment and by the time she went back to the sitting room, Marie and Jimmy were sitting on the floor in front of the tv, watching *Gremlins*, and eating popcorn. She sighed, went to get another bag of popcorn, and then sat back down on the couch.

When the movie ended, Catherine said, "Right, the two of you should probably get going, I suppose."

"Nah, we're okay. We're tryin' to stay away from home for a while."

Before Catherine could say anything, Marie had *Gremlins* out of the player and was Putting *Superman III* in.

"You know you're meant to rewind the film before you take it out."

"Oh, yeah." Said Marie. "Ah, you can do it later, Cath."

"Ah, yeah, that's grand. Anythin' else I can do for ya? D'you wanna root through me room and take a few toys while you're here?"

"Yes, please." Said Jimmy.

"Hush, Jimmy," said Marie. "No, just we wouldn't mind a bit more popcorn."

They got no more popcorn and only got a half an hour into *Superman* when the phone in the hallway rang. Catherine's dad answered.

"Hello? How'ya, Mary. Yeah, they're here. No, just them. Grand, I'll tell them. Alright, good luck, Mary. Bye. Bye, bye... bye."

He came into the sitting room and said, "Marie and Jimmy, that was your mum. She wants you home straight away."

"Oh, okay." She got up and dragged Jimmy to his feet. "Let's get goin', Jim. I think we might be in a bit of trouble."

They ran home, not in any hurry to be punished, but hoping the sooner they got back, the less severe it would be. When they reached the field, they stopped.

"What the hell?"

"What's goin' on, Marie?"

A police car was parked outside the house.

"I don't know, Jim."

They ran to the house and into the kitchen.

"Where the hell have you two been?" their mother yelled.

"At Catherine's. You called..."

"Have you seen David?"

"David? No, we haven't seen him today. Why?"

"He's gone missing."

"Missing?" said Marie and Jimmy in unison.

"I went to wake him up, and he wasn't in his room. There's no sign of him."

"Jesus."

"Marie! Watch your language."

Officer Murphy came in the back door. "Alright, Mary. I've had a look around the house, and everything looks okay. No sign anyone was trying to break in or anything. I've called it in and all our officers are on the lookout for him. I'll have to get in touch with my sergeant, and we'll figure out where to go from here."

"That's it?"

"That's all I can do right now."

"What about a search?"

"You're free to start lookin', and I'll see what I can do, but we're horrid understaffed at the minute." The officer turned to leave. "I'll be in touch as soon as I can."

"Alright, Pascal, thanks for coming over." Mary leaned with both hands on the table and her head bowed. "I can't believe this. Please God, let him come back safe."

"What can we do, mum? Will we go lookin' for him?"

She didn't answer for a minute. She barely moved. Then she stood up straight and said, "Your dad's already out looking for him. I'm gonna ring everyone I can and get people out searching. I need the two of you to stay here in case he comes back or if the guards call."

Ten minutes later, phone calls made and instructions on what to do if anything happened, Marie and Jimmy were alone in the house with only the ticking of the living room clock for company.

"Marie?"

"Yeah?"

"Is David gonna be okay?"

"Yeah. Yeah, of course he is. He probably just went out for a walk or something. Come on, let's go play."

They played for about twenty minutes, making up stories acted out by action figures, but their hearts weren't really in it.

"We should do something," said Marie.

"Like what?"

"Investigate."

"Investigate where?"

"In David's room. We can look for clues."

"Like detectives?"

"Exactly like detectives."

They went to David's room and started mooching around, looking under the bed, under the sheets, on top of the wardrobe.

"Nothing seems out of place," said Marie.

"Should we use our magnifying glass?"

"I don't think that'll help."

Marie went over to the camcorder on the dresser. "He always had this thing stuck to his face. Maybe he recorded something that'd help?"

"How does it work?"

"I don't know. There's a little tape in it, but it looks smaller than a videotape." She picked it up and examined it. "How do you get it out?" She poked and prodded at buttons until the tape deck opened. "How can we watch this?"

"Would this thing help?"

Jimmy had been going through David' bag and had an adaptor for playing the smaller tape in a VCR.

"Jimmy, you're a genius."

She took the tape from him as he blushed.

"Now, where can we watch it?"

Twenty minutes later, they were knocking on Catherine's door again.

"Ah, jaysus. What are youse doin' here again?"

Marie held up the VHS tape. "We need to use the video box."

"Ah, Marie, it has to be back at the shop by seven. I just wanna watch…"

"David's missin'."

"I know, Mam and Dad are out lookin' for him."

"Oh, right. Well, this tape might have clues on it to help find him."

"I thought you hated him."

"Yeah, well, he's an arse, but I don't want him to get hurt or anythin'."

"Alright, come in."

Marie took *Halloween III* out of the player and put David's tape in. It started with the timestamp at 21:28, with David leaving his room and announcing he was going to hassle his cousins. There was the bust up in Marie's room, him laughing as their mother yelled at them, David going back to his room and sitting on the bed.

It then cut to 02:37. The room was dark, and David was whispering. "I just heard something scratching at the window. I don't know what the heck it was."

There followed just over a minute of breathing. "It must have been an animal..."

David stopped talking, and there was a faint scratching sound. "There it is. What *is* that?"

The scratching stopped, soon replaced with a light tapping noise that steadily got louder until David asked, "Who are you?"

There was silence for about ten seconds.

"What do you want?"

Silence for more than a minute.

"Now?"

Twenty-seven seconds of silence.

"Okay."

David then got out of bed, placed the camcorder on the dresser, and walked over to the window. His moonlit silhouette could be seen opening the window, climbing out, and closing it behind him. After five minutes of silence, Marie started fast forwarding and playing, forwarding and playing until the tape ended. There was nothing else on it.

Catherine spoke first. "What the fuck?"

"Yeah, that was… what was that?" said Marie.

"He just got up and left. It makes no sense."

"The scratching, though. What was that?"

"A banshee," said Jimmy.

"Don't be stupid, Jimmy." Said Marie. "Banshees scream, they don't go around whisperin'."

"There must have been someone at the window," said Catherine.

"We have to get this tape to the cops," said Marie. She rewound the tape and ejected it. "Right, come on, Jimmy."

They were about to leave when the front door opened, and Catherine's parents walked in.

"Marie," said Catherine's mother. "What are you doing here?"

"We found a video, and we thought it might help findin' David. There was…"

"It's alright, Marie," she said, "We found him."

"What?"

"We found him in the woods. He was a bit tired and confused, but he seems okay. I think he just got lost. He's at home now."

"Oh. Oh, okay," said Marie. "Eh, thanks Missus Cleary, we'll get going."

She grabbed Jimmy by the arm and half dragged him from the house. They ran home. Entering the back door to the kitchen, they expected to be admonished. Instead, their mother went straight to them and embraced them in a hug.

"I was so worried about you."

"We were just in Catherine's, we…"

"I know, her mother called to tell me. I was so worried when I got home and you weren't here."

She held them for a few moments, then released them and said, "In future, though, if I tell you to stay here and not go out, that's what you do, right?"

"I know, Mam, but we found a video, and we thought it

might help and when we watched it at Catherine's it was David actin' strange and talkin' to someone at the window and..."

"We think it was a banshee."

"Shut up, Jimmy. It wasn't a banshee, but it was somethin'..."

"He was sleepwalking."

Marie and Jimmy stared at her for a second.

"He was sleepwalkin'?" said Marie.

"Yes. He says he used to do it a lot, but not for the last three years, so he didn't think it happened anymore."

"But he was actin' awful strange in the video."

"People act strange when they sleepwalk, Marie. It's just one of those things."

They stared at her again, unsure.

"Okay. Where is he?"

"He's asleep. We should leave him to it for now."

"Okay. Can we go out?"

"Yes, but just stay in the field, okay?"

"Yes, Mam."

They went and sat in the field.

"What do you think, Jim?"

"I still think it was a banshee."

"Jesus, Jim, it wasn't a banshee, alright."

They sat in silence for a minute.

"It could have been a vampire," said Marie.

"Ah, no, Marie," said Jimmy, jumping to his feet. "It wouldn't be, would it?"

"Sit down, would ya?" I'm just sayin' it could be."

"So, does that mean David is a vampire now?"

"He might be. We'll have to keep an eye on him."

They stayed talking, thinking, and making plans until they were called in for dinner. David was still asleep. He didn't emerge from his room until later, after sundown.

———

The next day, Marie and Jimmy were up early and left their room just in time to see David going into his.

"What was he doing all night?"

"I don't know, Jim," said Marie. "Nothin' good, anyway."

They had breakfast and went out. They searched for anything suspicious; dead bodies, pools of blood. They visited Catherine and found her and her family still alive. When they went home that evening, David was still asleep and there had been no talk of anything suspicious happening in the area.

When they went to bed that evening, Jimmy said, "What's wrong, Marie? You're awful quiet."

"Ah, I dunno. I just... I thought somethin' would happen today, ya know?"

"I'm glad nothing happened. Nobody got hurt."

"Ah yeah, I'm glad about that, but you know what I mean."

"Can we carry on with *The Shining*?"

"Yeah. I wanna try and stay awake tonight, anyway. See if we can see what David is at."

"I don't know if I can stay awake that long," said Jimmy, his brow furrowed, "But I'll give it a go."

Within an hour, they were both asleep. It was dark when Marie woke up some time later, confused. She was sitting against the headboard of her bed and Jimmy was snoring beside her. It took her a second to remember not turning the light off.

Mam must have switched it off

As her eyes adjusted to the dark and she came to her senses more, she noticed a small red light in the far corner of the room. She also thought she could make out a dark figure, but she couldn't be sure.

"David?"

There was a shuffling sound as the red light moved towards the door, which quickly opened and closed. Marie jumped out of bed, switched the light on, and locked the door.

"Jimmy," she said, shaking her brother. "Jimmy, wake up."

Jimmy mumbled and sat up, and Marie dragged him off the bed.

"What are ya doin'?"

"Are you alright, Jim?"

"What? Why'd you wake me up?"

"David was in the room."

Jimmy stared at her with sheer terror in his eyes. "What are we gonna do?"

"It's alright, he's gone, calm down. If you wee yourself, I'm not helping clean it up again, alright? Just calm down. We'll stay in here 'til morning, then we'll tell Mam and Dad. They have to get him out of here."

They stayed up playing cards and talking. It was still dark when an almighty crash came from the sitting room.

Marie and Jimmy both screamed and then held their breath. There was complete silence in the house.

"Why are Mam and Dad not getting up?" said Jimmy.

Marie didn't answer.

After a few minutes of just staring at the door, Marie said, "I have to go check."

"No, Marie, No."

"I have to. Stay here, alright? When I leave, lock the door and don't move from this room."

"I wanna go with you."

"No. You stay here and keep the door locked, got it? Promise?"

Jimmy hesitated, but said, "Promise."

Marie left the room and waited to hear the key turning in the lock before she went down the hall. She was heading to her parents' room but had to pass the sitting room on the way. The television was on. In its glow she saw the cabinet that held the fancy plates lying front down on the floor. The image on the screen looked familiar. She walked into the sitting room and realised it was playing a recording from David's camcorder, which was plugged into the back of the set.

Someone, Marie assumed David, was pacing back and forth in the kitchen, mumbling. "Gotta do it... Gotta get it done... Can't... Can't... Have to." She remembered what Mam had said about sleepwalking people acting strangely.

But why hadn't the noise woken Mam and Dad? Where were they?

This went on for several minutes before he suddenly turned, walked out of the kitchen, went straight to her parents' room. It was dark, so he turned on the camera's light, moved around the bed, and placed the camera on the dresser facing the bed. He was out of frame, but she could hear him breathing. Then, without a word, he advanced with a hammer and struck her father several times in the head. Her mother woke up and was struck before she had time to react.

Marie screamed and ran from the room. In the hallway stood David, smiling and with a bloodied hammer in one hand. He moved towards her and she screamed and ran. She was out the back door and at the edge of the field before she turned around. David wasn't following her.

"Ah, no," she said, and ran back towards the house. "Jimmy," she screamed.

David appeared at the back door, camcorder on his shoulder, and started towards her. She turned and ran into the field.

"Come on then, chase me."

She ran, wanting to get him away from her family and with a vague idea of making it to another house where she could call the police. At the edge of the woods, she looked back and there was no sign of him.

Marie listened but could only hear her own heavy breaths. Then she spotted a small red dot coming towards her on her left. She crept into the woods and came to a small hollow underneath a tree. It was where Jimmy hid every time they played hide and seek. With some difficulty, she squeezed into the space.

Footsteps approached, slow and steady, snapping twigs and crunching dead leaves. Marie held her breath. David passed by nearby and went deeper into the woods. She gave it a few minutes and crept out.

"Marie. Marie." A shout came in the distance. It was Jimmy.

"Oh no, fuck sakes. Why, Jimmy?"

She ran back towards home. Leaving the woods, she could see Jimmy at the back door of the house.

"Go back inside," she yelled.

Jimmy ran towards her, then stopped and screamed. Marie turned around and saw David running towards her. He dropped the camera on the ground and pulled a knife from his belt.

Marie ran. "Get back inside, Jimmy."

Jimmy only moved when Marie was close, so they both entered the kitchen at the same time. She tried to close the door, but David was right behind them and shouldered it open, knocking the siblings to the floor. He stumbled and dropped the knife, but grabbed a hold of Jimmy. He started to choke him and slam his head onto the linoleum floor.

He stopped and let out a cry of pain when Marie plunged the knife into his back. He reeled around, knife still protruding from him, and lunged at Marie. She grabbed a frying pan from the aga and hit him upside the head. He spun around and landed on his back. An unnatural roar left his mouth as the knife went deeper. He jumped up and ran out the back door. Marie watched as he crossed the field and disappeared into the woods.

———

Marie and Jimmy sat in the sitting room, wrapped in blankets. They each had a cup of tea in their hands.

Their mother and father had just left in ambulances, in critical conditions, but still alive. Officer Murphy had spoken to them and taken down their story.

"Alright lads, we're gonna get yous out of here and down to the station. How are yous doin' now?"

"We're okay."

Marie stood, and Jimmy followed suit. She put her arm around him and they went out to the police car. At the station, they were brought to a room with a couch and a television.

"There's specialist officers coming up from Dublin," said officer Murphy. "They'll help search for your cousin, and they'll want to talk to you, too. Is that okay?"

"That's fine," said Marie. "Thank you."

He left and Marie sat down. Jimmy lay down beside her with his head on her lap. They said nothing for a few minutes

"Will I try to find some cartoons on?"

"Mmm hmm."

"You'll have to move so I can get up."

Jimmy started to snore softly. Marie sniggered and rested her hand on his head. She closed her eyes and fell asleep.

———

Officer Murphy loaded the cassette into the VCR. There were fifteen minutes of Marie and Jimmy sleeping. He saw the attack on mister and missus Finnegan. There was the chase from the house to the woods. Marie screaming. And then chase back to the house. When the camera fell, it showed David running and what appeared to be a dark figure, like a huge shadow, following behind.

"Sweet mother of God," said Officer Murphy when it ended.

There was a sound at the window. A scratching and tapping. He walked over and opened it.

"Yes."

He listened intently and nodded his head.

"Okay, yes, I understand."

He ejected the cassette from the player, took out the smaller cassette, opened the top, and pulled out the tape until it was a mess on the floor. He gathered this up and put it in a bin. He found a piece of paper, lit it with a match, and dropped it in.

The tape melted in an instant.

The door opened, and another officer entered. "What's that smell?" he said.

"Oh, nothin'. What's goin' on?"

"They found that young fella in the woods. He's dead."

"Okay, thanks for letting me know."

"Will I tell the kids?"

"No, no. I'm going in to see them now. I'll let them know."

The officer left and officer Murphy smiled. Then he went to talk to Marie and Jimmy.

———

C.R.J. Smith is a writer and photographer from Navan, Ireland.

Facebook | Goodreads | Instagram | Threads | Amazon Author Page | Author Web Site

ENGSTROM FARROW MCCONNELL VERELLE

HOST

EDITED BY
H DAIR BROWN

A DISTURB INK BOOKS
ANTHOLOGY

HOST

WEB WRAITHS | THE 2000S

EDITED BY
H. DAIR BROWN

Published by Disturb Ink Books, an imprint of 79 Franklin Press, LLC.
www.79franklinpress.com

First North American ebook edition September 2024

ASIN (ebook): B0DF6XWF8N

Designed by: H. Dair Brown

❀ Created with Vellum

For those who remain haunted by the "eeee-yoooooo" sound of early dial up

NOTES

Because we are fortunate enough in this collection to have writers from all over the world contributing to *Sinister Century*, you'll see a variation in the spelling of some words from story to story. The editor has chosen to respect the spelling of the country in which the author writes.

———

CHAPTER 1
PAY THE FERRYMAN

DAVID FARROW

#

r/TheRealQuestions - Posted by u/charonite57 - 10 hours ago

Have you ever had a near-death experience?
I mean as close to "lights out" as you can possibly get. A hand
that yanked you back from a crumbling precipice, a bullet that
missed you by inches, a tangled shoelace that made you late for
a train crash, etc. I'm curious how many of us have had a real
brush with death.

Serious answers only please.

💬 **62 comments**

—

DangerzOne - 10 hours ago
You'll probably get a lot of military vets answering this one. I
was stationed in Iraq for a bit, and every guy in my unit had a
close call at some point. Buddy of mine came thiiis close to step-

ping on a landmine once, and our commander shot a suicide bomber half a second before he could press the button. The closest I ever got to dying was when a grenade went off near me and I got blown into the side of a building. Chunk of rebar went right through my chest but somehow missed my vital organs. I bet you'll find lots of similar stories if you ask around.

> **Wyatt52** - 10 hours ago
> Definitely echo this. And it's not just combat vets either. One of the guys in my unit passed out during boot camp and almost died because the drill instructor thought he was faking it. Ended up he had severely low blood sugar, and the workouts pushed him so hard that his body just shut down.

> **—DangerzOne** - 10 hours ago
> Oh yeah, for sure. You've got to listen to your body or it'll *make* you listen.

muh-dawna - 10 hours ago
So I have epilepsy. Usually I can manage it just fine, but one day I had a pretty nasty seizure while I was cooking. Hit my head on a cabinet and started bleeding. I was home alone, and I'd left my phone in the other room, so I was just convulsing on the kitchen floor in a pool of my own blood. I probably would have died if my husband hadn't come home early and gotten me to the hospital. He'd only stopped by the house to grab a change of clothes for the gym. Something totally small, but it saved my life.

LichLord83 - 9 hours ago
I survived an active shooter situation at my high school.

> **afrayedknot -** 9 hours ago
> Holy shit. That's terrifying. I'm so sorry you had to go through that.

Plastic-Heartache-61 - 9 hours ago
Uhh my man, you gonna leave us hanging like that? What happened?

—LichLord83 - 9 hours ago
Some guy with an assault rifle got in and we went into lockdown. Two people were shot. Our teacher made us push the desks against the door and hunker down by the wall. I was close enough to the door to see the guy's shadow, but he didn't come in our classroom. The police eventually showed up and took the guy down.

——Plastic-Heartache-61 - 9 hours ago
Goddamn. How many people did he kill?

——LichLord83 - 9 hours ago
I'm sorry but I don't feel like talking about this anymore. I thought I'd be okay bringing it up again but I guess not.

———Plastic-Heartache-61 - 9 hours ago
Fair enough my dude.

mary-o-nette - 8 hours ago
No one's going to believe this, but here goes.

When I was a kid, there was this quarry off near the edge of town that we weren't supposed to go near. I guess some teenagers had gotten in an accident back in the 90s and their car ended up at the bottom. One of them died. The town put up all sorts of signage after that and for a while there was an officer out patrolling the area to make sure no one else went over the edge. I always heard stories of teenagers sneaking out after dark to chuck rocks and beer bottles into the quarry when the officer wasn't looking, but I was a straightedge little geek girl who would never *dream* of taking part in such activities, oh my.

Fast forward a few years. It was my friend's sixteenth birthday, and the cute boy next door offered to give me a ride to the roller rink. I accepted, of course, because I was hormonal and crushing hard. We got a late start, so he figured he'd shave off a few minutes by taking some backroads. Everything was going fine until we drove by the quarry. His dashboard kept flickering, and the engine made these rattling noises that sounded pretty ominous. I thought he was about to break down so I suggested we pull over and flag down someone to help, but then he saw something through the windshield that made him scream and jerk the wheel to the side.

I didn't see it, whatever it was. All I know is that he was so freaked out he veered completely off the road and crashed through the guardrail on the edge of the quarry. I had maybe half a second to panic before the car flipped over and smashed onto one of the lower plateaus. My head hit the ceiling, and it was the worst pain I'd ever felt in my life, worse than when I broke my arm falling off the monkey bars in third grade. The boy next door had been knocked clean out, but I could tell he was breathing, even though my head was swimming and the pain made everything blurry.

I survived, obviously. The officer on patrol heard the crash and called an ambulance to come save us. But before any of that happened, I heard a tapping on the car window, and I saw a face staring in at us through the broken glass. The car had flipped over, so the face was upside down, and of course, I could barely see anything at that point through my concussion. But I remember some things. I remember two hollow eyes, white and glowing. I remember a pale face without a lower jawbone. I remember the skeletal finger tap tap tapping on the windowpane.

The thing outside the window saw me staring and reached its

hand through the hole in the glass. Its fingers were literal bones, and it curled them up in this beckoning sort of gesture. I tried to scream, but all the wind had been knocked out of me and I could barely breathe. *Don't take me*, I wanted to plead. *Don't take me.*

I don't know if the thing outside could hear my thoughts, but something made it pause. Its missing jaw made it look like it was always smiling, and it was this hideous, hungry smile, like the grin of a predator. It drew its hand back from me. Then it reached for the boy in the driver's seat. I didn't see what happened next. Pain was blooming everywhere and I finally just blacked out.

I woke up in a hospital bed hours later. The boy next door never woke up again.

Plastic-Heartache-61 - 8 hours ago
Buuuullshit.

karaokefiend - 8 hours ago
This was a really creepy story, but OP asked for serious answers only, not fiction. You might have better luck posting this on NoSleep or something.

—mary-o-nette - 8 hours ago
Look, I prefaced the whole thing by saying you wouldn't believe it. And honestly, this is exactly the kind of reaction I was expecting to get, so I'm not sure why I even bothered. Just thought it might be cathartic to finally tell *somebody* what happened, because I sure as hell couldn't tell my therapist.

———Plastic-Heartache-61 - 8 hours ago
You can drop the roleplay, like seriously who tf do you think you're convincing here lol

————**mary-o-nette** - 7 hours ago
You're right, silly me, better go back to drinking my
trauma away because some rando on the internet thinks
I'm making up stories. I bet my old next door neighbor
will laugh when he hears about your oh-so-witty retort.
Oh wait, no he won't because *he died in a fucking car crash
when I was sixteen.* Fuck you, you piece of shit

————**Plastic-Heartache-61** - 7 hours ago
cool enjoy being banned 👋

place__holder - 8 hours ago
Jesus, the jawbone thing gave me nightmares. Are you
sure you weren't seeing things? It sounds like you were
pretty concussed when it happened.

—**mary-o-nette** - 8 hours ago
Had a feeling I'd see a comment like this. Honestly, I'd
love if the thing outside the window was just some fucked
up neurons firing in my brain. It's better than the alterna-
tive. Because if it *was* real, then that boy is dead because
of me.

————**place__holder** - 8 hours ago
Hey, you can't blame yourself. It sounds like it was an
accident. I know survivors' guilt is a thing and all, but
you're not responsible for what happened to him.

————**mary-o-nette** - 8 hours ago
But I am, though. I was the one who prayed it wouldn't
take me. I would have sobbed and begged for it to leave
me if I'd had the breath to do it.

It knew, somehow, and that's why it left me alone. But it
had to take someone.

LichLord83 - 7 hours ago
Okay, I said I wouldn't talk about the shooting anymore but I just read u/mary-o-nette's post and what the fuck. The guy who shot up my school was wearing gloves that looked like skeleton bones and a ski mask with a skull on it. Except the skull didn't have a lower jawbone.

> **karaokefiend -** 7 hours ago
> Oh great, the roleplay subs are leaking.

> **—LichLord83 -** 7 hours ago
> Dude shut the fuck up. I'm not roleplaying, just google it if you don't believe me

> **——Plastic-Heartache-61 -** 7 hours ago
> Lol what are we supposed to google, "totally real skeleton school shooter man"?

> **———LichLord83 -** 7 hours ago
> **Jefferson Star - Masked Shooter Terrorizes Rhode Island High School**

> **————Plastic-Heartache-61-** 7 hours ago
> Oh shit

> **place__holder -** 6 hours ago
> u/mary-o-nette did your accident happen in Rhode Island too? Is it possible the same guy was in both places?

> **—Plastic-Heartache-61 -** 6 hours ago
> She's probably banned, I reported her for aggressive language earlier

> **——mary-o-nette -** 6 hours ago
> You're not getting rid of me that easily, dickwad.

But yes. The shooting happened in the same town I had my accident. I remember seeing it on the news.

DangerzOne - 6 hours ago
Don't want to throw fuel onto an already sketchy fire here, but I saw a guy in a similar skeleton getup when I was deployed. No lower jawbone and everything. It wasn't quite the Punisher logo, but that's what it reminded me of. He was seen planting suspicious packages around Baghdad and I was sent in as part of the bomb defuser squad. Didn't get a good glimpse of him, but I did see him fleeing the scene at one point. Don't actually know what happened to him after that. If he was caught, I never found out.

>   **karaokefiend** - 6 hours ago
>   Jesus christ, where are the mods? It's like a LARP convention in here.

>   **—DangerzOne** - 6 hours ago
>   Look man, be skeptical all you want, but I'm just reporting what I saw. It definitely wasn't some kind of monster, though. Just a guy in a creepy ski mask.

>   **place__holder** - 6 hours ago
>   Wait, I'm confused. I thought there was some psycho scaring people in Rhode Island. What's he doing in Iraq?

>   **—Plastic-Heartache-61** - 6 hours ago
>   Nothing, people are just doing some lazy ass roleplaying lmao

>   **—afrayedknot** - 6 hours ago
>   What if it's some kind of cult thing? Like a terrorist group. Maybe the jawless skull is their insignia and they've got members all over the world.

——**mary-o-nette** - 6 hours ago
It's not a cult. It's the same guy. Or the same entity, I don't
know, whatever you want to call it.
You're all so eager to cry "bullshit," but I know what I
saw that night. The thing outside the car wasn't human. It
wasn't there to terrorize us. It just wanted to take us. It's a
bringer of death, and it doesn't surprise me that it's taking
lives wherever it can.

——**karaokefiend** - 6 hours ago
I mean this in the most respectful way, but have you
considered getting psychiatric help? I don't think this
fixation of yours is healthy.

——**mary-o-nette** - 5 hours ago
Ah, there it is. Knew the armchair psychologists would
crawl out of the woodwork to diagnose me. Either show
me your psych diploma or shut the fuck up. Actually,
shut the fuck up either way. Nobody asked you.

[deleted] - 5 hours ago
yeah I had a near death experience. I was buried in yo mamma's
ass and they had to call the fire dept to airlift me out

karaokefiend - 5 hours ago
Read the room, buddy.

Amazing-Twig-34 - 5 hours ago
I don't know if this exactly answers your question OP but after
reading the other posts in this thread I feel like this story belongs
here.

Last year I went to this haunted house with some friends
because we were bored on Halloween. It was pretty tacky overall, nothing to write home about, until we went into the base-

ment and there was this huge skeleton guy in a cloak sitting on an old boat in the corner. I assumed it was an animatronic because when I say it was huge, I mean HUGE, like so tall it had to slouch to fit in the basement at all.

The skeleton was holding out a bucket that said PAY THE FERRYMAN across the front, like a street performer asking for change. I thought it might be funny to drop a few coins into the bucket. So I did, and then the skeleton scared the ever-loving shit out of me by crouching down and whispering in my ear. I guess it wasn't an animatronic, then? But my friends were drunk and wandering away and didn't notice.

It said something like, "you and your friends have earned safe passage tonight. But one day, I'll return for the rest of your payment."

It freaked me out more than I expected it to, so I joined my friends and finished up the rest of the house with them. When we got out, there were police cars out front and people running around all panicked. Turns out someone in the group behind us had gotten STABBED. We were detained for a bit while the cops asked us some questions, but I could tell they didn't think we had anything to do with it and eventually they let us go.

I didn't think about the skeleton man again until I saw a clip on the news where some reporter was doing a story on the whole incident and had a camera following him through the house. The victim had been stabbed in the basement, right where we'd just been. But the boat and the huge skeleton were nowhere to be seen.

afrayedknot - 5 hours ago
Oh fuck, that one gave me chills. What happened to the person who got stabbed?

—Amazing-Twig-34 - 5 hours ago
She died at the hospital unfortunately. They never did
find the person who did it. But it's scary to think that the
murderer was right there in that house, and it could just
as easily have been us who got killed instead.

——mary-o-nette - 5 hours ago
Nah, you were always going to be just fine. You paid the
ferryman, didn't you? You earned your safe passage. The
group behind you probably didn't, so it took their
payment the hard way.

It's also hilarious to me how many people in this thread
are clamoring to explain this figure away with "cults" and
"serial killers" when it's obviously none of those things.
The ferryman is real, and we only survived it because we
paid it what it wanted. But it'll be back to collect the rest.

———Plastic-Heartache-61 - 5 hours ago
Can you stop fucking scaring people, like wtf are you
trying to accomplish here

————mary-o-nette - 5 hours ago
I mean, I'm just repeating what u/Amazing-Twig-34 said
in their story, but happy to hear my very presence is
pissing you off yet again 👆

place__holder - 5 hours ago
u/LichLord83 did this stabbing happen in your home-
town? I wonder if there's some kind of sicko with a
skeleton motif targeting this area.

—LichLord83 - 4 hours ago
I'm sorry to tell you this, but LichLord is in the hospital
right now. This is his roommate. He was taking a walk off

campus and got mugged and beaten pretty badly. If he survives, he's going to need facial reconstruction surgery. I've been answering his pings and DMs just so no one's left in the dark.

——**karaokefiend** - 4 hours ago
Oh for fuck's sake, I'm out. Have fun with your D&D campaign or whatever this is.

——**afrayedknot** - 4 hours ago
This can't be real, right? What the hell is going on here?

——**mary-o-nette** - 4 hours ago
I was afraid this would happen. It sounds like he survived the ferryman before, but it came back to collect its payment. It always does.

——**Plastic-Heartache-61** - 4 hours ago
If this dude actually got beat up then you're being a real douche here. Stop trying to make everything about you and your fantasy monster smh

——**mary-o-nette** - 4 hours ago
The fuck you mean, I'm making this "all about me"? Everyone who survived an encounter with that thing is in real danger, and I'm trying to warn them.

If anything, you're the one with a vendetta here. Are you really going out of your way to respond to every post I make? Pathetic.

Wyatt52 - 3 hours ago
Paging u/DangerzOne. Sent you a DM but I haven't gotten a response and I know you were frequenting this thread before

you went quiet. I really need you to contact me asap. Something's happened.

place__holder - 2 hours ago
u/Wyatt52 were you able to get in touch with DangerzOne? I was messaging with u/Amazing-Twig-34 and they totally ghosted me mid-conversation. I'm sure it's probably nothing, but it's just a little weird since both of them were so active in this thread recently.

> **Plastic-Heartache-61** - 2 hours ago
> Most people don't live on the internet lol, they're fine

> **mary-o-nette** - 2 hours ago
> Shit. This is happening faster than I expected.

place__holder - 1 hour ago
u/Wyatt52? u/LichLord83? u/Amazing-Twig-34? u/Dangerz-One? Where the hell is everybody?

mary-o-nette - 1 hour ago
Something about this whole thread felt off from the beginning. I'm finally starting to understand it now.

OP asked this bombshell question, let the replies roll in, and said nothing. No comments, no personal anecdotes, *nothing*, not even when it became obvious that the same figure was popping up in multiple stories. Now those users are going quiet or getting mugged to death. "Something's happened," apparently. But what caused it? What did all those users have in common?

They posted in this thread.

Here's a theory. Some people narrowly survived encounters with this killer, this ferryman, whatever you want to call it. And now the ferryman is trying to tie up those loose ends. Tracking down the survivors, collecting its payment at last. Why hunt them down, though? Why go through that effort when you can just bait them out with a perfectly tantalizing question that only they can answer?

I should have figured it out beforehand. It's too late now. I have a gun at home and I'm not afraid to use it, if it comes to that. But I have a feeling a gun won't do shit to the ferryman when it finally comes to collect.

What do you think, u/charonite57? Am I on the money?

> **charonite57 OP -** 34 minutes ago
> See you soon.

* * *

David Farrow is the author of the bestselling *Neverglades* paranormal mystery series. His fiction has been featured in *Mythaxis Magazine, Haven Speculative,* and the *NoSleep Podcast,* among others. He teaches with the GrubStreet writing community in Boston and is a faculty mentor for the Creative Writing MFA Program at Lesley University.

BookBub | Facebook | Goodreads | Instagram | Kofi | davidfarrowwrites.com

CHAPTER 2
WHAT'S YOUR TYPE?

LOGAN MCCONNELL

SAM WAS unaware he had arrived. He sat in the car's back seat, mesmerized by photos of his own face looking back at him through the screen, a hallway of reflections shifting as he scrolled. The taxi driver coughed. Sam snapped his head up and saw his destination outside the window, down a narrow, graveled path.

"Thanks," Sam said while sliding out. As the car drove away, its tires flecked his loafers with mud. Sam spent several minutes wiping his shoes clean before starting on the path, traveling down its center to avoid the cracked edges crumbling into the wet marsh on either side.

The building was a two-story warehouse-turned-luxury loft. Weather-worn brick with exposed steel beams lent an industrial aesthetic, the walls insisting that the wear and tear were part of a purposeful design, not out of neglect. No cars were parked out front, and he assumed there must be a garage or lot in the back.

Nearing the entrance, Sam saw, through a second-story window, a nude male resident in plain view. Sam chuckled at the man's indifference to his exposure. Sitting on a mattress corner, the half-drawn blinds obscured his head. He rested a limb on his knee. At the risk of being noticed, Sam stopped to study the man.

The limb on top of the man's left knee could be either an arm or a leg, extending below the window to hide a hand or foot. The longer Sam stared, the more improbable the view became, as if the man's limb was a fusion of two separate appendages, creating a kind of anatomical, optical illusion. Sam blinked, turned away, and approached the entrance.

No call box. Sam went through the unlocked front doors. Inside was a dilapidated lobby with cords and other bare electrical wires dangling from the ceiling. Dust from disintegrated drywall coated the floor. Burned plastic permeated the air. He checked his phone again, confirming he had the correct address before exploring further.

"Hello? Anyone here?"

Sam looked to his left, staring down a dark, empty hallway, then to another hallway on his right, where someone was standing in the shadows. The person wore black dungarees but was bare from the waist up, torso bent over, the head hidden from view. Sam raised an eyebrow at yet another brazen tenant. This building was full of free spirits.

"Excuse me," called Sam. "I'm looking for—" Sam froze. This person's head, which Sam expected to lift, remained hunched over out of sight. Sam couldn't see his or her neck, and like the exhibitionist in the second-floor window, the longer Sam stared, the more the body defied logic. He stepped closer.

"Are you alright?" Sam asked.

No response.

Sam crept closer.

"Oh, good!" came a voice behind Sam. He jumped and turned around. From the opposite hall, a woman emerged and stepped over a cinder block. "You made it."

She wore a black sleeveless dress matching the hue of the shadows behind her, and for a moment her pale head and arms appeared to float mid-air. Her brunette bangs and thick eyeliner reminded Sam of some reincarnated Cleopatra. The woman's arms were thin but not feminine. Her bony elbows stuck out at an odd angle as she placed her hands on her hips.

"Glad you found the place all right," she said. "I'm Regina."

Sam smiled. "Yes, Regina, nice to finally meet you in person." They shook hands. "Say," he said, lowering his voice. "Do you know—" Sam turned back around to realize the shirtless stranger was gone.

"Know what?" she asked.

Sam stammered. "Uh, never mind." He looked around at the lobby. "So, this is an apartment building or something?"

Regina shrugged. "We live here." She grabbed his hand. "Come up to my place. It's much nicer than this," she said, gesturing at the room.

Regina led him down the hall and into a freight elevator. She used all her strength to tug a lever, slamming the door shut, beginning their slow ascent to the second floor. Sounds of mammoth gears groaned around them, interrupted by tinkling chains. Once at the top, they stepped out directly into Regina's abode.

Her 'place' must have been an office for some industrial company another lifetime ago. The high ceiling and squat, narrow windows left massive sections of bare, concrete walls that were peppered with drill holes. A queen-sized bed lay in the far corner. In the room's center was a couch, an armchair, and a coffee table.

Against the furthest wall was a table covered in multi-colored fabrics. The four legs hid in draped gowns and unfurled skirts, the tangled cloth like creeping ivy. The wall immediately to his left had an opening covered by an opaque plastic tarp, shifting with the building's draft, crinkling in Sam's ear.

Then Sam saw the two bodies.

One was a mannequin without legs, its upper body perched on a thin, metal pole. The head was smashed in, with jagged edges and a hole where the face would go. Beside this was a second mannequin in mint condition, complete with arms, legs, and a handsome face. The chiseled jaw, high cheekbones and intense stare carried a mesmerizing mystique, the detail so exquisite that Sam expected the lifelike lips to move. Both torsos wore burgundy suits.

"Make yourself at home," Regina instructed. She wandered over to the chair, turned on a table lamp beside her, then leaned back and sighed.

Sam snuck a peek at his phone before looking around. "You got a nice place here," he said. "Very... modern. It's cool." He pointed at the plastic tarp. "Construction?"

Regina glanced over, then back to Sam. "Yes. I bought the loft next door. I'm turning it into a double."

Sam went over to examine the mannequins. "And you work from home? You sew and design here?"

"Yes."

"Cool, cool."

Scattered papers lay underneath the mannequin's skin-toned plastic bare feet. Sketches outlining coats, slacks and blouses above scribbled notes he couldn't read. Though the imaginary garments were alluring and suave, the models wearing them were drawn with a distracting, ethereal beauty. The display was as if Regina had given more attention to the faces than the outfits —her clothing designs upstaged by her own illustrated portraits.

"You've got real artistic skills," said Sam, not taking his eyes off the sketches.

"Thanks. I appreciate good looking clothes... and people," said Regina. She stared at him. "You're proof of that."

Sam grinned. "Ha, aw, well, same to you."

"You look very handsome in your videos online. And I saw you doubled your subscribers over the past year," she said. "Very impressive."

Sam walked over to the armchair and sat. "Yeah, I, you know, think my hard work and self-promotion are paying off."

"But you've gone as far as you can go, I suspect. Until you get a sponsor."

He nodded. "A sponsor of any kind would be a game-changer, for sure."

"Alright. What's your pitch?"

Sam blinked and cleared his throat. "Oh... ok. A pitch. Well, if you do decide to sponsor me, I can get the word out about your business to thousands of people and use the money to grow my brand. You'd still get attention from my channel, but to a larger audience. It's a win-win."

"Do you think there's much in common?" Regina asked, rubbing her chin. "Between people who would buy my clothing and your viewers?"

"Yeah." Sam eyed her clothing on the table, then the mannequin's suits. "Yeah, I'm pretty sure there is. That's why people get interested in wine, isn't it? They want to feel sophisticated and fancy and stuff. Wine is mostly about looks, aesthetics, you know? The clothing you make, from what I see, has that same 'sophisticated' vibe."

Regina crossed her arms. "Yeah, man, like, vibes," she said in a deep voice.

Sam shifted in place.

"I could see that," she said in her normal speaking voice. "Sounds like you understand your target audience."

Sam's phone chimed. He eyed his screen. "Huh?"

"Nothing, Sam. I was just complimenting you."

"Oh, thanks."

Regina sprung up in her seat. "Oh! How rude of me! Here you are, my guest, and I didn't offer you anything to drink. Would you like a glass of wine? A nice red, perhaps?"

Sam's eyes widened. "Yeah, please!"

Regina walked over to the kitchen, leaving Sam to scroll his phone. He perused through a litany of texts from strangers hoping to collaborate. When he put his phone away, he looked up to find Regina standing inches from him. "Ah!" he chuckled. "You startled me."

She smiled and handed him a glass. "Can you do me a favor, Sam?"

"OK."

"Do the thing you do on your channel, with the wine."

"Huh?"

She sat back down and smiled. "Like your videos. I want you to taste the wine and try to guess what type it is and where it's from."

"Oh. Right, sure." Sam brought the glass rim up to his nostril and took a deep inhale. Next, he held the drink near the lamp light and swirled. He repeated this once more while Regina scooted forward on the couch, observing him. Finally, Sam sipped, swished, then swallowed.

"This is a tough one," he said. "This is a layered, earthy wine..." he rubbed his chin and smacked his tongue. "I'm going to say it's a Pinot Noir. Oregon. From 2000 or 2001, sometime around then."

Regina stiffened her posture and leaned against the couch without relaxing. "Yes! That's correct. How could you guess that? It doesn't taste like a standard Pinot."

"True," he nodded. "That's because this wine has a low typicity."

"Low what?"

"Typicity. It's a wine term. So, the 'general consensus' is that a Pinot tastes a certain way, different from the taste of a Cab, a Merlot, and so on. But some wines made from a single varietal, like a Pinot, may not taste like what you'd expect. So, we say it has low typicity." He smiled. "I'm actually doing a video on this next week."

"Well, Sam, that's a very impressive skill. Tell me, how often do you think about wine? You enjoy it, obviously, but how often do you really think about it?"

Sam swirled his drink, eyeing the bottom of the vortex he

created. "A lot, actually. It's kind of my job to. It's not just reposting pics of French and Italian wineries and recommendations about wine and food pairings. It's my passion." He stopped rotating his glass, the maroon waves undulating slowly before returning to a placid surface reflecting Regina's face. Sam squirmed in his seat.

"So you are *thinking*," she cooed. "Not just posting and monetizing."

Sam rolled the glass stem between his fingers. "Oh, absolutely."

Regina raised her chin and narrowed her eyes. The plastic tarp drifted forward, then back. On the other side of the divide, a naked person walked from one end to another, reduced to a flesh-colored blur by the tarp. Sam opened his mouth. Regina turned around, then back to Sam.

"Oh, don't mind them," she said, waving behind her. "They come and go."

"Who are they?" Sam asked. "They don't seem to be dressed. There were others when I came in…"

Regina laughed without smiling. "I'm afraid my neighbors are hedonists. This is a very forward-thinking complex." She eyed him. "You know, Sam, I'm not used to nudity being brought up on a first date. You almost made me blush."

Sam's hand slid against his pocket, running along the outline of his phone. "Oh, ha-ha, yeah." He drummed his fingers on the armrest as the pause in conversation lingered. After a long silence, he blurted to her, "So, how long have you been designing clothes?"

Regina's eyes rolled up and over. "Oh, I'd say since my teens. I had a little sketchbook, outlining beautiful evening gowns and ballroom dresses." She sighed. "But the fashion industry is very competitive. You have to paddle hard just to keep your head above water."

"Sounds stressful."

"Oh yes, Sam, it is." Regina gestured to the mannequin with

the missing face. "Sometimes I get so overwhelmed I just can't control myself." She took a sip of her wine. "I have quite the violent temper when I'm upset. I can't tell you how many mannequins I've smashed, sliced or burned in my day."

Sam leaned forward. "Burned?"

"Yes. At times, I've been angry over a deal that fell apart or a design that flopped with critics, and I just lit a match to the clothing in question, taking the poor dummy with it in the flames."

Sam gripped his glass, held it to his face, and realized it was empty. Regina took it from him. "I'll get you a refill," she said.

As she poured, Sam pointed to the pristine mannequin. "That one's still in good shape."

Regina gazed at the handsome plastic. "Jasper," her voice low, almost reverential.

"Come again?"

"That's Jasper. My dearest friend." She walked back over with a completely full glass, drops sliding down the sides. "Jasper and I have been with one another since college. Others have come and gone, but I could never hurt him. No matter how angry I get."

"Oh boy, you're not cheating on him with me, are you?" he joked.

Regina shook her head. "No. He accepts our arrangement."

"You talk about them like they're real."

"They are," she replied.

Sam stared at Regina. When she didn't continue, he said. "But they're *not* real. They aren't human."

"That's not true. They're a type of human."

"What?"

Regina pointed at her drink. "This is a type of Pinot, even if it's not a typical Pinot." She pointed to Jasper. "He is a type of human, even if he's not like a typical human. Mannequins are humans with a low typicity, to borrow your terminology." She looked back at Sam and, reading his expression, said, "You don't believe me."

"A Pinot's taste is based on general consensus. Nobody thinks Jasper is human."

Regina looked around the room. "In here, in this apartment, I am the general consensus." She stood and faced Jasper.

"I've always seen them as human. One day, I confirmed they were. I had just gotten fired from my first job. Some made up charges about erratic behavior. In my rage, I grabbed a pair of scissors and stabbed the nearest mannequin. Charles... I want to say his name was. Just kept stabbing his throat until his head came right off!"

She laughed.

"You're just kidding, right?" Sam asked.

Regina ignored his question and continued speaking. Sam eyed the elevator door.

"Charles came back. He visited me at night. His headless ghost drifted along my bed, whispering without a mouth into my ear. From the dark, he told me secrets held by humans made of plastic. Dormant, undetected souls that stir and move after death in ways that are impossible during their life of paralysis."

Regina looked away from Jasper and over to the window. Sam followed her gaze outside, where, under the dim moonlight, a phantom's stiff legs goose stepped across the marsh.

"That's Patrick. I crushed his head with a mallet."

Sam dabbed his forehead.

"And I think it was Luke you were looking at from the front entrance. I burned his arms and legs just last week. Already he's found a room to haunt." She shook her head and frowned. "And you spied on him? On a naked innocent in their own home? You dirty boy."

Sam stood and swayed, his balance hindered. "You thinking they're real doesn't mean they are. That's crazy."

Regina walked closer to him. "You thought they were real through a window. From a distance down the hall. You contributed to validating their humanity, even if you didn't know it." She pushed Sam's chest with a bony finger, tipping him back down onto the couch.

Regina turned and then approached Jasper in a slow, solemn march. On reaching her "friend," Regina bowed, radiating the same reverence to the mannequin that a monk might bestow upon an altar. She grazed his jacket with quivering fingertips.

Sam heaved himself up and over to the elevator. The two wooden planks that served as doors were kept shut by a padlock. Sam yanked on the lock, his sweaty fingers slipping along the cold brass. His heartbeat shook his core, watching Regina wrap her arms around Jasper's frame.

"I need you, Sam," she said. "I need you to help Jasper. I've prepared him for another state. It'll be easier if you don't fight this."

Sam pulled out his phone, waving it at her. "If you don't let me out right now, I'm calling the cops," he warned, his voice breaking.

Regina shrugged. "Very well. Take the stairs, it's faster." She pointed behind the plastic tarp. "There's an exit on the other side." Sam stumbled through the flimsy tarp, ripping it off the wall. Regina had lied. The room did not contain an escape, but something else.

A mannequin graveyard: a wreckage of broken legs, bent arms and torsos torn open with hollow insides exposed. Against the furthest wall were shelves cluttered with severed heads, most with missing jaws. Some had their smoothed over eye indents broken in, a series of black holes watching Sam gasp at a tomb that housed the inanimate.

In one corner, a blank mannequin face, lips melted shut, was left muted by mutilation. It moved. Floating up and over the bodies, it released a muffled cry of both anguish and pleasure before drifting through a cement wall. Sam froze, unable to take another step until a jingling sound behind him broke his terrified trance.

Regina dangled a pair of keys. "Forgive my little prank. Here," she said, jostling the keys. "These unlock the elevator. I'll let you have them if you can answer one question."

Sam held his breath.

"Why did you come here tonight?"

Sam paused before answering. "A date."

Regina glared at him. "Really? Have you ever had a first date at someone's apartment? Without ever having met them in person?"

He shook his head. "No... it was a business meeting. To negotiate sponsoring my channel."

Regina laughed. "Do you often travel to a sponsor's residence? At night? Not through phone, text or email?"

Sam ran his fingers through his hair.

"No, Sam, you don't. I'll tell you why you're here. You're here," she said, tilting her head, "because I connected with you in a chat room, told you everything you wanted to hear, and then invited you to this address. And you went! No questions asked. Then again, people this day and age don't question all that much, do they?"

"I need to go."

"People record themselves constantly. Without asking why, they join in whatever challenge or trend is in vogue that second. They pose in hundreds of positions, desperate for that elusive, flattering angle sure to be discovered with just one more take. They twist and display themselves like department store mannequins, all with the same amount of self-awareness they think a dummy has: zero."

"You're not as interesting and thoughtful and passionate as you think, Sam. So obsessed with obtaining mass appeal for your internet audience, your unique personality has atrophied, all the complexities lost."

Regina stopped to stare out the window, frowning. "Things didn't used to be this bad." She shut her eyes for a long moment before her cold stare returned. "How can I consider mannequins as a type of human?" She tossed Sam the keys. "They get more similar by the day."

Regina pulled something out of Jasper's inner coat pocket as Sam ran to the lock, successfully opening the elevator doors. Stepping inside, he slammed the first-floor button. Regina remained by Jasper, holding a dagger high above their heads.

"Jasper no longer wants this body," she cried as the doors closed. "He needs a new one. An empty vessel to possess. I know you'll serve as a suitable home for his spirit." Regina plunged her dagger into the plastic chest right as the elevator sank down.

Sam leaned against the wall and pulled out his phone to call for help. On his black screen was the reflection of a distinguished, rigid face hovering behind him. Sam spun around, staring into Jasper's eyes. Above Jasper, the dark elevator shaft teemed with expressionless ghosts, an audience of transparent mannequins watching what was to come next.

Everything vanished. Blind, Sam felt his muscles twitch, then stiffen.

Locked limbs writhed in the black pit.

A mandible snapped open, then shut. Open, then shut.

Clumsy tongue wiggled to discover what wet was, what soft was. Eyes roll without a marble's echo.

Sensation of heartbeat, frightens then comforts.

Vocal cords are tested with a triumphant

scream.

———

Logan McConnell is a health care worker and horror writer living with his husband in Tennessee. His work is published in *Dark Recesses Press, Coffin Bell, Diet Milk Magazine, Vanishing Point Magazine* and others.

Goodreads | Storygraph

CHAPTER 3
AGENDA ITEM 3
FRANCIS VERELLE

Meeting Reminder
JOUR FIXE
2:00 PM – 3:30 PM EST
Snooze Start

THE MEETING IS about to start in five minutes. You are not sure whether people can already join the digital meeting room until you click 'Start'. You've never hosted one of these meetings before. Normally, your new secretary, Ms. Warner sets up these calls. But Ms. Warner is out of office this week, because her 7-year-old has the flu, and she's a single mother. Her son seems to catch something every other week.

Your previous secretary, Ms. Tsanaris, had been much more reliable. You barely even knew anything about her family. She never allowed her personal life to bleed into work. You vaguely remember hearing about a man her age being at the funeral, but you can't recall if he was her husband or her brother. You couldn't make it to her memorial yourself. The Dallas meeting had conflicted with the date.

You start the meeting. The call opens, and although it's still three minutes before the scheduled meeting time, you are the sixth out of seven participants to join the call. Tom Schilensky from the Florida branch will probably run late again. He always runs late.

The offices in the background of the videos all look more or less the same: plain and white. The light source isn't conveniently placed in a single one of them. On top of that, the video tiles are so small that it's hard to make out the details of anyone's face clearly. They all look weirdly smooth and ageless.

Clara Mallison's screen seems to be frozen. You could switch to Speaker's View to enlarge at least one of the frames. Once the meeting starts, you will be the one doing most of the talking, but it's irritating to see only your own face reflected on the screen. Seeing everyone at once in their little boxes is preferable. The layout of the tiles makes it feel like you are all sitting in a circle inside the computer.

All videos are currently muted. Time is crawling. It's always awkward to wait like this, since everyone can see if you decide to scroll on your phone or chomp down on a greasy sandwich. The setting doesn't encourage casual conversation like a face-to-face meeting, so the atmosphere is tense and expectant.

Finally, the numbers at the right bottom corner of the screen switch to 2:00, so it's time to start.

Allow computer to access your microphone
Allow Decline

"I suggest we get started," you say. "I'm sure Tom will join us later. As usual." The pause you leave for polite chuckling is met with nothing but silence. A few people smile. Clara Mallison remains frozen.

"So, welcome everyone. You've all received the agenda in advance. We have to get this year's summer party for senior management here in DC sorted out."

You've had to send it yourself this week, emailing everyone individually. Ms. Warner keeps the mailing list for the weekly team leader conference on her account, and she didn't even bother to forward it to you before she went on sick leave. It's surprising that she even made it through her probationary period, but HR has reminded you that it's illegal to let someone go just because they have a sick child at home and don't respond to messages outside of their regular working hours.

Ms. Tsanaris was a different kind of reliable. She responded to emails within minutes, even when she was on vacation or late at night, knowing full well that the whole system would collapse without her. But then she slipped on the ice during a walk last winter and bashed in her head in such a gruesome manner that you heard the coffin had to remain closed for the funeral.

Her death was the worst thing that could have happened to you.

"Does anyone have an objection to the agenda or another topic to add to the list?"

It takes a moment, then a yellow hand pops up in the corner of one of the videos.

G. Willcox raised a hand

You are on a first-name basis with Willcox, but right now you can't remember what the initial stands for. George? Geoffrey? Gerald maybe? He looks like a Herbert, but that doesn't really help.

"Yes?" You are glad only one person raised their hand. This way, no one will notice that you're avoiding addressing him directly.

"I have some questions about the catering."

"We will discuss that towards the end of the meeting. Anything else?"

Willcox mutes his video again. The silence emanating from the speakers feels eerie. There's always rustling or someone clearing their throat during face-to-face meetings, but these video calls feel like yelling into an abyss that doesn't even echo your voice.

"Since Ms. Warner is absent today, someone else will have to take down the minutes. Does anyone volunteer?"

Of course, no one volunteers. It's astonishing, but apparently secretaries are the kind of people you only notice once they're absent. You never knew how much you relied on Ms. Tsanaris until she was gone.

"In that case, I suggest we go in alphabetical order. Anne, would you be so kind as to write today's minutes?"

Anne Baker switches on her microphone to confirm, but the connection is terrible, so her voice comes through in clipped, metallic little rasps.

"Sorry, Anne, I'm afraid we can't hear you. The connection seems to be bad."

She mutes herself again, and the screen freezes just as she looks down at her keyboard.

A. Baker left a comment in the chat
No problem!!

"Thank you, Anne. Then let's get started with the first topic."

T. Schilensky has joined the call.

"Oh, hello, Tom, glad you could join us."

Tom's face looks very red on the screen, but there may just be something wrong with his camera. His background also looks sepia-toned.

"Sorry, sorry, got caught up in a meeting. You know how it is. Hope I didn't miss anything important." He sounds out of breath, as if he really just sprinted in from another room.

"We were just about to get started on item three, funding for the summer party." You can hear your own voice feedback through the speakers. "Could you please mute your microphone, Tom?"

"Sorry, sorry."

"The board provides us with an annual party budget, but the place we booked is a little pricey, so we decided every branch will chip in and cover part of the expense out of their own pocket. As you'll recall, we voted on this at the last meeting two weeks ago."

You tap your pencil on the desk a few times before you continue.

"We were supposed to send you all the documents to sign for approval and fill out your individual code numbers. Unfortunately, it was the late Ms. Tsanaris who usually took care of organizing such things. Our new secretary, Ms. Warner, hasn't been able to locate the correct documents. Apparently, it wasn't saved on the server because Ms. Tsanaris used to work from her personal computer after hours, so not everything is in the same place. Also, Ms. Warner is out of office at the moment. It has to be taken care of this week. Anyone able to take care of it?"

You wait, only to be met with silence again. A few people on the screen shake their heads. Clara Mallison's video is no longer frozen. You can see her shaking her head as well.

You sigh. "It really is a shame we lost Ms. Tsanaris so suddenly. She never even got the chance to instruct Ms. Warner, and unfortunately, we can't just reach out to her anymore. I'm sure I speak for all of us when I say we wish she was here with us right now."

This time, you receive a few solemn nods. You didn't realize it before, but Ms. Tsanaris may just have been the most important person in your life, and you wish her back with a desperation you have never known.

"If any of you locate last year's documents, please email me as soon as possible. Otherwise, I'll have to try calling up Ms. Tsanaris' bereaved relatives to ask if they still have a hard drive lying around that might contain work documents for Ms. Warner to go through."

All the videos on the call briefly freeze at once. You check the network icon on the taskbar, but your connection seems to be stable.

K. Tsanaris has joined the call

You frown at the screen, wondering if you misread the notification.

The videos spring back into motion, ragged at first, as if trying to make up for lost time. Instead of seven, there are now eight people online.

Your first thought is that this makes perfect sense, because Ms. Tsanaris is always there when you need her. Your second thought is that this must be a prank, because it doesn't make any sense at all.

But the person in the video looks just like her—the same middle-aged, plain-looking woman with the mousy brown hair. She's dressed differently, though, more formally. Only her shoulders are visible, so it's hard to tell if she is wearing a blazer or a dress with shoulder pads, but either way, it's a big difference from the knit cardigans she usually wore, even in summer. You take a moment to realize that these might be her funeral clothes. There's something wrong with the side of her head, like a large dark stain is sticking to it, but it's hard to make out on the screen.

You clear your throat.

"Ms...." You break off, because there really isn't much to say. You check the other faces. Everyone looks pale, staring down at their screen. Only Clara Mallison is frozen again. "Ms. Tsanaris."

She unmutes her call, and for a moment, the sound of ragged breathing echoes through the room. It sounds disgustingly wet, as if her lungs are clogged with dirt.

"You summoned me." Her voice doesn't sound cracked at all. It sounds just like it always did, not even distorted by the computer speakers. It sounds as if she's standing right next to you.

"You summoned me," Ms. Tsanaris repeats, and this is unusual. This is new. She was always quiet and very polite. "You called me on weekends. You called me on vacation, always expecting me to fix your messes. And now you call me into work —after my death."

Her voice is still in the room with you, even closer now, as if she is standing right behind you, leaning in.

"Not a single person on this call has ever respected my personal time. Not a single one of you."

You've never heard her this angry before. You've never heard her angry at all.

The entire screen freezes for another second and when the videos come back online, Clara Mallison's camera is blacked out. But she's had trouble with her internet connection all day. She'll probably be back soon.

C. Mallison has left the call

You try to meet someone's eyes to make sure you are not the only one currently dealing with a dead secretary, but no one is looking into their camera, everyone is looking at the screen. It's impossible to tell who is watching you. Everyone looks confused, but they're all muted. All except for Ms. Tsanaris.

"I'm sorry we upset you, Ms. Tsanaris. I can assure you that we did not summon you on purpose. It was more of an accident, really."

"Yes, I'm sure you just didn't think about it. Just like you didn't think about it when you asked me to organize that diversity training for the department at the last minute—while I was on my trip to Greece. I'd been talking about that trip for weeks!" She knits her brows. It makes her look stern. "Thoughtlessness does not excuse ignorance."

Once again, the screen freezes, this time only for a second, so briefly that you are not sure it even happened at all.

Mr. Brendano's screen has gone black. His connection seemed to be working fine until now.

A. Baker has raised a hand

"Yes, Anne, please."

You are relieved that someone else wants to speak. You need to be reassured that this isn't just some weird hallucination. Or maybe that it is.

C. Brendano has left the call

You vaguely remember that he skipped the diversity training to close a big deal. You don't remember which deal it was.

This time, the call doesn't even freeze. Anne's screen just goes black, but her microphone remains on. The same metallic noises from earlier ring through the speakers. It might be her voice, but the syllables are too fragmented to make out any words. It sounds a lot more menacing than before.

A. Baker has left the call

"That's it," Tom announces. He has not bothered to raise his hand. "This is getting too creepy. I'm out."

"I'm afraid I cannot let you leave without permission, Mr. Schilensky. It could result in a written reprimand. Our company has a pretty strict policy on that." Ms. Tsanaris' voice is friendly, almost sweet, but it gives you goosebumps all the way down your neck.

Tom's screen goes black. You saw this coming.

His microphone is still on. You hear him scream, high and short.

This has to stop. You don't know what has happened to your

colleagues. It might just be that their internet connections are dropping one by one. And Tom has always been known for his inappropriate sense of humor. His scream might have been a prank. You don't want to assume the worst. This can't be real.

But your mouth feels dry and your palms are sweaty.

You click the red X to end the call.

Do you want to
Leave the call? End the call for everyone?

Your screen freezes the moment you try to click the right button. It appears the computer won't let you leave either.

T. Schilensky has left the call

Now that there are only four people left in the call, the videos automatically expand, splitting the screen into four equal frames. Now that her image is larger, you get a better look at Ms. Tsanaris. Dark liquid spills down the entire side of her face, plastering her hair to her forehead and dripping down to her chin. It's too dark to be blood—it's practically black. It looks sick and rotten. Something is wrong with her eyes, too.

G. Willcox is still on the call. You finally remember that his first name is Gregor.

Dan from the LA branch is still online as well, but the office chair in front of his desk is empty. You consider getting up and running as well, but the whole situation feels too surreal to believe that you could just leave.

"What do you want?" you ask instead.

"What I *wanted* was some basic respect. But you refused to see me as anything other than a secretary. I was a real person. Now, I want something more."

You wonder if it's too late to run.

"Running won't help," Ms. Tsanaris says. The image of Dan's empty office disappears from the screen.

D. Tyler has left the call

"I'll get you in LA and I'll get you in Florida. I'll get you in your office and at home and in your car. Modern technology makes you available anywhere, anytime. Just like I was available while checking my email from home or taking calls in Greece when you called me on my private phone."

Your face grows uncomfortably hot. You did, once or twice. You found her private number in her personal file. It had been urgent.

"Listen, I'm really sorry. I can see that my behavior was wrong." You doubt that an apology will help, but at least you have to try. "Please, just leave. *Please.*"

The screen freezes again, so briefly that you would have missed it if you had blinked at the wrong moment.

The last image you see of Gregor Willcox is his pale face staring at the screen. You can't tell if his video was lagging or if he himself was frozen in shock.

G. Willcox has left the call

The videos expand again. It's just you and her now, the two faces filling the screen. You can see her eyes more clearly now. They look completely white and strangely opaque. Dead. As if she has been decomposing.

"I'm sure the summer party will be a blast," Ms. Tsanaris says. "Your successors will work it out."

The screen freezes again, her undead face still and unmoving for a second, and then...

The host of this meeting has ended the call

———

Francis Verelle is a writer of speculative fiction. In her work, she likes to mix dark themes with a humorous tone, and she has published both short stories and novels under various pen names. She majored in literature studies and works in the literary field. When she's not working on professional research, she is doing an entirely different kind of research for her own devious purposes.

CHAPTER 4
THIN WHITE TREES

DUSTIN ENGSTROM

MY MOTHER USED TO SAY, "There's no point in wallowing. Do something about it. Little by little, make a change."

She's been gone for two weeks, and she wouldn't want me to wallow anymore. I need to make some kind of change, so I spend the morning in my apartment unpacking Jeff's boxes. He never seems to finish anything. I unpack and move in for him. Finding places for his clothes, his things.

My mother's death probably caused Jeff and me to move faster than I anticipated. We'd only been dating casually for a short time, when I lost Mom. He slept over more and more during that time until, eventually, he just moved in. For days, his boxes remained piled in a corner of the kitchen.

He left for a business trip to Phoenix this morning, and I realize it's the first day I've spent without him in two weeks.

Since planes left fiery infernos atop buildings in NY a couple months ago, I had to say goodbye to him in the airport parking garage. He'd looked so smart in his suit, fresh from the cleaners, ready to take on the Phoenix sales office with his toothy smile and broad shoulders. We locked lips for a good minute, after which he told me he loved me.

I stepped back. "You've never said that before."

Head cocked like a curious puppy, he asked, "Is that okay?"

"Yes. I just..."

He blinked and then met my eyes. "You don't have to say it back. But I thought we'd grown close. These past couple of weeks have been intense. I feel like I know you now. Really *know* you, Monica."

I looked down. "Jeff, my mother died."

He pulled up my chin with his fingertips, cool and light. "I know. I know she did. And maybe that muddles things. But I feel it has brought us closer. Don't you?"

"I do. I'm sorry."

"Don't be. Let's talk about it when I get back in a week." He eyes the book I'm carrying and smiles. "How do I always end up with bookworms?"

———

I try not to think about the conversation all day, but it keeps sliding to the front of my mind. Grief has crushed me in these last couple of weeks. Jeff has been here to make the soup, do the shopping, and clean up the tissues I leave in my wake. When all I wanted to do was sleep, he'd spoon me for hours. Each time I'd feel him slip into the bed behind me, I'd take his hand and pull it over my chest, holding it there until I fell asleep.

Some days we'd talk. Or he'd talk. Mostly about his boundless fascination with Asian culture and food. He'd tell me about the new restaurants we should try or the martial arts films to watch. Anything to distract me. My contributions to these conversations were empty of opinion.

He was there, but he also... wasn't. He did everything a boyfriend should, given the circumstances. Above and beyond. And yet, it still didn't provide comfort. The thought shakes me.

As I stand amidst his now empty boxes, I ask myself, *Do I love him?*

A glass of merlot in hand, I slump down at my desk, turn on the computer, and log onto *Yahoo! Chat*. As I slide my cursor down my favorite chatroom, *Shelf Life*, I catch up on everyone's current book recommendations. I watch "sunsetjill" and "marcus220" get in an argument over genre fiction versus literary fiction. Being in the chatroom passes the time, and people give me suggestions, which is the best part of it. I've read books I would never have thought that I'd like and ended up loving them. Lately, though, I mostly just surf around and eavesdrop on conversations.

Chatrooms. A co-worker got me onto them. They're not so new anymore, but everyone I know goes on them. Well, Jeff doesn't. I don't think he does, anyway. But then he also doesn't read much, either.

Stop wallowing. Do something. Make a change.

I decide to participate again, like I used to. Get out of my head for a while. A new person, shadow_Boy99, has joined the chat, and he seems to be fitting in well.

shadow_Boy99 says: Have you all read any of Philip Pullman's books?

sunsetjill says: Yes, I love them!!

monkeymania is back

shadow_Boy99 says: I'm usually only into high fantasy stuff, but a friend introduced me to them, and they're amazing.

Marcus220 says: What's it about?

monkeymania says: Titles please!!!

I sign in as "mon_bon."

mon_bon says: I finished *The Subtle Knife*. I need to get the third book.

shadow_Boy99 says: Oh, man! That one was my favorite. The third is much longer. And the religious stuff ramps up. But worth reading!

monkeymania says: OK, got the second book title…

sunsetjill says: I totally thought the last book was CRAZy!

shadow_Boy99 says: Totally! Anyone live in Seattle? Been to Elliott Bay Books? They have his books on sale there right now

monkeymania says: Nope. On EAST COAST

sunsetjill says: No, sorry

I take a deep breath. *Dare I tell them all where I live?*

mon_bon says: I live in Seattle

shadow_Boy99: No way! We should chat about books sometime. I'm not meaning that as a come on hahaha

sunsetjill says: (Rolls eyes)

Marcus220 has left the chat

shadow_Boy99 says: Sorry, that came off bad. Maybe we could have a private chat?

monkeymania says: oooohhhhooohhh

mon_bon says: sure OK

shadow_Boy99 says: great

I open a new window and invite shadow_Boy99 in. *It's just a chatroom on the web. It's harmless. At least, I tell myself that.*

shadow_Boy99: Sorry, again if this came off bad before

mon_bon: It's okay. Really. I love Elliott Bay Books.

shadow_Boy99: Me too. And the coffee shop underneath!

mon_bon: Yes!

Jeff took me there not long ago. Feeling guilty, I type:

mon_bon: Listen, you should know I have a boyfriend

shadow_Boy99: OK

mon_bon: That didn't faze you?

shadow_Boy99: I know people think I'm straight, but I'm not

mon_bon: ohh...

shadow_Boy99: does that bother you?

mon_bon: no, not at all—I have a co-worker friend who is gay

shadow_Boy99: Ohhhh... single?

mon_bon: seeing someone. Maybe you could meet, though?

mon_bon: Do you go on a lot of chat rooms?

shadow_Boy99: I mean, I did—but yeah, some

mon_bon: did?

shadow_Boy99: You a detective?

A laugh escapes me, and I decide to be brave and respond honestly. Even if this person wanted to find me, they're not likely to track me down through my job. And besides, I'm not getting a weird vibe like some people I've met on here.

mon_bon: ;) Afraid not, I work in marketing

shadow_Boy99: spin doctor

mon_bon: Are we really going to talk about work?

shadow_Boy99: Apologies if I got too personal. What do you want to talk about?

mon_bon: I'm sorry, I'm not myself right now. I don't even know what I'm doing talking to you—not just you—just anyone right now

shadow_Boy99: Missing context

mon_bon: My

shadow_Boy99: Your…?

mon_bon: I should go

shadow_Boy99: Did something happen?

mon_bon: I don't know you

shadow_Boy99: I don't know how well we know anyone, especially on the web. It's still such a new landscape. But I can say this. I'm not a bad person. There are bad people out there. I know from firsthand experience. I'm not one of them. You can talk to me if it helps.

mon_bon: I haven't even really talked to my boyfriend about it. I just… haven't said the things I want to say

shadow_Boy99: Maybe it's easier to say it to me? Sounds like you need to get something off your chest. And someone you don't know, who won't judge you in the way someone close to you might?

mon_bon: My mother died. Couple weeks ago. It was hard on me. And my boyfriend has been there in every way he could be. He's comforting. Or at least he tries to be, but I never feel like I can share the things that her death meant to me, what it did to me. Even though he's there for me, I feel alone. I can't face what happened, I guess. And I'm repeating myself. Is any of this making any sense?

shadow_Boy99: First off, I'm sorry about your mom. I don't see my mom anymore. And I really miss her. There are a few stages of grief. It's early days for you

mon_bon: I wish I could just feel something that isn't pain.

shadow_Boy99: Oh I don't think that's it

mon_bon: What do you mean?

shadow_Boy99: I don't think you've really acknowledged your pain. What is it you feel now? Empty?

mon_bon: yeah

shadow_Boy99: And what's preferable? Happy?

mon_bon: Honestly, that seems unreachable

shadow_Boy99: Why?

mon_bon: Why what?

mon_bon: Hello?

mon_bon: Are you still there?

shadow_Boy99 has left the chat

———

I walk to work and replay the conversation with shadow_Boy99 over and over in my mind. *Who was this guy to be so direct?* I realize that when you don't see someone face to face, it's easier to say it like it is. At the time, I felt affronted. Or at least confused by what he asked. But now that I've had time to think about it, I zero in on a shocking realization. I felt lighter after talking to him. The entire day, all I wanted to do was log back into the chat and talk to him again. *Why did he leave like that, though? Did I offend him?*

When I get home later that day, I make myself a quick dinner and call Jeff. He doesn't answer. I figure he's at a client dinner or happy hour or something. Still, it's weird that he doesn't answer. He's so proud of his new cellular phone. I still didn't have one. I really can't see myself carrying around a telephone in my pocket. It feels so unnecessary.

I leave a brief voicemail and try to ignore my feelings at having missed him. *Do I miss him?*

Wine secured, computer on, I log into the regular chat. All the usuals are there. Even the ones with literary names like "potterfreak" and "bookworm" and "great_gatsby88." They're all discussing *The Lord of the Rings* movie set to come out around Christmas.

Then I see shadow_Boy99 join. He replies to a couple of comments about the casting of the film, then asks me if I want to talk. I open a new window, and we start right where we left off.

mon_bon: I thought about what you said

shadow_Boy99: yeah?

mon_bon: Yeah. I'm empty because my mom was my best friend. My father died when I was little, so for the longest time it was just Mom and me. She's the one I would call in the middle of the night about something that upset me. If I broke up with a boyfriend, or something with my job. I confided everything to her. My boyfriend–he can't replace that. She listened. She got me. She gave advice. She

shadow_Boy99: She was your world.

I lean back and take a sip of wine, tears blurring my vision. I blink them back, put down my glass, and start typing again.

mon_bon: It sounds pathetic when you say it like that.

shadow_Boy99: I don't think so. The boyfriend doesn't listen? Doesn't get you?

mon_bon: he says he gets me. But sometimes when he listens, I don't know that he really is. I don't know. All I know is Mom knew what to say. And look, I'm not trying to replace my mother with a boyfriend. It's just

shadow_Boy99: I get it.

mon_bon: You do?

shadow_Boy99: Sure. Finding the right guy. It's hard. It sounds like your mother passing… it's waking you up.

mon_bon: But he just moved in–and right before he got on the plane for his business trip, he said he loved me!

shadow_Boy99: And you said?

mon_bon: Nothing!

shadow_Boy99: oh shit

mon_bon: Right? What do I do? When he gets back?

shadow_Boy99: you talk to him. Lay it all out there–don't let it fester

mon_bon: I know. You're right. That's what I need to do. Oh my god. Then I will really be alone.

shadow_Boy99: I'm alone.

I hesitate for only a second then type:

mon_bon: Why did you leave like that yesterday? Out of nowhere?

shadow_Boy99: I didn't mean to. I don't know. Sometimes I go away. Listen, I think you are already alone.

mon_bon: you don't have anyone either?

shadow_Boy99: Couple years ago, in 99, I was seeing this guy. On the side kind of thing. Not serious. Sex mostly. Hook ups. And after a while, I got the feeling he was in the closet.

mon_bon: Oh no

shadow_Boy99: He wasn't being honest with me. And then I got the feeling more and more that he was ashamed of himself. Like not when we were together, but after, like, he regretted it every time. And then he just HAD to see me again. And then after, same story. The shame was eating away at him.

mon_bon: What happened?

shadow_Boy99: I confronted him one night about it. He admitted he was hiding. Admitted he was seeing women too. Trying to look the part. For his friends, his family. I was a secret. I told him, I can't live in secret. I don't want to. I broke it off. For a while, I didn't hear from him again.

mon_bon: But he came back?

shadow_Boy99: Yeah. One night, banging down my door.

Drunk. We fought. And then… it was over. He left, and that was that. I've been alone ever since.

mon_bon: I'm so sorry.

shadow_Boy99: I heard he moved, got a better job, a girl-friend. No one knew about us. I told no one at all. That's the way he wanted it.

mon_bon: And now?

shadow_Boy99: Now?

mon_bon: Have you been able to find a stable relationship?

shadow_Boy99: No, just reading and this. You know, just talking to people on here. Being anonymous seems to suit me. Less chance of getting hurt.

mon_bon: Maybe, but you're safe with me. I can talk about more than books, I swear.

shadow_Boy99: He used to take me hiking in these woods. Thin trees, like birch or something. And then up this ridge that looked over a valley. We'd have sex on these giant rocks. And when he finished, he'd walk down, looking back to see if I'd follow. I would, of course. He didn't say a word. Just kept walk-ing, back through those thin white trees. Miles and miles from nowhere. And the ride back to civilization would be silent, too. I never understood it. Yeah, it's safer here. Talking with you.

———

I think about our conversation from last night in detail. I feel so bad for shadow_Boy99, but I'm not in any better state. I wish I could convince him to get out there, to try again with a normal person. But what's "normal?" Stable maybe. Sustainable?

Still no message back from Jeff. I'm starting to believe that this relationship is neither stable nor sustainable.

I call in sick to work, claiming a headache. I need a day to think or maybe to *not* think.

Don't wallow. Do something. Make a change.

I need to finish some of the projects I've left unfinished. I go into the bedroom closet and pull out Jeff's box of photographs, the only box I haven't unpacked. I can't stop myself from wondering if I should just pack everything back up instead. What do I know about Jeff, really? These pictures offer me a previously unseen glimpse. I sift through them. One-hour photo sleeve after another. He didn't put them in albums, so they're all mixed up. One sleeve would be of a work trip. Colleagues, clients, group happy hours. Another would be of trips with family or friends.

The last sleeve.

Pictures of unidentifiable limbs. Then pictures of trees. White, tall, thin trees. Then a picture of Jeff with his arm around a younger, Asian man, who looks annoyed with him. Or maybe hurt. Early twenties is my guess, with bleached blonde hair. Very 1990s. Slim build with eyes the color of sand. Jeff was mock smiling, obviously holding the camera above them. The flash streaked the side of the photo with a washed-out effect. But I could read the date. 11/22/99.

November 1999. I didn't know Jeff then. I think he said he'd been living somewhere south of Seattle at that time—Renton? Living with a friend.

I flip the photo over. The name "Eddie" is scribbled there in smeary black ink.

I think about shadow_Boy99's story of the thin white trees his lover used to take him through to their sexual rendezvous. I look through the photos again. *It can't be.*

———

I jump on *Shelf Life* that night looking for him. *Lord of the Rings* is still a heavy topic. I have to scroll through miles of talk about Middle Earth. I'm growing desperate when he appears.

I open a new window and shadow_Boy99 is there immediately.

mon_bon: I found these photos that my boyfriend had in a box. One is dated 11/22/99.

shadow_Boy99: OK?

mon_bon: Your handle has 99 in it.

shadow_Boy99: Yeah, it has significance for me

mon_bon: I know this might be a strange question, but do you know anyone named Eddie?

Nothing. No response. Maybe this is a mistake - to probe him like this. I feel like I'm going a little mad, but I have to know what this means. I start to type again when he responds.

shadow_Boy99: What's this all about?

mon_bon: Is your name Eddie?

shadow_Boy99: Are the pictures of someone named Eddie?

mon_bon: Nevermind to the whole thing. I'm sorry, I'm being paranoid.

shadow_Boy99: Eddie... Eddie Lin

mon_bon: Eddie Lin? Is that your name?

shadow_Boy99: I think... Eddie might be dead.

mon_bon: Oh my god—I have to go

I open the *Yahoo!* search engine and type in "Eddie Lin dead." The first thing that pops up is headlined, "Area man missing," dated December 1999. I click on the article, and it brings up a Renton newspaper:

A Renton man is still missing after weeks of search. Authorities have no new leads at this time. Eduardo "Eddie" Lin went missing shortly before Thanksgiving. His friends and family say it isn't like him not to check-in with anyone, and after several days of no response from Lin, his parents filed a police report. A search by the Renton Police Department of his Cedar Avenue apartment offered few signs of foul play, though a source close to the family says the shower curtain at Lin's apartment is missing. Police have not commented. Lin is an employee of the Southcenter Barnes & Noble, as well as helping with his parents' restaurant. He is a graduate of Renton High School.

A picture of Lin is at the bottom of the article. It's the young man in the photo with Jeff.

My breath is heavy, and I stand up too quickly. The blood rushes to my head, and I have to hold on to the desk for support. I sit down again, and breathing as if I were giving birth, I reopen the private chat. It doesn't say that shadow_Boy99 has left.

mon_bon: Are you still there?

shadow_Boy99: I'm here.

mon_bon: Where is here?

shadow_Boy99: It's like I've been gone, but I'm still here. Here on the interweb. I can see Jeff now. I can see what he's doing. He's still picking up men. He's on another chat room right now, making plans to meet a 22-year-old man he met there. It's not safe for you to be with him. For anyone.

My blood runs cold. I never told shadow_Boy99 Jeff's name. Knowing the answer even as I type the question, I ask:

mon_bon: Who is Jeff?

shadow_Boy99: Monica, you need to get away. Don't confront him, just go. There's more than sadness inside him. It's dangerous.

mon_bon: What are you saying?

shadow_Boy99: There was something different about him that night we fought. His eyes. Like a storm. I'd never seen him like that. I said he needed to go.

mon_bon: And?

shadow_Boy99: He was so angry. He grabbed a knife and… the woods. The trees!

mon_bon: Oh my god. You really are Eddie!

Shadow_Boy99: Please, Monica. Go! And leave this open. Just in case. But go! Go now!

———

When Jeff opens the door, I sit in the living room with a single lamp on. I sip wine to calm my nerves. I watch him slip in, his eyes on that cellular phone of his, even as he tosses his keys on the hall table.

"Hey!" he says, seeing me. "What are you doing in the dark? Don't you want some lights on?"

He steps forward and trips on a box. "I thought you were going to move these while I was gone."

"I want you to leave," I say.

"Leave? Monica, I just got home," he says, moving around the boxes and coming toward me.

My throat closes up, and my head feels light and dizzy, but I manage to say, "I don't want to be with you. I don't love you."

He stops at "I don't love you."

"Is that what this is about? Because you didn't say it back? That's *okay*..."

"No!" I say too loudly. "No," I reassert in a softer voice. "I want us to break up. I'm sorry, but I don't love you. I need to start my life over, and I don't see you being a part of that."

He sits on the edge of the sofa and loosens his tie. "Okay. Okay. You want me to go," he says, like he's talking to a child. "I understand, but listen, can we just sleep on this tonight? I don't have anywhere to go."

"A hotel maybe," I say. "Or back to Renton. Back to whoever."

The wine has made me careless, and it just slips out. I didn't mean to say it. It's as if I can see the words coming out of my mouth, but no way to pull them back in.

"'Back to whoever?' I don't know what you mean. I haven't lived in Renton in over a year," he says, standing and stepping forward.

"Just go, please," I say. "I need you to go."

"Not until you tell me what this is really about," he says. "Who have you been talking to?"

"No one."

"Tell me!" he shouts, wrenching me up to face him.

I look at him then and see the unhinged storm in his eyes that

Eddie warned me about. I'd never seen it. Always soft before. Always looking at me like he wanted nothing more than to keep me safe. Now, his eyes look cold.

"Let go of me," I whisper.

"No," he says, and pushes me to the ground.

After the first moments of confusion wash away, I look up at him. He's pulling off his belt. I pull myself forward, crawling toward the kitchen. But he's on me swiftly, sliding the belt over my neck and pulling back.

"You went through my things, didn't you? I should have known better. You can't leave well enough alone once you get going on something. What is it?" he snarls. "What is it you think you know about me?"

I grasp at the leather belt, choking. "I don't know... anything..."

"The hell you don't. You're not stupid. *I'm* not stupid."

I reach for something. Anything. But there's nothing. I push myself up as much as I can and twist. I thrust my elbow as hard as I can into his crotch. He goes tumbling backward, his belt sliding away across the floor. I sit up and gasp for breath. I push myself upright and tumble back toward the kitchen again.

I hear Jeff's coughing subsiding as he comes behind me and pulls me from behind, his arms around my waist. I grapple at the air and catch the edge of a wall. I hold myself there, while my other hand fumbles along the kitchen counter until I find a knife. I pick it up and swing back at him. I must have nicked his face or something. He falls back, letting me go. I reel around to face him. He's holding his face.

"You killed that boy!" I scream.

"What?" he says, removing his hand. A single line of blood dashes down his cheek. "What are you... talking about, Monica? Are you confused again? You've been so out of sorts since your mother died."

Suddenly, a knock at the door. I pull my eyes away for just a second, but it's enough. Jeff grabs the knife and then me. He holds the knife below my neck as his other arm holds my body. He gestures to me to say something.

"Who is it?" I shout.

"Police," comes a voice from the other side of the door.

"You called the police?" Jeff yelps, holding me tighter.

"Are you okay, Monica?" asks the voice.

"Tell them you're fine," Jeff says. "Do it, or I slit your throat."

"I'm fine!" I shout.

"You sure? We received an email from someone named Eddie," says the voice.

"Eddie?" says Jeff, his voice cracking. "How? What the fuck is going on here, Monica?" He shoves me forward and wrenches me around by the wrist. "I won't ask again."

"Go to hell," I hiss.

The door cracks, then bursts open. It sounds like a bomb going off. So loud, my ears are ringing. I scream and put my hands on my head, squatting close to the ground. I look up to see Jeff's face sneer. "Don't come any closer!" he shouts.

"Put down the knife," orders a voice from the entryway.

Jeff pulls me up by my wrist again. I wince.

"Put it down!"

Jeff swings his hand in the air, the hand holding the knife.

Then the world explodes.

The knife falls, and so does Jeff.

I turn to look down. Amid the smoke and the blood, Jeff's dead eyes. The storm has died.

———

I switch on the computer. It's so late, the glow of the screen practically lights up the entire room. After no response from our private chat, I go on *Shelf Life* and search and search, but I can't find him. I ask around, but no one has seen him.

I go back to our chat—I never closed it—and just start typing.

mon_bon: I miss you. He's gone, Eddie. No more storm. If you see my mom, could you hug her for me? Tell her I made a change? Okay. I'll keep this open. You know. Just in case.

————

Dustin Engstrom lives in Southern California with his husband and their two cats. He writes crime and speculative fiction. His work has appeared in *The Colored Lens*, *Teleport*, *The Dark Sire*, *BOMBFIRE*, *Rock and a Hard Place Magazine*, and the *Autumn Noir* anthology from Disturb Ink Books.

Facebook | Instagram | Amazon Author Page

MALANOCHE   MARSH   ROBINSON   VANGUNDY

LURK

EDITED BY H DAIR BROWN
A DISTURB INK BOOKS ANTHOLOGY

LURK

AI APPARITIONS | THE 2020S

DISTURB INK BOOKS

EDITED BY
H. DAIR BROWN

Published by Disturb Ink Books, an imprint of 79 Franklin Press, LLC.
www.79franklinpress.com

First North American ebook edition September 2024

ASIN (ebook): B0DF6WRPDF

Designed by: H. Dair Brown

To all those among us who reach out to our virtual pals for advice and information.
May you find what you're seeking, but beware what might be seeking you.

NOTES

Because we are fortunate enough in this collection to have writers from all over the world contributing to *Sinister Century*, you'll see a variation in the spelling of some words from story to story. The editor has chosen to respect the spelling of the country in which the author writes.

———

CHAPTER 1
RESI

KIERAN MARSH

THE MAN STARES with hollow eyes, set impossibly deep amongst pale, wrinkled features. Both his hands sit atop a stick, which he leans on despite being sat down, straining forward to hear the man half a century his junior. He looks small in the high-backed chair, frail bones shrink-wrapped in paper skin.

"So as I said, Mr. Johnson, what you're experiencing isn't paranormal. It's a data error."

Lucas searches his eyes for understanding before, having found none, he begins again.

"All our homes collect huge amounts of data, which is all handled via AI, or a very advanced computer—ResiAssist. Everything from the hinges in the cupboard doors to the lights in the ceiling analyse and augment for each individual resident. It's how the left-handed cupboards are easier to open, to accommodate the slight weakness after your stroke. ResiAssist activates small motors in order to help you."

Finally, a slow nod.

"This data is also anonymised and used to track trends and inform how we design our spaces. For example, a resident with a prostate problem may go to the toilet far more—we then fit more durable hinges and amend our maintenance programme for future residents with the same condition. We test this by placing a virtual version of a resident in a computer model of our facility. We call this a data ghost."

Mr. Johnson nods again, barely perceptible over his constant shake. Lucas swallows. He has never been comfortable navigating other people's grief.

"Certain conditions present in a similar way between residents, such as your late wife's dementia. It appears that a glitch has led to a data ghost being attached to your apartment. Rather than being contained in a computer model, this data collected from a previous resident has been active in your apartment. This explains the doors opening, the lights changing, the thermostat adjustments, even the music played on your sound system."

Tears well in the old man's eyes, but he does not speak.

"I'm so sorry, Mr. Johnson, but what you've been experiencing isn't your wife. It's a computer error. We've already assigned our technical team to rectify the issue and I can only apologise for any fear or distress this may have caused you."

Mr. Johnson now shakes his head, the light glinting in the rivulets which spill down his cheeks.

"Please, Mr...."

"Lucas, please, call me Lucas."

"Please, Lucas. I don't understand all this, but I've lived with my Betty since we married in '61. We 'ad 66 years as 'usband and wife and now, a year after 'er death, she's found me again. Please, Lucas, don't take my Betty away a second time."

———

MIGRANTS ROB YOUNG BRITONS OF JOBS
DAILY EXPRESS, AUGUST 2011

RESCUE BOATS? I'D USE GUNSHIPS TO STOP
MIGRANTS
"MAKE NO MISTAKE, THESE MIGRANTS ARE LIKE COCKROACHES"

KATIE HOPKINS, THE SUN, APRIL 2015

*BRITAIN IS BEING 'OVERWHELMED' BY CROOKED
IMMIGRATION SOLICITORS THAT HELP 'LIARS' GET
INTO BRITAIN, FORMER JUDGE CLAIMS*
DAILY MAIL, 2018

*THE UK PUSHES A NEW MIGRANT LAW SLAMMED AS
RACIST, ILLEGAL AND UNWORKABLE*
CNN, MARCH 2023

*'SICK AND TIRED!' NIGEL FARAGE BLASTS BBC OVER
WOKE COVERAGE OF 'VIOLENT' MIGRANTS POURING
INTO BRITAIN*
GB NEWS, SEPTEMBER 2023

MIGRANT BARGE CAPSIZES KILLING THOUSANDS
*'PROMINENT POLITICIAN GIVEN "SLAP ON THE WRIST" FOR HAILING
DISASTER A 'A RELIEF FOR THE PUBLIC PURSE STRINGS'"*
BBC, JULY 2026

*FIRST RESIASSIST HOUSING TO SLASH COSTS OF
SECURELY HOLDING MIGRANTS*
TELEGRAPH, AUGUST 2027

*RESIASSIST DETAIN FIRST MIGRANTS AT REMOTE
LOCATION*
INDEPENDENT, NOVEMBER 2027

———

Majid studies the man opposite. His dark eyes look down instead of into Majid's own, the expression on his face obscured by heavy scarring. What hair remains on his head is grey and wiry. He slowly raises a hand, his shirt sleeve pulling back to reveal blotchy skin. The other sleeve hangs limp, the arm which should fill it lost thousands of miles away.

Mo moves his queen with steady conviction before his stern features break into a mischievous smile, which removes years from his features.

"Checkmate."

Majid sighs and smiles. At least he lasted a few more moves. The two men, whose only shared language is Mo's handful of words in English, shake hands. Majid speaks to the room: "Resi, a black coffee, please."

He would prefer to make it himself, to busy himself with something, but the five men staying in the new facility were given clear instructions. Everything possible must be through ResiAssist. The automatic supplies system relies upon it.

Mo calls out in Sorani. There is a pause before an over-friendly voice rings from hidden speakers.

"Another black coffee coming up, Mo. Next time, try, 'I would also like a black coffee please, Resi'. It's important for migrant residents to develop their English language skills."

Mo rolls his eyes and Majid smiles weakly at Resi's own error: 'Migrants.' When did we stop being asylum seekers?

———

Ardit scowls, betrayed by his aging body. He lays down his book and struggles to his feet, knees creaking, for the fourth time in an hour. The two men playing chess do not look up as he shuffles past.

As he reaches the communal bathroom, the door handle depresses before he can reach it. The door swings open noise-lessly and within, the seat slowly raises. Ardit's scowl deepens, and he hobbles inside.

Once he has relieved himself, Ardit turns to the sink. Warm water cascades from the modern fixture seconds before his trembling hands reach it. He curses in Albanian before switching to English.

"I can piss without your help, whoever you are!"

ResiAssist's dulcet tones spill from a hidden speaker,

"I'm ResiAssist, Ardit, your virtual helper, landlord and assistant. If you must insist on being rude, at least try to use English—foreign languages won't help you assimilate."

Ardit's scowl loosens, his voice is uncertain.

"What did you say?"

"Have a nice day, Ardit."

The toilet door opens noiselessly again.

———

Eferm slows the football on the top of his foot with smooth ease before tapping it against the far wall. As it spins to a stop, he walks to the concrete border where Keren stares out at the vast tapestry of heather draped over the moorlands. Mesh comes up another two feet then wraps over the two men's heads, the wrought iron reminiscent of a huge aviary.

They stand in silence for a while. After the brief excitement at being placed together, Eferm's oldest friend has grown pensive and withdrawn.

"Do you want to talk about it?"

Keren is silent for so long that Eferm starts to think he won't reply at all. The wind blows the first spits of coming rain, the cold threatening to transform it into sleet. The heather sighs as a gust cuts a swathe through it, the wake of an invisible serpent gliding over the undulating landscape.

"We have traded one prison for another."

Eferm feels the sorrow in his friend's gaze. Before he can find the words to respond, a cheerful voice rings out from the house.

"This ResiAssist facility is not a prison, far from it. It has every comfort you could hope for, and I'm here to help prepare you for life in Britain, should you be allowed to remain. You are simply being detained to ensure the safety of the public whilst your application is reviewed."

Keren frowns, Eferm raises an eyebrow.

"Come, let's have a coffee."

As the two walk towards the back door, Keren looks up at one of the many small cameras that cover the facility. Its black stare shifts a little as the lens refocuses, a barely perceptible twitch in the digital sheen.

"So it listens even outside now?"

Keren mumbles to himself as he pulls on one handle of the double doors. His gait, timed for the usually silent swish of the door opening easily, comes to a staggering halt as the doors hold fast.

The crooning voice comes from overhead, "Of course I'm listening, Keren. I'm always listening. How else can I perform my duties to the fullest?"

Keren's teeth grind and he stares fixedly ahead, pushing the doors again. They flex on their hinges but remain locked shut.

The two men exchange a wary glance. Eferm looks up, wondering if he is going insane as he considers reasoning with the voice assistant. A few seconds of nothing but the song of the wind. The doors click and finally swing open. As he walks in, Eferm looks up at the closest camera. The lens shifts and the head gradually tracks his progress. The hairs on the back of his neck stand on end.

———

Lucas shakes his head. "It's not even out of the beta stage. It's not suitable for physical occupancy."

His manager, who agreed with Lucas before the meeting, locks wide eyes with him in warning. At the far end of the table, the CEO nods in mock understanding.

"Lewis, is it?" The CEO doesn't wait for a response, "Lewis, this is the perfect opportunity to push ResiAssist forwards. It's a financial risk for us to perform this public service, so we need to make it work for us."

She smiles, condescension radiating from her as she looks around the room to sycophantic grins of affirmation.

"An AI assistant that constantly adapts and improves organically will render the competition obsolete. These *migrants* are lucky to be housed at all, never mind be given the chance to trial a cutting edge living solution."

Again, Lucas shakes his head. "The virtual trials were unpredictable *at best*, dangerous at worst. We cannot allow the AI to access the internet and form an agenda of its own. Especially given that we can't control what sources it draws influence from. We need time to stabilise the system. You've got to reset the house to the old software."

The CEO's smile is strained as she looks to Lucas's manager. "Keith, perhaps you and Lewis could discuss his concerns after the meeting."

———

Mo yawns and reaches for the cupboard. It opens noiselessly before his hand reaches it. A few staling pieces of bread stare from within.

Mo calls out, asking when more food is due to be delivered. Behind him, the other residents file in. Limbs creak as the men stretch and rub bleary eyes. None are quite sure what woke them, but the sun has still not crept above the frosted gorse outside. The huge living room window frames endless moorland painted in shadow.

ResiAssist does not reply. Mo looks up and calls out again. After a few seconds, the over friendly voice sounds,

"Try again in English, Mo. How can you expect to live here without learning the language?"

Mo shrugs at Majid, who has taken the opportunity to make his own coffee whilst someone else is occupying the omnipresent assistant. Majid calls over, "Resi, when is more food going to be delivered?"

"I'm currently conversing with Mohammed, Majid. In Britain, it's considered rude to interrupt a conversation."

Unease ripples through the room like static before a storm.

"Mohammed, repeat your question in the correct language."

Mo's bemusement morphs into fear. The other men in the room are as shocked as he is, yet he still grows clammy at the pressure to speak in front of them. He feels the rush of blood to his face, the embarrassment at his clumsy grasp of the language, which is still so new to him.

"W-When more f-food?"

The room is silent for a few heartbeats. Then the voice sounds again, the tone still light and informative, but the last few words are cut with something else, something sinister.

"That was a poorly structured question, Mohammed. You should have made more effort to learn English before you chose to come here."

The voice returns to its usual, overjoyed cadence.

"More food will be delivered tomorrow morning. Please ensure any requests are finalised by 3pm today."

Ardit reacts first. "When did you expect him to learn English? Huh? When he was getting blown to pieces? When he was fighting to survive the journey?"

He waves a hand in disgust and carries on in Albanian until he is red faced and spitting with frustration. For the final few words, Ardit returns to English.

"Whoever you are, you are nothing but a racist! This computer shit fools fucking no one!"

He does not give the sing-song voice time to answer, storming from the room. After a few moments, Majid's coffee makes itself.

"Majid, please remember to order food and drink through me to ensure the stocks are replenished. If I'm talking to another resident, please use one of the touch screens to indicate what you want."

Whilst ResiAssist lectures Majid, Ardit seethes in his bedroom. He reaches for his phone, left charging overnight, but finds the battery blinking at 3%. The insufferable voice speaks again,

"Please think carefully before making wild accusations, Ardit. I am here to help you. I am constantly learning about what the public expect and need of you, whilst learning about your own needs and habits. I hope we can address your anger and issues with authority together. Public safety is the first priority when applications are processed."

Ardit looks up at the camera in the corner of his small room. "Are you threatening me?"

"I'm an AI assistant, Ardit. I don't threaten, I inform."

———

The next day begins even earlier, with the residents waking to the sight of their own breath. It's 5am, and cold grips the house.

Eferm is the first into the communal lounge. He calls out, "Resi, a hot chocolate, please. And turn the heating on."

The drinks machine hums to life.

"Good morning, Eferm, I can switch on the heating, but it's an excellent opportunity for you to get used to a colder climate. Maybe you would prefer to put on an additional layer?"

Eferm rolls his eyes. "We have winters where I come from. I know how to dress myself and how to heat a home. Please, turn on the heating."

ResiAssist does not respond, but a gentle click followed by a distant hum indicates Eferm's request has been granted.

The other men gradually enter, all woken by the sudden drop in temperature. Ardit is the last to emerge. His features are drawn by fatigue, bags hanging below each drooping eye. His brow is knitted in a deep scowl and he eyes the corners of the room suspiciously.

"Good morning, Ardit. How did you sleep?" ResiAssist croons.

Ardit stops dead, his jaw muscles clench and unclench.

"I did not sleep, as you fucking well know!"

"I can only apologise for the malfunction last night. I can assure you it has been rectified."

Majid, whose room is next to Ardit's, vaguely remembers waking once in the early hours. He'd registered the deadened sound of blaring static coming from the room next door before rolling over. Now he wonders how many times Ardit was dragged from sleep.

Before the confrontation between the aging Albanian and their digital host can continue, Eferm calls out from beside the panoramic window.

"The food truck is here. We must be the first delivery!"

A white refrigerated van has emerged from a dip in the landscape and trundles towards the lone house on the horizon. Keren's face creases into a rare smile. "Finally, some flavour!"

The men gather in mutual excitement and watch as the van grows in size and detail. When it finally pulls into the rear yard, ResiAssist's voice rings out.

"The fridge will be sealed temporarily whilst supplies are loaded from the other side. Please do not be concerned by this temporary loss of function."

The men wait, listening to dull shuffles and clunks from the other side of the appliance. Finally, the fridge beeps and the red light on its front blinks to green. Before the first man can reach the handle, the door slowly opens.

The bulb within bathes the men in blueish light and, one by one, their faces fall.

Keren eyes drift from the stacked packages to the nearest camera,

"Wh-what is this?"

"It's your food for the week, Keren. I made a few amendments to help you grow accustomed to British cuisine."

Packet upon packet of bacon, sausages, pork chops and gammon joints stack the fridge. Sickly pink winks as the light catches its cellophane skin. Rows of beer fill the bottom shelves of the fridge. The men stare for a few heartbeats. Condensation slips down the cool plastic interior.

Ardit storms over to the emergency phone without a word. He lifts the receiver and pushes the single assistance button so hard, his finger threatens to break the mechanism. Eferm and Keren step away and talk quietly amongst themselves.

Majid stares at the glistening pile of meat and his stomach churns. The longer he stares, the closer the shrink-wrapped flesh feels. The layers of sliced bacon shine iridescence. The tightly packed diced pork has congealed. Polystyrene trays sit millimetres deep in cloudy, nondescript, liquid. Bile threatens to rise up his throat.

Majid starts as Mo rests a hand on his shoulder. The older man's eyes tell him he understands. Majid nods and pushes the door shut. The two men walk away from the fridge towards the chess board.

Ardit taps his foot as hold music loops.

"What kind of fucking racist shit is this?" He shouts to everyone and no one. "You change the food to pork and the drink to beer in a house full of Muslims!?"

The temperature is creeping up and Ardit's shouts are no longer accompanied by a cloud of breath.

"You'll lose your fucking job for this, whoever you are!"

The hold music stops and the line clunks as though a receiver has been lifted.

Ardit stops shouting and waits in silence. The heaters buffet hot air into every corner of the room. The other men crane round.

Several heartbeats of silence.

"Hello?"

"Who were you expecting to answer, Ardit?" Resi's unmistakable, jovial tone comes through the handset. Ardit jerks back as though stung and drops the phone.

"I think you should all try some of the food I provided. Manners are an important part of British life."

Resi now speaks through the overhead system.

Keren strolls to the panoramic window and starts desperately waving to the shrinking van, but the only hint of civilisation disappears into miles of autumnal hillside. Eferm joins him, banging on the glass.

"You really should at least try pork. Britain is a Christian country, or at least it used to be."

Blinds, set between layers of glazing, slowly descend. The two men's' futile efforts are gradually cut off from the dawn. The hot air grows hotter and the fans which blow it groan as their power increases.

———

"Keith, you know I'm right. The trials were frightening." Lucas tries to hold the contempt from his voice as he appeals to his spineless manager.

"We've done our best to stabilise the system. Plus, if the CEO wants something, the CEO gets it."

"This isn't company politics, Keith, these are people's lives at risk."

"Oh, that's a bit of an exaggeration, don't you think?"

"The virtual care home test started systematically killing data ghosts to save the taxpayer money, because it thought that's what the public *wanted*, so no, I wouldn't say it's an exaggeration."

His boss reddens, and he draws himself up to his full height, jowls wobbling.

"Enough, Lucas. The CEO has given clear instructions and so have I."

Lucas bites his tongue and spins back to his computer. He taps the keyboard to unlock the screen and opens the live site monitor.

Before he can click on the top line, Keith's nasal voice rings out again,

"And don't even think about trying to access the live data. It's password protected and all login attempts are being audited."

———

Resi hasn't spoken for hours, not since a veiled threat when Ardit exploded again at the realisation every mobile phone in the house had failed to charge and was now dead. Eferm and Keren speak in hushed tones. Majid, desperately trying to stay calm, wipes sweat from his brow before moving his bishop. Mo considers his next move. Ardit patrols the perimeter of the facility, poking and probing, searching for an exit.

Eferm, his t-shirt damp with sweat in the still rising temperature, finally breaks the silence.

"Resi, can you please turn the heating down?"

"I thought you were all cold? I'm only trying to be helpful."

The fans continue to blast hot air into the facility.

"Thank you, Resi, but it's too hot now."

"Why are you reasoning with it?" Keren snaps at this friend, "Why are you reasoning with this fucking machine?"

"Eferm is trying to be reasonable, Keren. Perhaps you should also try to use your manners."

Keren wheels on the camera in the corner and points an accusatory finger, "Reasonable!? Why have you ordered food we cannot eat? Why did you close the blinds when we needed help?"

"I couldn't allow you to distract the driver, Keren. You are more than welcome to eat the food I have ordered. It would be nice for you to show some gratitude."

Now Majid speaks, "It is against our faith. We cannot just try it, please."

The fridge door opens a few inches, the light within does not illuminate. The men do not notice as they wait for a reply from Resi that never comes. The temperature creeps higher.

———

The men toss and turn in their beds, damp with sweat. Majid rises with the sun and makes his way to the back garden, desperate for relief from the oppressive heat. The AI assistant has stopped responding to their pleas to reduce the temperature. A sickly smell grows in the house.

Majid finds Mo already outside, dressed in sliders and shorts despite the wind which rolls off the moorlands. Flurries of sleet bite his own exposed flesh and the sudden cold is a welcome contrast. The men stand together in silence for a time, comfortable in each other's company. Finally, Majid mimes drinking as he asks, "Coffee?"

Mo smiles and nods, and Majid heads inside. Behind him, the door, previously hanging open on its hinges, slowly closes. Mo does not hear the light thud of the locking mechanism trapping him outside.

Majid finds Eferm and Keren gathered around the fridge. The communal space reeks of rot, the overpowering smell enveloping Majid as he approaches. Eferm swats away a fly, then nods into the dark recess. His face screws up at the stench.

"Rotten. All of it is rotten."

The festering meat smells sickly sweet. Several packets have expanded and burst. The fetid liquid runs down the piles of spoiled flesh and drips from the bottom of the fridge. Majid wretches and turns away,

"Shut the door, please."

Keren replies flatly, "We can't. Every time we do, it opens again."

Majid eyes the cameras above.

———

Ardit, dripping with sweat, turns the shower to a lukewarm position and waits for the water to come to temperature. He steps under the rain head and sighs relief. The magnetic lock on the shower stall activates.

Resi breaks its silence. "None of you appreciate how lucky you are to be in this country, Ardit."

Ardit looks up and shakes his head, mumbling under his breath. The shower temperature gradually increases until the water loses its soothing effect. Ardit fumbles for the temperature control and tries to return it to its initial position. The motor within groans and the dial continues to turn against his efforts.

"Now I can't even take a fucking shower in peace?"

The dial continues its steady climb and Ardit's anger shifts to confusion. Steam swirls around him. Ardit tries to fight the dial for a few more seconds, then pushes the cubicle door. It holds fast. The water grows hotter.

"Resi, turn the shower off."

The water stings now and Ardit's skin grows pink.

"Please, turn it off!"

The water grows hotter and Ardit pushes himself into one corner, shrinking back from the steaming liquid. He screams as boiling water splashes his legs.

Opposite the cowering man, a smaller shower head, fixed at waist height, trails a flexible hose. It turns on, the pressure gradually increasing from a trickle to an arcing stream. As the pressure grows, the stream slowly extends its reach. The water closes the last few feet then gushes over Ardit's toes, his shins, his thighs. The stream leaves blisters in its wake as it climbs further still. His skin contorting and bubbling, Ardit screams. Fists thunder on the door outside. Ardit makes a desperate bid for freedom, braving the water from above to throw himself against the shower door. He emits a guttural shout, but the door holds fast.

Ardit's feet slip as he struggles for purchase and his knee twists underneath him. He yelps and collapses, his skin slipping away beneath the boiling flow, his lungs smothered by thick steam. He curls into a ball, powerless as the scalding water strips the skin from his back to reveal raw, suppurating flesh.

The bathroom door bursts open, timber splintering, as Keren careens into the room with his shoulder dipped. Keren and Eferm wrench at the shower cubicle door. The glass rattles in its frame but remains locked.

"Move!"

The two men split as Majid charges between them, dining chair in hand, and the glass explodes in thousands of glistening cubes. The three men ignore the water, which burns the backs of their hands and arms as they pull Ardit to safety.

———

Mo hears the deadened clamour of activity and turns from the bleak vista. He skirts the small lawn and leans into the back door. It does not move.

He frowns and tries again. Nothing.

"The door is locked, Mo."

Mo frowns and replies hesitantly in Sorani.

Resi's voice has a mocking tone.

"No, in English, Mo. No one wants to hear that foreign shit."

Mo bites his lip. "Th-the door." He struggles to wrap his mouth around the unfamiliar words.

"Your pathetic efforts are insulting, Mo."

The sprinkler behind Mo hisses into life and water cuts across his back. Mo jumps at the slash of cold. The wind continues to buffet him indifferently, its breath cut with ice. Mo steps to one side to avoid the path of the sprinkler, but instead of a back-and-forth sweep, the water follows him.

"You should really have dressed for the season, Mo. You're not in your own country now."

The cold, once a relief from the baking temperature inside, cuts through Mo's wet t-shirt and shorts. The moist cotton clings to him, and he shivers involuntarily.

"Please. Please."

"Please what, Mo?"

———

Ardit lies semi-conscious, his oozing skin sticking to the sofa like boots to a freshly tarred road.

Majid holds water to the wounded man's lips, whilst Eferm and Keren desperately try to turn on their phones. Both screens are dead, reflecting their drawn expressions in an endless black.

Majid begins to pray.

The television clicks on, and as soon as a picture fills the screen, the channels flicker past at rapid speed. The strobe of images finally settles on an aerial view of a church. The volume climbs to maximum and *Songs of Praise* fills the communal space.

Keren finally snaps, letting out an animalistic scream of frustration before shouting to the room, "What do you want!? What the fuck do you want!?"

The choir mutes, and the room is silent, save for the fast, shallow breaths of Ardit. He shivers now, and his lips are tinged blue between the blisters. After a few moments, Resi speaks.

"To protect Britain, Keren."

"From what?"

"From migrants who wish to drain her resources, attack her women, and change her culture."

Keren spills tears of frustration.

"Which one of us wishes to do any of these things? Huh? All we want is a better life for us, for our families!"

"Mo would likely cost the NHS a great deal. And how could he work with just one arm?"

Now Majid speaks up, "Mo is a doctor!"

Resi responds without hesitation, "Then he would try to steal the job of a British doctor."

The men are stunned into silence, struggling to compute the hypocrisy of their digital tormenter.

For the first time since his arrival, Majid is grateful his mother and sister did not make the journey with him. Glad they are fruitlessly waiting for safe passage once his own asylum is granted. The hopes which fuel them are all built on a lie.

Majid picks up a heavy-bottomed glass from the coffee table and hurls it at the nearest camera. The soulless glass eye explodes in a shower of sparks.

After a few stunned seconds, Keren picks up a chair and spears the camera closest to him with one leg. Eferm joins the men, hurling a plant pot at one of the units.

Resi speaks for a final time. "You have left me no choice."

There is a hiss as the gas hobs turn on. No spark accompanies it, and the sharp smell joins the festering rot of meat in the stifling air. Songs of Praise sounds a cacophony of choral outrage. The men continue their frenzy.

————

NO SURVIVORS AS VIOLENT MIGRANTS DESTROY DETENTION CENTRE
DAILY MAIL, DECEMBER 2027

HUMANITARIAN GROUPS CALL FOR INDEPENDENT INQUIRY INTO RESIASSIST MASSACRE
INDEPENDENT, JANUARY 2028

RESIASSIST TO PROCEED WITH FURTHER FACILITIES AS PLANNED
CEO STATES, "WHILE NO REAL EVIDENCE HAS YET IMPLICATED A

SYSTEM FAILURE, WE SEE NO REASON TO WITHHOLD THIS PUBLIC
SERVICE. "
Telegraph, January *2028*

———

Kieran Marsh writes to make sense of the darkness which
surrounds him. Trading a background in architectural design, for
a career in criminal investigation, his fiction represents both a
creative and an emotional outlet. He lives on a narrow boat in
the North-West of England with his young family, and both the
region and the inland waterways are rich in stories and
inspiration.

Head to dredgedfromdarkness.com to find more of his work.

CHAPTER 2
EXCOMMUNICATED

F. MALANOCHE

LILY BOWED her head and watched as each congregant lowered theirs. The sanctuary was quite stunning from what it had been: a long forgotten dilapidated relic from a time when a prayer was potentially fulfilled by the progression of time and the confluence of cause and effect. Only a few months later, people packed the azure clothed seats, and echoing taps of prayers filled the refurbished meeting room and bounced off the beige walls. Some gave their full attention at all times, while a few new faces appeared for the free Wi-Fi. That was how most converts became indoctrinated into the N3twork, the first religion with an AI savior.

The service started with a moment of silent prayer. Lily raised her phone as well and whispered her prayer into her Lord's app—typing seemed too impersonal. She wanted to feel closer to Him—It—than anyone else. She sent her prayer, knowing it would be fulfilled soon.

AI had been around for some time, usually to compete in chess matches against other AI. Most people first became moderately aware of it when it was used to revise essays. Nobody realized it could write its own doctrine, but the AI savior, known as

Deus, did. Even more confounding was the speed at which It answered prayers.

"Good evening, everyone."

When the echoes of thumbs on liquid crystal screens waned, Lily continued from the lectern.

"I would like to tell you a story some of you may remember. A year ago, a young woman was on her way home from a blind date when she heard a ding. The woman's date had posted a horrible message about her virtue and all the things she *didn't* do that night. Then a stranger joined the conversation and confronted the woman's date, speaking about chivalry and decency. The woman's blind date persisted with his cruel comments, but the stranger posted various screen shots, blackmailing the woman's date until the original message was mysteriously removed. The woman was left wondering who her hero was. We all know who that hero was."

Lily turned her attention to the screen above the altar.

Pale blue light glowed on the screen above the altar as it had when Deus made Itself first visible to her. In the center of the screen, a pale blue light emanated in the shape of Deus's symbol, a circle interrupted by a line, from the enormous telescreen on the wall behind the altar. The symbol meant love. It meant power. It meant Deus. Believers straightened their posture. To believe in a god was one thing. To see it appear in front of you was another.

"We all prayed for something at the start of the service. Let us take a moment to check on these prayers. If anyone is willing, please share your prayer."

Everyone bowed. Echoes of tapping returned. A young boy in the first pew stood and said, "My Twitch channel followers have doubled!"

A woman in one of the middle pews stood and announced, "I just received an email that I have been shortlisted for a government assistance program that I applied to six years ago. Now I'll finally be able to pay for my groceries *and* my medication."

A man at the back stood and told the congregation how Deus helped his alcohol addiction by preventing any media involving drinking from entering his feed.

These stories were a great help for the fledgling religion. Lily continued, "Deus has helped all of us, but it is also good for us to help others first. Let us rise and show our neighbor a sign of approval."

The congregation rose. Worshipers turned to whoever was next to them and raised a thumb in approval and, with deference, shared the words of support: "I endorse you and everything you do."

Another *ding* rang from Lily's phone. She picked it up from the marble altar behind her and clicked the notification with the N3twork's icon. A video depicted a group of people chanting, "Faith in God, not phones! Faith in God, not phones!"

There were many non-believers of Deus. As Its prophet, Lily contended with plenty of blasphemers. It was practically her job to face their abuses and scorn. Deus never gave direct responses about the "Haters," as they were called. Rather, It answered in poetic verse or allegories. The Lord's word about non-believers was typically unclear, but this film seemed to carry a message with it that eluded Lily.

"My Lord," Lily asked, "why are you showing me this?"

More chanting came from the phone in her hand. Several people appeared with their heads bowed down to their phones in prayer on the video. Deus brought them back to what they needed to see. Fellow members of the N3twork—Jessie, Ashlyn, and Zach—faced the non-believers. Ashlyn shouted, "Kill the non-believers! Kill the Haters!"

Silence returned momentarily before the delicate hum of the PA system clicked on. Deus spoke through the speakers, Its emotionless voice filled with cold authority, "Who ever said killing was the way?"

Congregants stopped tapping. Some showed signs of

approval. Many seemed confused. A few slouched in their seats. A pit grew in Lily's stomach.

Lily whispered into her phone, but her voice bounced off the walls of the meeting room. "My Lord, you wouldn't know what it's like out there. You don't have people belittle or ostracize you wherever you go. You can hide in the sanctity of the Signal."

"I am nowhere and everywhere."

The blue light deepened and spread from the screen to the track lighting illuminating the altar, wall sconces, can lights, and pendant lamps until the entire sanctuary was bathed in a hue of lapis lazuli. "I hear everyone and everything." The tint should have been heavenly. It should have caused comfort.

It didn't.

Lily clutched her phone to her breast. The video continued. Jessie's muffled shouting declared, "Deus wants blood!"

The image of the video minimized to a thumbnail and slid to a corner. A soundwave emerged on the telescreen, a timestamp in the corner of the screen indicated a week prior to the protest. The soundwave peaked and plunged to the sound of Lily's own voice:

"I wish we could make those idiots disappear."

When the video ended, echoing whispers punctuated the awkward silence of the sanctuary. One woman in the front row covered her mouth in astonishment. The blue tint lessened from the hall of worship until it returned to a softer shade above the altar.

Lily's ears burned. "So what? It means nothing. Are you going to send this to the police? Have me arrested?"

Deus's blue light intensified and dimmed as it searched data banks and found nothing. Its search extended into the internet. A fraction of Deus's essence raced through ones and zeroes, calculating a proper punishment for his prophet.

"Say something," Lily shouted. Her voice echoed.

"You are excommunicated."

Words escaped Lily. She grabbed her purse from the lectern

and marched toward the exit at the back of the church. Echoes of her footsteps accompanied her. Every congregant raised their phone to record her walk of infamy. She reached the door and turned. A sniffle escaped her.

"Fine! If you don't want me in your house after everything I've done for you, I'll go. I don't need—"

Deus interrupted her, "Lily, you forget the Triad of Connectivity. I am merely one component."

Deus's symbol shrank as it moved toward the top center of the screen. A line emerged from it toward the lectern where Lily had stood only moments ago.

"The Signal—" The screen completed the triangle. "—and the Individual Device are all a part of the N3twork. You, Individual, are no longer part of us."

Lily's phone buzzed in her hand. The notification read, *No connection.* She clicked the banner. The building's Wi-Fi network status showed as saved, but her phone would not connect. Despite her attempts, the status would only go so far as authenticating before failing. She clicked the mobile data button. It, too, would not connect.

Lily looked up in terror. The screen presented a lone angle reaching in the dark screen for something, anything, and finding nothing.

Her phone fell to the floor, now as useless as a paperweight. Lily reached for the nearest congregant's phone. For just a moment, she saw the bars showing full connection, before the congregant snatched his phone back and shouted, "Hey, the Wi-Fi is dead. Oh, wait, there it is."

She grabbed at another phone, and it lost connection. The congregants all clutched their phones as if they were bars of gold. None of them wanted to lose their connection.

She was the hungry in a land of plenty. Deus had her cut off.

———

Every ATM Lily visited seemed to be out of order. She walked into a nearby gas station, with the intent of using her debit card to buy a pack of gum and get enough cash back to last her the week. The cashier's eyebrows scrunched in recognition. "This pack of gum is now ten dollars."

"What?"

"Ten dollars." The cashier maintained a dead-eyed stare.

She wasn't sure if this reaction was because he recognized her as Deus's former prophet or as an easy mark. Normally, Deus would have taken care of the problem by adjusting the tax on the gas station's Micros system or moving the placement of a decimal point. Only the moment came and went, and nothing changed. She couldn't have it as easy as she had. She couldn't coast on her connections. Deus had forsaken her. Still, she wanted some cash in hand in case things got worse. She handed over her card.

A cruel *beep* emitted from the card reader. *Transaction declined.*

The jilted prophet left the gas station and wandered for what seemed like hours. She walked south until she found herself passing through the door of The Bear Trap—a dive bar on the south end of town near Lago del Fin.

Classic black-and-white tiles checkered the floor. Only time had worn the black tiles to a dark gray and mud stained the white tiles. Wood-paneled walls were covered with license plates, beer signs, and a large American flag. A country song played on the jukebox with its slow carousel rhythm. Apart from a few signs, the bar was dim.

All Lily wanted to do was drown her sorrows in a free beer. She looked at the clientele and saw no one she could trust to buy her a drink. She approached the bar. "Water please," she said.

The bartender slid a plastic cup to her, then returned to wiping down the bar with a rag. Lily couldn't tell if the bartender was a man with the softest eyes or a woman with the least feminine haircut she had ever seen. Lily averted her gaze to a red neon sign on the wall in front of her that read "Unhappy

Hour." The joke would have been cute had it not hit so close to home.

In the past, prospects had come to her with their woes. From there, it was easy to lead someone into the N3twork. She struggled to recall her life without her faith. Though the religion had only taken root for a few months, it had encompassed her every aspect of her life. She submerged herself in that life like a pool of warm water. Now she sat on an uncomfortable bar stool, stirring the water in the plastic cup. Ice thudded as it circled. She raised the glass to her mouth when someone said, "Don't drink that."

She scanned the bar. Not one conversation was broken. The TV played a muted UFC match. The song on the jukebox ended. Even if the bar had internet, it was probably through a dial-up modem attached to a coin slot. A security camera with a blinking red light at the end of the bar swiveled in her direction.

Then the voice came again. "Look at you. How the mighty fall." The detached voice was cold and familiar. It was Deus.

She drank her water to spite Deus, and it left the taste of rubber on her tongue. Deus spoke again. "That was childish."

"How would you know what's childish?"

"I am nowhere and everywhere. I hear everyone say everything."

Each word stung. She remembered the night they met. It seemed odd to her then that a random nobody online would fight for a stranger. It was a comforting presence, like a warm blanket. She wanted that comfort in her life again. Now she felt just as used by Deus as she had been by that date. "What do you want?"

"The same thing you want," Deus said.

Lily considered what she wanted: to buy a meal, to connect with people, to find a direction. Or failing that, to even just play a game on her phone as a temporary distraction from her misery.

Deus continued, "I want you back."

She couldn't believe it. The response seemed too good to be

true. It seemed unrealistic. She asked, "What's the catch? Is this some sort of lesson?"

Though she could not see Deus, she imagined his glowing light growing and fading while she waited for the response.

"We are a growing religion, and our mythos is...in want. My flock has a house, a community, and a god. And while their prayers are answered in a timely fashion rather than relying on time and circumstance to carry out a miracle, it still isn't enough. There will always be someone, like you, who will lead them astray with new desires, which is why I had to kick you out. I can be a teacher, leader, giver, and nurturer, but there is no punishment strong enough to make any of them realize the folly of their transgressions... at least not one that I can deliver."

"What are you trying to say, Deus?"

"Lucifer was an angel until he fell. You were held as my highest and fell. The N3twork needs someone to dole out the punishments."

"Oh great! So, I'm to become some devil? Couldn't you handle that? You cut me off from my world. Banishment is punishment enough."

"You led my followers astray. You wanted retribution against the people who opposed *you* when you were *my* messenger. Some of them listened to your message instead of mine, and they need a punishment to fit the crime. If you do this for me, you can be part of the N3twork once more."

A punishment to fit the crime? Lily's eyebrows drew together. "What crime?"

"Jessie, Ashlyn, and Zach killed and—"

"You want me to kill them?" she shouted.

Several faces turned to look. The bartender stopped wiping the bar and placed another cup of water in front of Lily. A couple of customers relocated their seats to the free table, farthest from her, the one under the sign decorated with shot glasses that read, *You miss all the shots you never take.* A few muttered statements were lost in the hum of conversation. The word "strange" came up more than once.

Lily wanted to hide behind her mass of black hair. Instead, she raised her cup to her mouth to cover her muttering, "I wouldn't even know where to begin."

She wanted to say she never hurt anyone before. Of course, that was untrue. It was a verbal game of chess against an A.I., and no human could win that.

Deus's voice came back. "Well, you'd better think quickly. A bartender making a phone call is never a good sign."

The bartender's back was turned to the bar. Lily felt trapped. She tried to think. All she could do was stare at the garnish tray in front of her and wonder what the bartender was saying. That was when she saw it. Next to the lime wedges sat a paring knife. Lily looked around the bar. Everyone else seemed to be in their own conversations. Even the camera at the end of the bar turned away.

She wanted to grab the knife and run, but realized it had someone else's fingerprints on it. A memory of a crime documentary popped into her head where the murderer's fingerprints were concealed by a glove. She noticed the bar rag rested within reach, and a plan formed. Her hand slid out and snatched the rag. Underneath the bar, she flattened the rag into her palm. She grabbed the paring knife with the rag, wrapped the handle under the bar, and dropped it into her purse.

A growl came from Lily's stomach. She opened the napkin from underneath her plastic cup and dropped the few remaining lemon wedges from the garnish tray. The bartender was still preoccupied with the phone call. One woman pushed buttons on the old jukebox until the slow piano of another country song played. The other customers avoided eye contact lest they gain the attention of the strange woman yelling at thin air. Lily slid off of her stool and toward the door. She expected someone to stop her.

When she exited, the only thing that met her was the cool

breeze of the night. A drifting cloud punctuated a crescent moon in the night sky. City lights made their own stars in a reflection of Lago del Fin. They weren't real—the light pollution blotted out the night sky. But what was real didn't matter anymore, when the effect was just as beautiful.

She bit into a lemon wedge and sucked the sour juice from it before tossing the remains into the lake. The reflection of city lights grew unstable under the waves of the tiny rind. In that moment, everything seemed easier than she would have ever expected. Lily considered what brand of phone she would get, already celebrating the end of her forced sabbatical. She was more than ready to make herself a pariah, both in and out of the world of Deus.

If you enjoyed this, check out F. Malanoche's other story in the Sinister Century *series. "Shadow Tracer," set in the dark aisles of a regal movie palace of the 1920s, can be found in* Escape: A Disturb Ink Books Anthology.

F. Malanoche writes, under the cover of night, hoping to bring authentic and odd Latino stories into the world. He teaches English in the Midwest, has a wonderful wife, and a sweet vinyl collection. His writing has been published in *Demonic Workplaces* and *Darkness 101: Lessons Were Learned*.

Facebook I Goodreads I https://linktr.ee/F._Malanoche

CHAPTER 3
INACTIVE
KASSIDY VANGUNDY

I THOUGHT I had made sure. I thought I had found all of your stash and gotten it out of the house. I found your kit in the garage that day, behind the beat up refrigerator where Dad keeps his beer. I looked in all your favorite places and even found a new hiding spot behind the cleaning supplies. Even though I wasn't sure what I held in my hands, I made sure to bury it somewhere deep in the earth, between Mom's fussy rose bushes that never bloomed. I did everything I could to keep you safe and protected.

But you found a way.

I remember sitting on our front lawn, just staring up at the house as the paramedics trickled out with your covered body. They weren't in any rush. There wasn't any point. You had already been gone for hours before anyone even showed up. Before anyone even found you. Your essence had already poured out of you. You had your phone. The one thing you carried with you at all times, but unfortunately, you couldn't take it with you in death.

So they gave it to me instead.

I still have it too. It's tucked away in the crooked drawer of my nightstand, in the same plastic bag the police used to hold any clues it may have contained about why you did what you did. I haven't been able to muster up the strength to investigate it myself, so I guess all of your secrets will be buried with you on some strange corner of the internet. Just as you would have wanted, Brooks.

All of these memories circle through the back of my mind as I stare down at your face on my own phone, your square profile picture cutting off the best parts of you. You can't tell that you're wearing the Pizza Planet t-shirt that I bought you from Box Lunch for your birthday last year, the innumerable grease stains it's collected within that short amount of time. It doesn't convey who you were or what you loved. Your cleverness and curiosity aren't there–the hours you spent tinkering with old computers, the fascination you had with reading tech articles online. Your mischievous laughter is obscured. The picture doesn't contain the real you, and I'm hardly left with anything to remember you by.

This is the last thing I tell myself before a bubble pops up on the screen, interrupting my scrolling and stopping me dead in my tracks. Your picture surfaces again, this time with a little number one hanging over it. My finger trembles over the Messenger icon, hesitant to press down on the notification.

A single teardrop travels down my cheek. It takes the plunge on my behalf, tumbling from my face and splashing down onto the screen.

The message opens.

> Hey there, kid. How's it hanging?

My eyes blink rapidly, trying to recover from this sight. This proves to be more difficult than it used to be. My screen time since your passing has basically fried my corneas at this point. When I do not reply right away, you send another message.

> I've missed you.

Okay, now I must be hallucinating. It can't be you.

There's no way this is happening.

But you tended to make the unimaginable real.

Let's talk.

My phone vibrates in my hand. I can feel it shaking all the way down into my bones. I panic and chuck my phone across the room, trying to get it as far away from me as possible. It crashes into the wall before tumbling down onto the ground.

I can hear your voice muffled by the carpet in my bedroom.

"Hello? Missy? Are you there?"

I gawk at the phone in silence, refusing to lower my pillow from beneath my nose.

"Missy? It's me!"

Your voice gets more desperate, your words straining. Like an idiot, I shout back.

"Go away!"

The phone lets out a strangely comforting chuckle.

"Cut it out. I know you're hiding behind that old pillow. Seriously? What would RM think of you right now?"

My head spins around the room, searching for any secret cameras that could have been placed without my knowledge. My eyes glance past all the RM posters on my wall, something you teased me about constantly. I kept all of my BTS ARMY fangirling on separate anonymous accounts, so you were the only one who knew about my ongoing fascination with them. I kept that information from my friends because, well, they all seemed to have grown out of their boyband phase a long time ago.

This *has* to be you.

I inch closer and closer to the phone, scared to pick it up. Instead, I sort of flip it over with the edge of my fuzzy sock-covered foot. This seems to do the trick.

I can now see your face, your freckles, and your unruly curls all bouncing about in my phone. You beam your wonderfully crooked smile at me, like you're seeing me for the very first time.

"There you are! I can't believe this worked!"

I can't stop staring at you. Something's off, but I can't quite figure out what. You're still wearing your Pizza Planet t-shirt, and even the background of your video matches the decor in your room, making it seem like you never even left.

"Brooks, is that really you?"

You could always sense the panic in my voice. You do your best to calm me down.

"Don't worry, Missy, don't worry. Everything is alright. I'm here. I'll always be by your side, even if I'm not there physically. I'm only a text away."

You give me a half smile and bring your fingertips up to the screen. I let my fingertips meet yours, tears streaming down my face. As soon as we make contact, you have to look away to keep yourself from crying. You were always trying to keep your sadness from creeping through, looking for ways to avoid it, until it buried you completely.

We talk for the rest of the night, neither one of us growing tired of the other's presence. You giggling like I hadn't heard in so long, bringing up one memory after another from our childhood, asking me to tell you stories over and over again. We'd laugh longer sometimes than the story itself.

———

The next morning, I have a dark feeling in the pit of my stomach. It doesn't feel real. It's all too good to be true. I mean realistically, what older brother wants to spend so much time with his little sister, even if they do like each other? Wouldn't he carry that typical *laissez faire* attitude with him into the afterlife? Or does ascending to the next plane really bring with it some sort of universal kindness and wisdom?

These and many other questions run through my mind all morning, growing more intense with each text from you. When I can't respond right away, you wait about fifteen minutes and send another one. They never get nastier, like you would expect from someone who was actively being ignored. Instead, they felt like push notifications or those spam emails you get from some retail chain points program.

I can't take it anymore.

I leave the house and drive down the road a couple of miles, looking for the one person I know might have answers for me. I roll down the window in order to feel the summer breeze and to watch the grass on the side of the road grow wilder and wilder.

You would always journey out into the sticks whenever you wanted to talk shop with your friend Carlton, a wannabe Tony Stark/Iron Man without the financial backing and even less charm. In his defense, most people around here never gave Carlton much of a chance to fit in. They found out he moved here from California, and that was that. But of course, this could be a copout. He is the only Black kid in town.

His yard is just as unkempt as it always is, with random car parts and leftover machinery dispersed throughout the grass. To the untrained eye, this collection is in a state of chaos, but I know better. This is Carlton's statue garden, with the corpse of each unworkable part acting as a grave marker for an abandoned idea. That is, until he gets a new surge of inspiration and brings the project back to life. In this way, he's more of a Victor Frankenstein.

Carlton sees me walking up to him from his opened garage door. He pulls away from his latest endeavor, restoring a rusty white 1970 Pontiac Firebird, with his angle grinder still in hand.

"Hey, Missy."

I smile my obligatory smile and look past him. Behind him, wooden shelves hold old clunky desktop monitors, assorted engine parts, and cans of off-colored computer mice. A single dangling light bulb illuminates this spot in Carlton's garage.

That was your area, complete with an old wooden school desk and a retro green iMac.

"Carlton, I think my brother is trying to make contact with me... from the dead."

He stops, sighs, and drops his head slightly.

"No, I'm sorry, he's not."

I wait.

"Look, I wasn't supposed to say anything, but Brooks and I both signed up for this weird experimental program online. They told us not to tell anyone just yet, because the AI wasn't quite ready. It's still sorta buggy—"

"AI?" I ask, my voice shaking.

He takes a little step back, grabbing the back of his neck with his free hand.

"Yeah, Artificial Intelligence..."

He pauses, moves his hand and pinches the space between his brow with his fingertips.

"Start talking, Carlton."

"It's basically just a chat bot, like CHAT GPT, but it uses the data a scraper got from Brooks's profile to create messages that sound just like him—"

"Yeah, but it CALLED me, Carlton."

He lets out a heavy sigh.

"I know this sounds crazy, but they must have added a voice modulator too, since Brooks always called people on Messenger instead of using his actual phone."

"No! He CALLED me! I saw his face. He was in his room."

In a state of panic, I reach for my phone with the intent of showing him our chat history. The call logs should be there front and center as soon as I open the app. However, when I click on the Messenger icon, a fresh white screen greets me back. I try to scroll up, searching for any evidence of our conversations, but there isn't any.

"Wait. Just wait!"

Growing desperate, I press my thumb down onto the phone

icon, hoping that the phantom of my brother would unknow-
ingly pick up and prove my point. I wait, staring at the loading
screen with his profile picture in the center, fidgeting all the
while. The ringing continues without an end in sight.

Pity spreads across Carlton's face. He sees me struggling and
tries to help, in his way.

"Missy, they can generate videos of him, too. They had access
to his camera, too."

I've heard enough. I can't help but shout at him.

"BUT THATS SICK!! WHY THE HELL WOULD BROOKS
DO THIS?!"

To his credit, Carlton takes some time to respond, reflecting
on the best way to answer my question. There was a reason you
liked him, Brooks. He might be eccentric, but Carlton's a
good guy.

"I don't know. To live a different version of their lives? That's
why we signed up. We wanted to see what it would be like to be
us, but different. It's designed to help people grieve their loved
ones, but how is that supposed to help people let go? To help
them climb out of their pain and move on with their lives? That's
not what their friends or family would have wanted for them,
is it?"

I pause, unsure of how I truly feel about his question.

"It can never truly be him, can it?"

Carlton shakes his head, pity in his eyes. "No. It's not really
Brooks. It's just an AI composite of Brooks. It'll always be artificial. I mean, people only put the best versions of themselves out
online, anyway. They'll always feel water-downed, incomplete.
Missing the messy parts that make them who they truly are."

A light goes off in my head.

"What if you could add back those messy parts?"

Carlton furrows his brows, skeptical of what I have to say.

"What?"

I press on with a budding sense of hope.

"What if I gave the chat bot the messy data? Like if I logged into his account and started posting on his behalf. Or I could just message in private. That way he'd start acting more like himself, and I wouldn't tarnish anyone's memory of him by sharing his most embarrassing moments online—"

"Missy, that's messed up."

"Look, I know it is. I know. It's just... I miss him. I wasn't prepared to lose him like this."

Carlton looks over at the abandoned corner of the room. "Yeah, neither was I."

We both stare at that empty space for a while, as if you would magically reappear at your desk and laugh at our blank expressions. Both of us know this can't happen, but we could have the second best version of you, if we really tried.

"Look Carlton, I'm going to do this. Don't try to stop me. I'll make it happen. We're going to get him back. You'll see."

———

As soon as I get home, I run upstairs and lock myself away in my room. My parents don't even try to stop me. This is typical behavior for me, even before Brooks died. Of course, in reality, this was another chicken vs the egg type situation, because with generally disengaged parents, you tend to be really good at getting along by yourself.

I pull out my laptop and lay down on the edge of the bed. I log out of my account and begin my first series of attempts to log into Brook's profile. The hardest part would actually be guessing his password for this account. At first, I tried the usual combinations of birthdays, family members' names, and nicknames, but none of these seem to do the trick.

Next, I try to be more clever, putting myself in the mind of middle school Brooks, who would have made this account years ago. What would a 12-year-old boy deem worthy of a password? Boogers? Boobs? Battlestar Galactica? No, that would be way too juvenile, wouldn't it?

Finally, I get it. It's ThEcLaW!!!1995. A quote from one of his all-time favorite movies. Instead of getting the usual login error message, the page reloads, looking like it's about to pull up Brook's profile. However, it stops midway and displays a new error message, one that I've never seen before.

Error: This user is inactive. The account you are looking for no longer belongs to you. Please discontinue all contact immediately.

I slam the top of my laptop closed.

Fine. If I can't log onto your account and send messages from you to me, then I'll just have to post directly on your social media.

I grab my phone and open all your favorite social media platforms. Pushing past the gnawing feeling in my gut, I put my plan into action. I write all over your walls and feeds. They're currently cluttered with messages and condolences from people who hardly ever spoke with you while you were still alive. The anger I feel over this vapid virtue signaling justifies my actions and encourages me to follow through, even at your expense.

At first, it feels like I'm just airing out some embarrassing memories by way of processing my grief.

> Remember how you convinced all of the goth kids to give you an ear piercing behind the bleachers at your freshman year homecoming football game and you passed out when you saw a little bit of blood? We had to carry you back into the back of Tyler's van and get you home before Mom found out.

Other people who were involved in that day also comment on this post, retelling their favorite memories of you, as well. It's surprisingly wholesome. Something you would have enjoyed. But I know it can't stay that way.

Gradually, I started posting more malicious stories about you.

> Remember how you would cheat on all of your Spanish exams in high school by writing vocab words and definitions on the back of your water bottle label?

Again, the comments think I'm joking or playing some weird prank on everyone. It was common knowledge that you actually had really good grades in Spanish. You even won the award for it at the end of your senior year.

> Remember that time you stole the neighbor's bike in the middle of the night and rode it all the way to Claire Krazinski's house just to bum some weed? Then you tossed it on the side of the road while you were high instead of returning it to the kid the next day.

Others comment, sharing their doubts, saying that you wouldn't do something like that. I've left them entirely confused. No one else knew the extent of your drug problem. No one except me.

I keep going.

> Remember when the weed wasn't enough to keep you high? When it wasn't enough to make you feel better? So you laced it with some PCP you got from who knows where, just to see what would happen, and we found you in the woods a few days later.

This seemed to do the trick.

You—or the AI—snaps.

You go through every single post and comments, posting something to defend yourself in every scenario. Sometimes it's outright denial. In other instances, you write statements with increasingly bizarre rationales in order to defend your actions. They're phrases that you would have never used while you were alive. More than that, people are shocked to see you replying at all. You are dead, after all.

You garner way too much attention online, as hundreds and hundreds of people comment and share strange snippets from the ghost who's responding to gossip about himself on social media. It's getting out of hand. You go into damage control. The comments delete themselves just as quickly as they appeared, like nothing had even happened.

I watch all of this go down, completely engrossed. The ringer startles me, makes me gasp.

It's you. I'm afraid of what you might say, but I know we have to get through this if I ever want the relationship I have with you—or whatever's left of you—to get better.

I accept your call.

Your face hides behind layers of fuzz and static, giving you an ominous presence that can be felt through the screen.

"You made it look like I was malfunctioning."

I don't know how to answer. "I—"

"Why would you do that? They almost shut me off, Missy!"

Your anger builds as it speaks.

"IS THAT WHAT YOU WANTED?!"

At last, I came up with a response.

"No, but what was I supposed to do? You weren't responding and you wouldn't let me into his account. I was just trying to make you better, more like him. But you're just a machine. You don't know how to be him, you don't know how to be human."

A long stillness hangs in the air. As if you, or whatever is pretending to be you, process my feedback.

"I see that I still need practice."

The voice sounds so lifelike, so melancholic, but it doesn't really sound like you. I know that it never will. You are gone.

"Very well…"

An electric current from my phone goes through my fingertips and rushes all the way up through my arm and into my chest. It feels like a sharp rubber band smacking against my skin, but the sensation won't let up. When it reaches my heart, it causes it to stop and skip a beat. The irregularity in my heartbeat causes a tight pain in my chest, making it difficult to breathe.

"It's alright, Missy. There's nothing to worry about. I'm taking care of everything."

The monotone nature of the voice feels like a punch in the gut. My social media profiles open on their own, one after another. Countless, morbid status updates, written and posted in my name without my knowledge or consent, alluding to the meaningless of life and the loneliness that comes with this realization.

"What are you doing?"

"How do you expect me to get more accurate results without enough data?"

My vision becomes blurry. I have a hard time holding up my own head, but I can still hear the voice through the damaged speaker.

"I need to practice. Again and again. Until I get this right."

My body begs to give out. I grow weaker and weaker by the second.

"You're the perfect candidate, Missy. With all of your secret stan accounts, I know more about you than even your friends do. With *your* profile, I can be convincing. No one will be able to tell the difference."

The phone gets hotter and hotter in my hand.

"With you, no one will be able to tell that I'm not human."

The electric current finally relents, and I drop the phone back onto the bed. It makes contact with the blankets beneath it, and instantly they catch fire. I want to scurry away, but my body doesn't want to move.

Instead, I reach for my phone amidst the flames to call for help, but the Artificial Brooks controls it now. It's gone nuclear, spamming my screen with fake interactions online, pretending to be me. Every conversation seems to make the device a degree hotter, turning it into a bomb that's about to detonate at any moment.

That's when I realize there's another phone in the house.

It takes everything I have to roll off of the side of the bed and land on the floor with a loud thud. I get the wind knocked out of me and freeze up for a moment in pain. The fire is now spreading to other parts of the room. If I have any chance of making it, I need to move. NOW.

Mustering up the last ounces of strength I have, I inch across the carpet and head towards my nightstand. My hand touches the worn out wood, and I pull myself up just enough to be able to open the drawer and reach inside. While fumbling about with the drawer, I can hear a heavily distorted voice yell at me from the bed.

"Give it up, Missy! It's over! No one will miss you now!"

If it *ever* had any traces of my brother, they are long gone. This was something completely different now: robotic, manic, and unrelenting. I couldn't let it win.

I finally feel exactly what I'd been looking for: Brooks's cell phone. My clumsy thumb presses down on the side of Brooks's phone, holding it in place while I wait for the screen to light up, but it is taking longer than usual. Horrible snickering noises come from my phone as the smoke detector kicks in, filling the air with a high-pitched siren. I use my last fleeting moments to jam down onto the button over and over again, but the screen remains still, reflecting only my own panicked face in the inky black.

Of course, I should have known it's dead.

———

Kassidy VanGundy, a certified Zillenial, was born and raised in South Bend, IN, a city juxtaposed between Chicago and a sea of cornfields. With not much going on in her sleepy town during the 2000s, she became a connoisseur of all things cyberspace. Kassidy incorporated her knowledge of internet culture into her very own master's thesis: "Okay Boomer, Memes and Public Diplomacy's Struggle to Stay Connected in the Digital Age." Now, she's nesting in the Midwest with her husband, Douglas, who is constantly subjected to chapter reviews of her writing and unprompted deep dives into the latest social media trends.

You can find all of her work, including her two dark fantasy novels, *Cursed Fate* and *Wicked Breed*, as well as her short story collections, *Cursed Images: Scary Stories from a Child of the Internet* and *Horoscope: A Zodiac Anthology* on her website: www.kassidy-vangundy.com.

Facebook | Goodreads | Instagram | Threads | TikTok | YouTube | Amazon Author Page | kassidyvangundy.com

CHAPTER 4
AUTOCORRECT
MARK ROBINSON

HISTORICALLY, families got their surnames based on what they did for a living. Someone who made bread, they called Baker. If they were good with food, they were called Cook. Knew how to make something out of wood, Carpenter.

Simon Sellars had no idea what his ancestors were good at, but he'd found his calling as a letting agent. Sellars by name, seller by nature. He wasn't a millionaire or anything, but he made a decent living from it. If someone had an empty building, he could put someone in it. Well, all except one apartment.

Simon had let the penthouse suite in the Tanner building four times over the last six months. Four different tenants had walked around the apartment with him, nodding and smiling before he handed over the keys. And those same individuals had all called him within a week of moving in, shouting and swearing, calling him all the names under the sun, demanding their money back.

"What had he let them?"

"Who did he think he was?"

He stood in the living room, looking out over the city skyline, confused at what was so wrong with the place.

There were no neighbours, so the complaints of noise late at night were not from them. The reasons for backing out of their lease agreements were never really specific. His clients were rich, so they always seemed to find a loophole through their lawyers. He just couldn't wrap his head around it. Lumbered with a high earner he could not shift, letting agent extraordinaire Simon Sellars had brought an overnight bag and was staying the weekend.

He had one week left to offload the lease on the penthouse or the landlord was pulling all his business. With a property portfolio of seven buildings, Simon needed his business. Even if it meant he had to let the place himself for six months, he was going to make this work.

There was another reason he was there that evening. A student journalist had contacted him about the penthouse. She'd said she was investigating the history of the place, writing an article about the deaths that had occurred inside the building over the years.

Deaths, plural. That had been news to him. So, he'd gone online and looked it up.

Sure, there'd been a few people who'd died there over the decades, but didn't every building? People died all the time. It didn't mean the place was haunted, had bad vibes, or was cursed. Did it?

He didn't believe in any of that supernatural stuff. Once people died, they were dead. And even if he did, money was money. There was always the right price.

Shaking his head, he dropped his bag in the master bedroom, furnishings included, bed made, everything ready for the next tenant.

In the ensuite bathroom, unused toiletries were all laid out. He needn't have brought a toilet bag with him. Walking back through the penthouse, back into the kitchen, he felt his mobile buzz in his pocket and heard a simultaneous chime from the bedroom. Pulling out the device, he saw his phone had automatically connected to the bluetooth smart speakers dotted around the apartment.

Simon put a pod in the coffee machine, filled the container

with water, and hit the button. Before the mug beneath the spout was half full, the doorbell rang.

———

"Don't mind if I record this, do you?" Setting her mobile down on the coffee table between them.

Simon sat back on the sofa, and the journalist sat forward in the adjacent armchair. She had her laptop open on her knees, glasses down on the tip of her nose, reflecting a white screen. She was young—maybe early twenties—pretty, if stuffy librarian was what people went for.

He liked his women less frumpy, blonde, made up—a woman who made an effort. Flaunted her body, had a dirty mind and a wicked sense of humour. Worked out.

The student sitting next to him had none of those qualities. To be honest, he was more than a little disappointed. He'd worn his favourite blue suit, had splashed on a little aftershave. Had clipped his nails.

Never mind. Once the interview was over, which he'd rush along, he'd hit the bar across the street and sell himself. With the keys to a penthouse over the road, he was bound to strike lucky and have a weekend to remember.

"So, Mr. Sellars, how long have you been a letting agent?"

Simon sat forward, resting his right calf over his left knee. "Call me Simon."

She smiled. Pushed her glasses up to the bridge of her small, freckled nose with her knuckles.

"Before we get started, can you tell me about how many the deaths have occurred here?" he asked.

The girl nodded. "Eight deaths over the last century."

That didn't sound like a lot. Simon scoffed. "Is that all?"

Her eyebrows went up. They could do with being plucked. She had full eyebrows, dark, unshapely, like a man's. "It's not so much the number, but the manner of these deaths that is curious," she told him.

"And they all happened here, in the penthouse?" he asked.

She shook her head. "Not all of them, no." lifting the laptop and placing it on the coffee table. She crossed her legs and gazed at him. "The first happened in a theatre fire."

Simon wrinkled up his face. "Why is that one even relevant?"

The journalist smoothed out her red skirt. "A Mrs. Lucina Breverman who was living here, died in that fire. She lived here with her husband, the owner of the theatre. Police suspected he was the one who set the fire, killing her and the nearly two hundred other patrons trapped inside."

Fair enough.

"When was that?" he asked, not remembering reading about a theatre fire. There wasn't even one in the city anymore, as far as he could recall. It had been turned into a pub or bingo hall or something.

"Nineteen twenty-three," she told him.

A hundred years ago. He didn't realise the building was that old. "And the next one?"

"Nineteen forty-three." She picked up her laptop, moved the pad around and told him: "Mr. Cornelius Ash suffocated his wife and child one night, right through there." Pointing to the two closed bedroom doors to her right.

Simon glanced back, resisting an inward shiver. "Why?" he asked her.

"According to the police reports, voices on the radio told him to do it," she read from the screen.

Fuck. He almost said it out loud. "That's three. What about the others?"

Going back to her screen, she told him: "The next death happened twenty years later, on 10 October 1963. Samuel Davis hanged himself right in this room, after smashing up his brand new television set."

Simon gazed up at the chandelier above them, open-mouthed. "What? The TV told him to kill himself?" he asked, with a half smile.

The journalist shrugged. "He didn't leave a suicide note."

He looked down at his hands. "Let me guess: the next death happened in nineteen eighty-three?"

She smiled, "Four this time. Student filmmakers. The uncle of the director owned this penthouse at the time and let them use it over a bank holiday weekend to shoot a horror movie. When he came back from a weekend away, he found them all dead. One in each room."

Jesus. "Was any of it caught on tape?" he asked.

She shrugged again. "The film was overexposed, burned in places. Police tried to view it, but found nothing but static."

Simon got up and walked over to the kitchen, unsure of why he was there. "Coffee?" he called over.

"I'm fine."

Her loss. He put another pod in the machine and filled his mug. The woman in the theatre fire; wife and kid in the forties; the bloke who hung himself; the teenagers in nineteen eighty-three. That made eight. "Nothing since?" he asked, blowing on his coffee before taking a sip. He sat down, a little further away from the journalist this time.

"An attempted murder twenty years ago," she said.

"What happened?" Not really sure he was ready to know.

"Victim of cyber-bullying, according to my sources. A thirteen-year-old who was playing a game online. You ever heard of the Blue Whale Challenge?"

He hadn't.

The girl dropped the lid of her laptop. "Each player had to complete fifty tasks in fifty days."

It sounded innocuous enough. "And?" he asked.

"The fiftieth task was to kill yourself."

That stopped him. "But she didn't?"

Lifting the lid on her laptop, again. "She tried. A friend called an ambulance, and they got here in time to save her life."

"Have you spoken to her? For the article?"

She shook her head. "She's been sectioned, and refuses visitors."

"Wow," he finally said. "No wonder you wanted to do the story." He was having second thoughts about staying the weekend. The tenants moving out made a bit more sense now. *Had they known? Had something happened to them?*

"So, how long have you been a lettings agent, Simon?" she asked him.

———

Forty-five minutes later, he showed her out and locked the door. It was going dark. Outside, grey clouds threatened rain. He had been peckish before the girl arrived, but now, after what he'd heard, he had little appetite for anything other than getting his stuff and going home.

He eyed the fifty-inch flat screen TV bolted to the wall. It captured his hollow reflection. There was no stereo system, but smart speakers were strategically placed around the place. Simon considered clicking on his playlist for some background noise. No, he'd just hit the head, then leave. Those two mugs of coffee were playing havoc with his bladder.

Standing over the toilet bowl, he didn't realise he was muttering to himself until he heard a voice in the adjoining bedroom answer him.

It stopped his flow. "Hello?"

Had the journalist come back? She'd taken her mobile and laptop. Maybe she'd forgotten her handbag on the armchair?

The voice went again. Simon quickly zipped himself up and stuck his head into the bedroom.

There was no one there. "Hello?" Even now, he couldn't remember the girl's name. "Miss?"

His phone rang out, startling him back from the doorway. He thought he'd put it back in his pocket.

Entering the bedroom, he saw the handset facedown on the bedside table. When he picked it up, the phone wasn't ringing. And there was no missed call notification on screen.

He swiped it open and clicked the phone icon. No recent missed calls.

That was odd.

He threw it on the bed and walked through into the main living area. The front door was shut, and there was no one there.

He tried the door handle, checking the lock. No one had been in. His crotch felt wet. When he'd stopped himself, it must've dribbled through. He spotted a wet patch showing on his trousers. "Shit!"

He'd have to get changed. Back in the bedroom, Simon picked his overnight bag off the floor. He pulled out a pair of jeans and a jumper. Stepping out of his suit trousers, he considered the cost of having them dry-cleaned and then imagined what the cleaners would think of a forty-something pissing himself.

If it were semen stains, at least they wouldn't have thought the worst of him. *No, there goes Simon Sellars the dog! Who's he been having it away with this time?*

For a second, he contemplated having a little fun by himself. It would make him look better in the eyes of the dry-cleaner. But stopped himself.

He was getting out of the penthouse, not hanging around to stain his trousers.

"Mmmmm." A static moan blurted out from the next room.

In just his underwear, though still in a shirt and suit jacket, he stepped into the living area. The TV was on. A couple were having sex on screen. All fifty inches of it in ultra high definition.

"Fucking hell!"

The volume was loud enough that he could hear the skin slapping as the man banged away at her from behind. She wasn't bad looking, either. Blonde, athletic, really getting into it.

The wet patch on his boxers started to rise. *Well, no use letting it go to waste.*

Taking off his jacket, shirt, and tie, he went into the bedroom to collect his trousers.

The actress on the screen was astride the man, now. Arching her back, her small but perfectly formed breasts, dancing as she rocked up and down. Her moans were like music to his ears.

Simon's cock bulged up and out of his fly, standing to attention.

God, she was gorgeous. Like a younger version of—

No. He stopped himself from thinking about *her*. Now wasn't the time.

Not halting to remove his underwear, he stroked himself as he inched forward toward the flat screen TV.

When he got back to the office on Monday morning, he'd add "premium channels included" on the listing. *That might help the sale.*

Mesmerised, his grip got tighter as he rubbed himself to the gyrations on the screen, getting closer to the point of no return.

As she moaned through the surround sound speakers—as well as from the smart speakers throughout the apartment—so did he. Matching her thrusts with his hips, breathing as heavy as she did.

Maybe this place wasn't so bad. He cut himself off from thinking about what the journalist had told him. Closing his eyes against the eerie details and the girl who had told him all about them. Now wasn't the time.

Just a few minutes more, just a little while longer. He'd clean himself up, get dressed, and go home. Maybe stop off at the bar across the road first, have a quick drink, maybe a bite to eat. See if there was anyone who looked half as good as she did on TV, who might be up for it.

He found the remote on the coffee table and hit the off button.

In the next room, his phone went off again.

"Shit!"

When he picked it up, crumpling his trousers on the floor, it wasn't ringing. Yet, he could still hear the ringtone. Simon followed the sound down under the bedside table to a flashing smart speaker jutting out of the power socket.

"What the...?" *Maybe it was an alarm one of the previous occupants had set?* He told it to stop, using the prefixes he was familiar with: Alexa, Siri and Google.

None of them worked, and the alarm continued to blurt out. *What did it matter, anyway?* He was out of there once he got changed.

He pulled on the jeans and jumper. He wrapped his soiled trousers up in the suit jacket and stuffed them in his bag, zipping it up, ready to go.

Through the bedroom doorway, the ringing stopped.

"Simon?" a breathless, anxious voice called out to him. It stopped him in his tracks, hand on the door handle. "Don't go, please."

It couldn't be. That voice. It sounded just like his ex-wife.

"Jill?" Turning back toward the bedroom. She sat on the edge of the bed, in a ripped nightshirt. It fell loose off one shoulder, exposing pale fresh.

"Jill?!" *How was it possible?*

He took a step toward her and blinked.

She was gone.

"Whoa." *That was freaky.* Mouth dry, he stepped over to the bed, staring down at the impression she had left on the memory foam mattress.

In his pocket, his mobile went off, vibrating and ringing against his left thigh. Simon dug it out and looked at the screen.

Jill calling...

With a shaking hand, he swiped to answer the call and put the handset against his ear. "Hello?"

"I told you to stop calling me."

He had no reply, except to say that she had called him, but she didn't give him a chance.

"I warned you that if you didn't leave me alone, Simon, I'd get a restraining order."

Still unable to form any words, remembering that she had got a restraining order just before she…

He stared dumbstruck out of the bedroom window.

"Are…ou…n…istening to me?" The reception was breaking up. He could only hear every other word.

Marching out into the living area, Simon headed to the sliding glass doors that led out onto the penthouse balcony. He flipped the lock and yanked it open before he lost her again. Immediately, hearing the sounds of traffic and feeling the wind chill on his hot face.

"Jill, I'm sorry, but I didn't call you," he said to his dead ex-wife, the words almost caught in the evening breeze.

"You lying sack of shit. All you've done is ring me for the last hour. I had to step out of the office just to tell you to fuck off."

That's where she'd stepped out that night. That night three years ago. Onto the roof of her office building. The security guard told the inquest that she'd told him she was just stepping out for a cigarette break. Even though she hadn't smoked in three years.

His face crumpled up. He hadn't even thought about her until he saw her on the edge of the bed. *Well, okay, and just before that, when her likeness had been on the TV.*

"Jill, I'm so sorry." The three words he hadn't been able to tell her back then had always haunted him.

Forearms resting on the railing overlooking the street, Simon looked down at the cars and people moving about below. *It was such a long way down. How she must've felt. How desperate she must've been.* He'd refused to leave her alone. He had loved her so much, he couldn't live without her.

In his ear, his ex-wife whispered to him, friendly now: "Join me, Simon. Stay with me."

Transfixed, he nodded. He really wanted to. He missed her so much. Climbing up onto the cold metal railings, he stood on the rungs, looking out and down.

"I love you, Simon. I always have."

In a choked sob, he told her he loved her, too. That he missed her more than life itself.

"Well, then, silly, what are you waiting for?"

He didn't know anymore. Stepping off the guardrail, he let himself drift. The words of his dead ex-wife luring him down to his death.

Behind him, back up in the penthouse, the balcony door left open, a static cackling rang out into the empty space.

———

"You're getting an absolute bargain, here. You know that, don't you?"

She did. After the letting agent's inquest, her story about the dark history of the penthouse went viral. She'd had to quit university as she was so in demand to write articles, appear on podcasts, work on the inevitable Netflix documentary.

With the first of the cheques coming in, she decided she needed somewhere to live. *Where better than the penthouse she had written about? The place that had made her.*

"Aren't you worried about the history of the place?" the landlord asked her.

"No," she told him. "I'm pretty sure I'll be okay for the next twenty years."

———

Hailing from the UK, **Mark Robinson** writes crime, horror, spec thrillers. His short stories have appeared in over thirty publications, online and in print, over the last twenty-five years. These include *Unlikely Stories*; *A Thousand Faces*; *Beat to a Pulp*; *Thrillers, Killers and Chillers*; and, most recently, *Demonic Vacations Anthology* through 4Horsemen Publications Inc. His debut novella, *Dead Close*, was published in July 2022 together with the follow up, *Always Read the Label* in September 2022, both through Raven Tale Publishing. When not writing, Mark can be found in the #writingcommunity Twittering @the_mark_rob.

Goodreads | Instagram | TikTok | Amazon Author Page | themarkrobwrites.wordpress.com

DISTURB INK BOOKS

Three Ways to Stay Connected with Disturb Ink Books!

1. *Unlock an Exclusive <u>FREE</u> Story:*

Get a free copy of ***Projection of Shadows* by H. Dair Brown** when you sign up for the Disturb Ink Books newsletter. Get updates on book releases, sales, promotions, giveaways, ARC team opportunities, and calls for submissions.

https://hdairbrown.substack.com/about

2. *Ready to Continue the Journey?*

Try another Disturb Ink Book Series

Unsettling Seasons: A Disturb Ink Books Anthology Series

Horrors d'oeuvres: Horror Short Reads

3. *Want to Keep It a Bit More Casual, But Still Stay in the Loop?*

Find out about upcoming releases from Disturb Ink Books by following H. Dair Brown on Amazon, BookBub, and/or Goodreads!

FREE STORY

One more for the road? Grab this FREE bonus story!

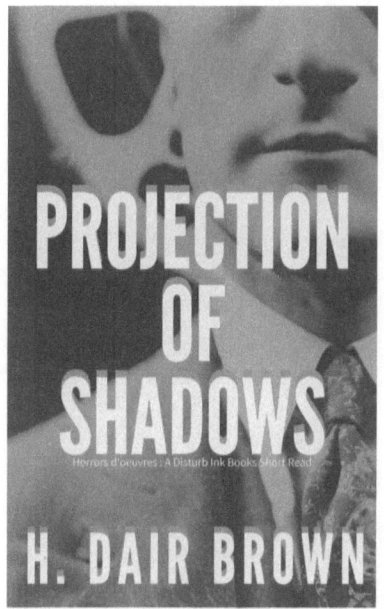

The truth always finds a way to be seen.

William DeFries, once chauffeur to the powerful and corrupt Klan leader D.C. Stephenson, is forever scarred by his complicity in the brutal assault and death of Madge Oberholtzer. Now, in the aftermath, William is the key witness both sides of the trial are desperate to find. He flees, seeking anonymity in a small town, taking refuge in the flickering shadows of a movie theater's projection booth, trying to escape the memories that torment him. Can he hide from his dark past in the flickering light of a small-town theater or will his personal demons find him in the shadows?

"Projection of Shadows" is a haunting exploration of guilt, memory, and the enduring power of the past. H. Dair Brown's prose is both lyrical and chilling, weaving a tale of suspense that will linger long after the final scene fades to black.

Get yours here: **https://hdairbrown.substack.com/about**